A Spinner in the Sun

Myrtle Reed

Contents

A SPINNER IN THE SUN

BY

Myrtle Reed

I
"The Fire was Kind"

The little house was waiting, as it had waited for many years. Grey and weather-worn, it leaned toward the sheltering hillside as though to gather from the kindly earth some support and comfort for old age. Five-and-twenty Winters had broken its spirit, five-and-twenty Springs had not brought back the heart of it, that had once gone out, with dancing feet and singing, and had returned no more.

For a quarter of a century, the garden had lain desolate. Summers came and went, but only a few straggling blooms made their way above the mass of weeds. In early Autumn, thistles and milkweed took possession of the place, the mournful purple of their flowering hiding the garden beneath trappings of woe. And at night, when the Autumn moon shone dimly, frail ghosts of dead flowers were set free from the thistles and milkweed. The wind of Indian Summer, itself a ghost, convoyed them about the garden, but they never went beyond it. Each year the panoply of purple spread farther, more surely hiding the brave blooms beneath.

Far down the path, beside the broken gate, a majestic cypress cast portentous gloom. Across from it, and quite hiding the ruin of the gate, was a rose-bush, which, every June, put forth one perfect white rose. Love had come through the gate and Love had gone out again, but this one flower was left behind.

Brambles grew about the doorstep, and the hinges of the door were deep in rust. No friendly light gleamed at night from the lattice, a beacon to the wayfarer or a message of cheer to the disheartened, since the little house was alone. The secret spinners had hung a drapery of cobwebs before the desolate windows, as though to veil the loneliness from passers-by. No fire warmed the solitary hearth, no gay and careless laughter betrayed the sleeping echoes into answer. Within the house were only dreams, which never had come true.

A bit of sewing yet lay upon the marble-topped table in the sitting-room, and an embroidery frame, holding still a square of fine linen, had fallen from a chair. An open book was propped against the back of the chair, and a low rocker, facing it, was swerved sharply aside. The evidence of daily occupation, suddenly interrupted, was all there--a quiet content, overlaid by a dumb, creeping paralysis.

The March wind blew fiercely through the night and the little house leaned yet more toward the sheltering hill. Afar, in the village, a train rumbled into the station; the midnight train from the city by which the people of Rushton regulated their watches and clocks. Strangely enough, it stopped, and more than one good man, turning uneasily upon his pillow, wondered if the world might have come to its end.

Half an hour afterward, a lone figure ascended the steep road which led to the house. A woman, fearless of the night, because Life had already done its worst to her, stumbled up the stony, overgrown way. The moon shone fitfully among the flying clouds, and she guided herself by its uncertain gleams, pausing now and then, in complete darkness, to wait for more light.

Ghost-like, a long white chiffon veil trailed behind her, too securely fastened to her hat to be blown away. Even in the night, she watched furtively and listened for approaching footsteps, one hand holding the end of her veil in such a way that she might quickly hide her face.

Outside the gate she paused, irresolute. At the last moment, it seemed as if she could never enter the house again. A light snow had fallen upon the dead garden, covering its scarred face with white. Miss Evelina noted quickly that her garden, too, was hidden as by chiffon.

A gust of wind made her shiver--or was it the veiled garden? Nerving herself to her necessity, she took up her satchel and went up the path as one might walk, with bared feet, up a ladder of swords. Each step that took her nearer the house hurt her the more, but she was not of those who cry out when hurt. She set her lips more firmly together and continued upon her self-appointed way.

When she reached the house, she already had the key in her uncertain fingers. The rusty lock yielded at length and the door opened noisily. Her heart surged painfully as she entered the musty darkness. It was so that Miss Evelina came home, after five-and-twenty years.

The thousand noises of an empty house greeted her discordantly. A rattling window was answered by a creaking stair, a rafter groaned dismally, and the scurrying feet of mice pattered across a distant floor.

Fumbling in her satchel, Miss Evelina drew out a candle and a box of matches. Presently there was light in the little house--a faint glimmering light, which flickered, when the wind shook the walls, and twinkled again bravely when it ceased.

She took off her wraps, and, through force of habit, pinned the multitudinous folds of her veil to her hair, forgetting that at midnight, and in her own house, there were none to see her face.

Then she made a fire, for the body must be warmed, though the heart is dead, and the soul stricken dumb. She had brought with her a box containing a small canister of tea, and she soon had ready a cup of it, so strong that it was bitter.

With her feet upon the hearth and the single candle flickering upon the mantel shelf, she sat in the lonely house and sipped her tea. Her well-worn black gown clung closely to her figure, and the white chiffon veil, thrown back, did not wholly hide her abundant hair. The horror of one night had whitened Miss Evelina's brown hair at twenty, for the sorrows of Youth are unmercifully keen.

"I have come back," she thought. "I have come back through that door. I went out of it, laughing, at twenty. At forty-five, I have come back, heart-broken, and I have lived.

"Why did I not die?" she questioned, for the thousandth time. "If there had been a God in Heaven, surely I must have died."

The flames leaped merrily in the fireplace and the discordant noises of the house resolved themselves into vague harmony. A cricket, safely ensconced for the Winter in a crevice of the hearth, awoke in the unaccustomed warmth, piping a shrill and cheery welcome, but Miss Evelina sat abstractedly, staring into the fire.

After all, there had never been anything but happiness in the house--the misery had been outside. Peace and quiet content had dwelt there securely, but the memory of it brought no balm now.

As though it were yesterday, the black walnut chair, covered with haircloth, stood primly against the wall. Miss Evelina had always hated the chair, and here, after twenty-five years, it confronted her again. She mused, ironically, upon the permanence of things usually considered transient and temporary. Her mother's sewing was still upon the marble-topped table, but the hands that held it were long since mingled with the dust. Her own embroidery had apparently but just fallen from the chair, and the dream that had led to its fashioning--was only a dream, from which she awoke to enduring agony. With swift hatred, she turned her back upon the embroidery frame, and hid her face in her hands.

Time, as time, had ceased to exist for her. She suffered until suffering brought its own far anodyne--the inability to sustain it further,--then she slept, from sheer weariness. Before dawn, usually, she awoke, sufficiently rested to suffer again. When she felt faint, she ate, scarcely knowing what she ate, for food was as dust and ashes in her mouth.

In the bag that hung from her belt was a vial of laudanum, renewed from time to time as she feared its strength was waning. She had been taught that it was wicked to take one's own life, and that God was always kind. Not having experienced the kindness, she began to doubt the existence of God, and was immediately face to face with the idea that it could not be wrong to die if one was too miserable to live. Her mind revolved perpetually in this circle and came continually back to a compromise. She would live one more day, and then she would free herself. There was always a to-morrow when she should be free, but it never came.

The fire died down and the candle had but a few minutes more to burn. It was the hour of the night when life is at its lowest--when souls pass out into the great Beyond. Miss Evelina took the vial from her reticule and uncorked it. The bitter, pungent odour came as sweet incense to her nostrils. No one knew she had come. No one would ever enter her door again. She might die peacefully in her own house, and no one would know until the walls crumbled to dust--perhaps not even then. And Miss Evelina had a horror of a grave.

She drew a long breath of the bitterness. The silken leaves of the poppies--flowers of sleep--had been crushed into this. The lees must be drained from the Cup of Life before the Cup could be set aside. Every one came to this, sooner or later. Why not choose? Why not drain the Cup now? When it had all been bitter, why hesitate to drink the lees?

The monstrous and incredible passion of the race was slowly creeping upon her. Her eyes gleamed and her cheeks burned. The hunger for death at her own hands and on her own terms possessed her frail body to the full. "If there had been a God in Heaven," she said, aloud, "surely I must have died!"

The words startled her and her hand shook so that some of the laudanum was spilled. It was long since she had heard her own voice in more than a monosyllabic answer to some necessary question. Inscrutably veiled in many folds of chiffon, she held herself apart from the world, and the world, carelessly kind, had left her wholly to herself.

Slowly, she put the cork tightly into the vial and slipped it back into her bag. "Tomorrow," she sighed; "to-morrow I shall set myself free."

The fire flickered and without warning the candle went out, in a gust of wind which shook the house to its foundations. Stray currents of air had come through the crevices of the rattling windows and kept up an imperfect ventilation. She took another candle from her satchel, put it into a candlestick of blackened brass, and slowly ascended the stairs.

She went to her own room, though her feet failed her at the threshold and she sank helplessly to the floor. Too weak to stand, she made her way on her knees to her bed, leaving the candle in the hall, just outside her door. As she had suspected, it was hardest of all to enter this room.

A pink and white gown of dimity, yellowed, and grimed with dust, yet lay upon her bed. Cobwebs were woven over the lace that trimmed the neck and sleeves. Out of the fearful shadows, mute reminders of a lost joy mocked her from every corner of the room.

She knelt there until some measure of strength came back to her, and, with it, a mad fancy. "To-night," she said to herself, "I will be brave. For once I will play a part, since to-morrow I shall be free. To-night, it shall be as though nothing had happened--as though I were to be married to-morrow and not to--to Death!"

She laughed wildly, and, even to her own ears, it had a fantastic, unearthly sound. The empty rooms took up the echo and made merry with it, the sound dying at last into a silence like that of the tomb.

She brought in the candle, took the dimity gown from the bed, and shook it to remove the dust. In her hands it fell apart, broken, because it was too frail to tear. She laid it on a chair, folding it carefully, then took the dusty bedding from her bed and carried it into the hall, dust and all. In an oaken chest in a corner of her room was her store of linen, hemmed exquisitely and embroidered with the initials: "E. G."

She began to move about feverishly, fearing that her resolution might fail. The key of the chest was in a drawer in her dresser, hidden beneath a pile of yellowed garments. Her hands, so long nerveless, were alive and sentient now. When she opened the chest, the scent of lavender and rosemary, long since dead, struck her like a blow.

The room swam before her, yet Miss Evelina dragged forth her linen sheets and pillow-slips, musty, but clean, and made her bed. Once or twice, her veil slipped down over her face, and she impatiently pushed it back. The candle, burning low, warned her that she must make haste,

In one of the smaller drawers of her dresser was a nightgown of sheerest linen, wonderfully stitched by her own hands. She hesitated a moment, then opened the drawer.

Tiny bags of sweet herbs fell from the folds as she shook it out. It was yellowed and musty and as frail as a bit of fine lace, but it did not tear in her hands. "I will wear it," she thought, grimly, "as I planned to do, long ago."

At last she stood before her mirror, the ivory-tinted lace falling away from her neck and shoulders. Her neck was white and firm, but her right shoulder was deeply, hideously scarred. "Burned body and burned soul," she muttered, "and this my wedding night!"

For the first time in her life, she pitied herself, not knowing that self-pity is the first step toward relief from overpowering sorrow. When detachment is possible, the long, slow healing has faintly, but surely, begun.

She unpinned her veil, took down her heavy white hair, and braided it. There was no gleam of silver, even in the light--it was as lustreless as a field of snow upon a dark day. That done, she stood there, staring at herself in the mirror, and living over, remorselessly, the one day that, like a lightning stroke, had blasted her life.

Her veil slipped, unheeded, from her dresser to the floor. Leaning forward, she studied her face, that she had once loved, then swiftly learned to hate. Even on the street, closely veiled, she would not look at a shop window, lest she might see herself reflected in the plate glass, and she had kept the mirror, in her room covered with a cloth,

Since the day she left the hospital, where they all had been so kind to her, no human being, save herself, had seen her face. She had prayed for death, but had not been more than slightly ill, upborne, as she was, by a great grief which sustained her as surely as an ascetic is kept alive by the passion of his faith. She hungered now for the sight of her face as she hungered for death, and held the flaring candle aloft that she might see better.

Then a wave of impassioned self-pity swept her like flame. "The fire was kind," she said, stubbornly, as though to defend herself from it. "It showed me the truth."

She leaned yet closer to the glass, holding the dripping candle on high. "The fire was kind," she insisted again. Then the floodgates opened, and for the first time in all the sorrowful years, she felt the hot tears streaming over her face. Her hand shook, but she held her candle tightly and leaned so close to the mirror that her white hair brushed its cracked surface.

"The fire was kind," sobbed Miss Evelina. "Oh, but the fire was kind!"

II
Miss Mehitable

The slanting sunbeams of late afternoon crept through the cobwebbed window, and Miss Evelina stirred uneasily in her sleep. The mocking dream vanished and she awoke to feel, as always, the iron, icy hand that unmercifully clutched her heart. The room was cold and she shivered as she lay beneath her insufficient covering.

At length she rose, and dressed mechanically, avoiding the mirror, and pinning her veil securely to her hair. She went downstairs slowly, clinging to the railing from sheer weakness. She was as frail and ghostly as some disembodied spirit of Grief.

Soon, she had a fire. As the warmth increased, she opened the rear door of the house to dispel the musty atmosphere. The March wind blew strong and clear through the lonely rooms, stirring the dust before it and swaying the cobwebs. Suddenly, Miss Evelina heard a footstep outside and instinctively drew down her veil.

Before she could close the door, a woman, with a shawl over her head, appeared on the threshold, peered curiously into the house, then unhesitatingly entered.

"For the land's sake!" cried a cheery voice. "You scared me most to death! I saw the smoke coming from the chimney and thought the house was afire, so I come over to see."

Miss Evelina stiffened, and made no reply.

"I don't know who you are," said the woman again, mildly defiant, "but this is Evelina Grey's house."

"And I," answered Miss Evelina, almost inaudibly, "am Evelina Grey."

"For the land's sake!" cried the visitor again. "Don't you remember me? Why,

Evelina, you and I used to go to school together. You----"

She stopped, abruptly. The fact of the veiled face confronted her stubbornly. She ransacked her memory for a forgotten catastrophe, a quarter of a century back. Impenetrably, a wall was reared between them.

"I--I'm afraid I don't remember," stammered Miss Evelina, in a low voice, hoping that the intruder would go.

"I used to be Mehitable Smith, and that's what I am still, having been spared marriage. Mehitable is my name, but folks calls me Hitty--Miss Hitty," she added, with a slight accent on the "Miss."

"Oh," answered Miss Evelina, "I remember," though she did not remember at all.

"Well, I'm glad you've come back," went on the guest, politely. Altogether in the manner of one invited to do so, she removed her shawl and sat down, furtively eyeing Miss Evelina, yet affecting to look carelessly about the house.

She was a woman of fifty or more, brisk and active of body and kindly, though inquisitive, of countenance. Her dark hair, scarcely touched with grey, was parted smoothly in the exact centre and plastered down on both sides, as one guessed, by a brush and cold water. Her black eyes were bright and keen, and her gold-bowed spectacles were habitually worn half-way down her nose. Her mouth and chin were indicative of great firmness--those whose misfortune it was to differ from Miss Hitty were accustomed to call it obstinacy. People of plainer speech said it was "mulishness."

Her gown was dark calico, stiffly starched, and made according to the durable and comfortable pattern of her school-days. "All in one piece," Miss Hitty was wont to say. "Then when I bend over, as folks that does housework has to bend over, occasionally, I don't come apart in the back. For my part, I never could see sense in wearing clothes that's held by a safety-pin in the back instead of good, firm cloth, and, moreover, a belt that either slides around or pinches where it ain't pleasant to be pinched, ain't my notion of comfort. Apron strings is bad enough, for you have to have 'em tight to keep from slipping." Miss Hitty had never worn corsets, and had the straight, slender figure of a boy.

The situation became awkward. Miss Evelina still stood in the middle of the room, her veiled face slightly averted. The impenetrable shelter of chiffon awed

Miss Mehitable, but she was not a woman to give up easily when embarked upon the quest for knowledge. Some unusual state of mind kept her from asking a direct question about the veil, and meanwhile she continually racked her memory.

Miss Evelina's white, slender hands opened and closed nervously. Miss Hitty set her feet squarely on the floor, and tucked her immaculate white apron closely about her knees. "When did you come?" she demanded finally, with the air of the attorney for the prosecution.

"Last night," murmured Miss Evelina.

"On that late train?"

"Yes."

"I heard it stop, but I never sensed it was you. Seemed to me I heard somebody go by, too, but I was too sleepy to get up and see. I thought I must be dreaming, but I was sure I heard somebody on the walk. If I'd known it was you, I'd have made you stop at my house for the rest of the night, instead of coming up here alone."

"Very kind," said Miss Evelina, after an uncomfortable pause.

"You might as well set down," remarked Miss Hitty, with a new gentleness of manner. "I'm going to set a spell."

Miss Evelina sat, helplessly, in the hair-cloth chair which she hated, and turned her veiled face yet farther away from her guest. Seeing that her hostess did not intend to talk, Miss Hitty began a conversation, if anything wholly one-sided may be so termed.

"I live in the same place," she said. "Ma died seventeen years ago on the eighteenth of next April, and left the house and the income for me. There was enough to take care of two, and so I took my sister's child, Araminta, to bring up. You know my poor sister got married. She ought to have known better, but she didn't. She just put her head into the noose, and it slipped up on her, as I told her it would, both before and after the ceremony. Having seen all the trouble men make in the world, I sh'd think women would know enough to keep away from 'em, but they don't--that is, some women don't." Miss Hitty smoothed her stiff white apron with an air of conscious virtue.

"Araminta was only a year old when her ma got enough of marrying and went to her reward in Heaven. What she 'd been through would have tried the patience of a saint, and Barbara wasn't no saint. None of the Smith family have ever grown wings here on earth, but it's my belief that we'll all be awarded our proper plumage in Heaven.

"He--" the pronoun was sufficiently definite to indicate Araminta's hapless father--"was always tracking dirt into the clean kitchen, and he had an appetite like a horse. Barbara would make a cake to set away for company, and he'd gobble it all up at one meal just as if 't was a doughnut. She was forever cooking and washing dishes and sweeping up after him. When he come into the house, she'd run for the broom and dustpan, and follow him around, sweeping up, and if you'll believe me, the brute scolded her for it. He actually said once, in my presence, that if he'd known how neat she was, he didn't believe he'd have married her. That shows what men are--if it needs showing. It's no wonder poor Barbara died. I hope there ain't any brooms in Heaven and that she's havin' a good rest now.

"Araminta's goin' on nineteen, and she's a sensible girl, if I do say it as shouldn't. She's never spoke to a man except to say 'yes' and 'no.' I've taught her to steer clear of 'em, and even when she was only seven years old, she'd run if she saw one coming. She knows they 're pizen and I don't believe I'll ever have any cause to worry about Minty.

"I've got the minister boarding with me," pursued Miss Hitty, undaunted, and cheerfully taking a fresh start. "Ministers don't count, and I must say that, for a man, Mr. Thorpe is very little trouble. He wipes his feet sometimes for as much as five minutes when he's coming in, and mostly, when it's pleasant weather, he's out. When he's in, he usually stays in his room, except at meals. He don't eat much more 'n a canary, and likes what he eats, and don't need hardly any pickin' up after, though a week ago last Saturday he left a collar layin' on the bureau instead of putting it into his bag.

"I left it right where 't was, and Sunday morning he put it where it belonged. He's never been married and he's learned to pick up after himself. I wouldn't have had him, on Araminta's account, only that there wasn't no other place for him to stay, and it was put to me by the elders as being my Christian duty. I wouldn't have took him, otherwise, and we've never had an unmarried minister before.

"Besides, Mr. Thorpe ain't pleasing the congregation, and I don't know that he'll stay long. He's been here six months and three Sundays over, and I've been to every single service, church and Sunday-school and prayer-meeting, and he ain't never said one word about hell. It's all of the joys of Heaven and a sure reward in the hereafter for everybody that's done what they think is right--nothing much, mind you, about what is right. Why, when Mr. Brewster was preaching for us, some of the sinners would get up and run right out of the church when he got started on hell and the lost souls writhin' in the flames. That was a minister worth having.

"But Mr. Thorpe, now, he doesn't seem to have no sense of the duties of his position. Week before last, I heard of his walkin' along the river with Andy Rogers--arm in arm, if you'll believe me, with the worst drunkard and chicken thief in town. The very idea of a minister associatin' with sinners! Mr. Brewster would never have done that. Why, Andy was one of them that run out of the church the day the minister give us that movin' sermon on hell, and he ain't never dared to show his face in a place of worship since.

"As I said, I don't think Mr. Thorpe 'll be with us long, for the vestry and the congregation is getting dissatisfied. There ain't been any open talk, except in the Ladies' Aid Society, but public opinion is settin' pretty strongly in that direction." Miss Hitty dropped her final g's when she got thoroughly interested in her subject and at times became deeply involved in grammatical complications.

"Us older ones, that's strong in the faith, ain't likely to be injured by it, I suppose, but there's always the young ones to be considered, and it's highly important for Araminta to have the right kind of influence. Of course Mr. Thorpe don't talk on religious subjects at home, and I ain't let Araminta go to church the last two Sundays. Meanwhile, I've talked hell to her stronger 'n common.

"But, upon my soul, I don't know what Rushton is comin' to. A month or so ago, there was an outlandish, heathen character come here that beats anything I've ever heard tell of. His name is Tom Barnaby and he's set up a store on the edge of town, in the front parlour of Widow Simon's house. She's went and rented it to him, and she says he pays his rent regular.

"He wears leather leggings and a hat with a red feather stuck in it, and he's gone into competition with Mrs. Allen, who's kept the dry-goods here for the last twenty years.

"Of course," she went on, a little wistfully, "I've always patronised Mrs. Allen, and I always shall. They do say Barnaby's goods is a great deal cheaper, but I'd feel it my duty to buy of a woman, anyhow, even though she has been married. She's been a widow for so long, it's most the same as if she'd never been married at ail.

"Barnaby lives with a dog and does for himself, but he's hardly ever in his store. People go there to buy things and find the door propped open with a brick, and a sign says to come in and take what you want. The price of everything is marked good and plain, and another sign says to put the money in the drawer and make your own change. The blacksmith was at him for doing business so shiftless, and Barnaby laughed and said that if anybody wanted anything he had bad enough to steal it, whoever it was, he was good and welcome to it. That just shows how crazy he is. Most of the time he's roaming around the country, with his yellow dog at his heels, making outlandish noises on some kind of a flute. He can't play a tune, but he keeps trying. Folks around here call him Piper Tom.

"Of course I wouldn't want Mrs. Allen to know, but I've thought that some-time when he was away and there was nobody there to see, I'd just step in for a few minutes and take a look at his goods. Elmiry Jones says his calico is beautiful, and that for her part, she's going to trade there instead of at Allen's. I suppose it is a temptation. I might do it myself, if 't want for my principles."

The speaker paused for breath, but Miss Evelina still sat silently in her chair. "What was it?" thought Miss Hitty. "I was here, and I knew at the time, but what happened? How did I come to forget? I must be getting old!"

She searched her memory without result. Her house was situated at the cross-roads, and, being on higher ground, commanded a good view of the village below. Gradually, her dooryard had become a sort of clearing house for neighbourhood gossip. Travellers going and coming stopped at Miss Hitty's to drink from the moss-grown well, give their bit of news, and receive, in return, the scandal of the coun-tryside. Had it not been for the faithful and industrious Miss Mehitable, the town might have needed a daily paper.

"Strange I can't think," she said to herself. "I don't doubt it'll come to me, though. Something happened to Evelina, and she went away, and her mother went with her to take care of her, and then her mother died, all at once, of heart failure. It happened the same week old Mis' Hicks had a doctor from the city for an opera-tion, and the Millerses barn was struck by lightning and burnt up, and so I s'pose it's no wonder I've sorter lost track of it."

Miss Evelina's veiled face was wholly averted now, and Miss Hitty studied her shrewdly. She noted that the black gown was well-worn, and had, indeed, been patched in several places. The shoes which tapped impatiently on the floor were undeniably shabby, though they had been carefully blacked. Against the unrelieved sombreness of her gown. Miss Evelina's hands were singularly frail and transparent. Every line of her body was eloquent of weakness and well-nigh insupportable grief.

"Well," said Miss Hitty, again, though she felt that the words were flat; "I'm glad you've come back. It seems like old times for us to be settin' here, talkin', and--" here she laughed shrilly--"we've both been spared marriage."

A small, slender hand clutched convulsively at the arm of the haircloth chair, but Miss Evelina did not speak.

"I see," went on Miss Hitty, not unkindly, "that you're still in mourning for your mother. You mustn't take it so hard. Sometimes folks get to feeling so sorry about something that they can't never get over it, and they keep on going round and round all the time like a squirrel in a wheel, and keep on getting weaker till it gets to be a kind of disease there ain't no cure for. Leastwise, that's what Doctor Dexter says."

"Doctor Dexter!" With a cry, Miss Evelina sprang to her feet, her hands tightly pressed to her heart.

"The same," nodded Miss Hitty, overjoyed to discover that at last her hostess was interested. "Doctor Anthony Dexter, our old schoolmate, as had just graduated when you lived here before. He went away for a year and then he came back, bringing a pretty young wife. She's dead, but he has a son, Ralph, who's away studying to be a doctor. He'll graduate this Spring and then he's coming here to help his father with his practice. Doctor Dexter's getting old, like the rest of us, and he don't like the night work. Some folks is inconsiderate enough to get sick in the night. They orter have regular hours for it, same as a doctor has hours for business. Things would fit better.

"Well, I must be going, for I left soup on the stove, and Araminta's likely as not to let it burn. I'm going to send your supper over to you, and next week, if the weather's favourable, we'll clean this house. Goodness knows it needs it. I'd just as soon send over all your meals till you get settled--'t wouldn't be any trouble. Or, you can come over to my house if you wouldn't mind eating with the minister. It seems queer to set down to the table with a man, and not altogether natural, but I'm beginning to get used to it, and it gives us the advantage of a blessing, and, anyway, ministers don't count. Come over when you can. Goodbye!"

With a rustle of stiffly starched garments Miss Mehitable took her departure, carefully closing the door and avoiding the appearance of haste. This was an effort, for every fibre of her being ached to get back to the clearing house, where she might speculate upon Evelina's return. It was her desire, also, to hunt up the oldest inhabitant before nightfall and correct her pitiful lapse of memory.

At the same time, she was planning to send Araminta over with a nice hot supper, for Miss Evelina seemed to be far from strong, and, even to one lacking in discernment, acutely unhappy.

Down the road she went, her head bowed in deep and fruitless thought. Swiftly, as in a lightning flash, and without premonition, she remembered.

"Evelina was burnt," she said to herself, triumphantly, "over to Doctor Dexter's, and they took her on the train to the hospital. I guess she wears that veil all the time."

Then Miss Hitty stopped at her own gate, catching her breath quickly. "She must have been burnt awful," she thought. "Poor soul!" she murmured, her sharp eyes softening with tears. "Poor soul!"

III
The Pearls

A rap at the door roused Miss Evelina from a deadly stupor which seemed stabbed through with daggers of pain. She sat quite still, determined not to open the door. Presently, she heard the sound of retreating footsteps, and was reassured. Then she saw a bit of folded paper which had been slipped under the door, and, mechanically, she picked it up.

"Here's your supper," the note read, briefly. "When you get done, leave the tray outside. I'll come and get it. I would like to have you come over if you want to.--Mehitable Smith."

Touched by the unexpected kindness, Miss Evelina took in the tray. There was a bowl of soup, steaming hot, a baked potato, a bit of thin steak, fried, in country fashion, two crisp, buttered rolls, and a pot of tea. Faint and sick of heart, she pushed it aside, then in simple justice to Miss Hitty, tasted of the soup. A little later, she put the tray out on the doorstep again, having eaten as she had not eaten for months.

She considered the chain of circumstances that had led her back to Rushton. First, the knowledge that Doctor Dexter had left the place for good. She had heard of that, long ago, but, until now, no one had told her that he had returned. She had thought it impossible for him ever to return--even to think of it again,

Otherwise--here the thread of her thought snapped, and she clutched at the vial of laudanum which, as always, was in the bag at her belt. She perceived that the way of escape was closed to her. Broken in spirit though she was, she was yet too proud to die like a dog at Anthony Dexter's door, even after five-and-twenty years.

Bitterest need alone had driven her to take the step which she so keenly regretted now. The death of her mother, hastened by misfortune, had left her with a small but certain income, paid regularly from two separate sources. One source had failed without warning, and her slender legacy was cut literally in two. Upon the remaining half she must eke out the rest of her existence, if she continued to exist at all. It was absolutely necessary for her to come back to the one shelter which she could call her own.

Weary, despairing, and still in the merciless grip of her obsession, she had come--only to find that Anthony Dexter had long since preceded her. A year afterward, Miss Hitty said, he had come back, with a pretty young wife. And he had a son.

The new knowledge hurt, and Evelina had fancied that she could be hurt no more, that she had reached the uttermost limits of pain. By a singular irony, the last refuge was denied her at the very moment of her greatest temptation to avail herself of it. Long hours of thought led her invariably to the one possible conclusion--to avoid every one, keep wholly to herself, and, by starvation, if need be, save enough of her insignificant pittance to take her far away. And after that--freedom.

Since the night of full realisation which had turned her brown hair to a dull white she had thought of death in but one way--escape. Set free from the insufferable bondage of earthly existence. Miss Evelina dreamed of peace as a prisoner in a dungeon may dream of green fields. To sleep and wake no more, never to feel again the cold hand upon her heart that tore persistently at the inmost fibres of it, to forget----

Miss Evelina took the vial from her bag and uncorked it. The incense of the poppies crept subtly through the room, mingling inextricably with the mustiness and the dust. The grey cobwebs swayed at the windows, sunset touching them to iridescence. Conscious that she was the most desolate and lonely thing in all the desolate house, Miss Evelina buried her face in her hands.

The poppies breathed from the vial. In her distorted fancy, she saw vast plains of them, shimmering in the sun--scarlet like the lips of a girl, pink as the flush of dawn upon the eastern sky, blood-red as the passionate heart that never dreamed of betrayal.

The sun was shining on the field of poppies and Miss Evelina walked among them, her face unveiled. Golden masses of bloom were spread at her feet, starred here and there by stately blossoms as white as the blown snow. Her ragged garments touched the silken petals, her worn shoes crushed them, bud and blossom alike. Always, the numbing, sleepy odour came from the field. Dew was on the petals of the flowers; their deep cups gathered it and held it, never to be surrendered, since the dew of the poppies was tears.

Like some evil genius rising from the bottle, the Spirit of the Poppies seemed to incarnate itself in the vapour. A woman with a face of deadly white arose to meet Miss Evelina, with outspread arms. In her eyes was Lethe, in her hands was the gift of forgetfulness. She brought pardon for all that was past and to come, eternal healing, unfathomable oblivion. "Come," the drowsy voice seemed to say. "I have waited long and yet you do not come. The peace that passeth all understanding is mine to give and yours to take. Come--only come! Come! Come!"

Miss Evelina laughed bitterly. Never in all the years gone by had the Spirit of the Poppies pleaded with her thus. Now, at the hour when surrender meant the complete triumph of her enemy, the ghostly figure came to offer her the last and supreme gift.

The afterglow yet lingered in the west. The grey of a March twilight was in the valley, but it was still late afternoon on the summit of the hill. Miss Evelina drew her veil about her and went out into the garden, the vial in her hand.

Where was it that she had planted the poppies? Through the mass of undergrowth and brambles, she made scant headway. Thorns pressed forward rudely as if to stab the intruder. Vines, closely matted, forbade her to pass, yet she kept on until she reached the western slope of the garden.

Here, unshaded, and in the full blaze of the Summer sun, the poppies had spread their brilliant pageantry. In all the village there had been no such poppies as grew in Evelina's garden. Now they were dead and only the overgrown stubble was left.

"Dust to dust, earth to earth, and ashes to ashes." The solemn words of the burial service were chanted in her consciousness as she lifted the vial high and emptied it. She held it steadily until the last drop was drained from it. The poppies had given it and to the poppies she had returned it. She put the cork into the empty vial and flung it far away from her, then turned back to the house.

There was a sound of wheels upon the road. Miss Evelina hastened her steps, but the dense undergrowth made walking difficult. Praying that she might not be seen, she turned her head.

Anthony Dexter, in the doctor's carriage, was travelling at a leisurely pace. As he passed the old house, he glanced at it mechanically, from sheer force of habit. Long ago, it had ceased to have any definite meaning for him. Once he had even stripped every white rose from the neglected bush at the gate, to take to his wife, who, that day, for the first time, had held their son in her arms.

Motionless in the wreck of the garden, a veiled figure stood with averted face. Doctor Dexter looked keenly for an instant in the fast gathering twilight, then whipped up his horse, and was swiftly out of sight. Against his better judgment, he was shaken in mind and body. Could he have seen a ghost? Nonsense! He was tired, he had overworked, he had had an hallucination. His cool, calm, professional sense fought with the insistent idea. It was well that Ralph was coming to relieve his old father of a part of his burden.

Meanwhile, Miss Evelina, her frail body quivering as though under the lash, crept back into the house. With the sure intuition of a woman, she knew who had driven by in the first darkness. That he should dare! That he should actually trespass upon her road; take the insolent liberty of looking at her house!

"A pretty young wife," Miss Hitty had said. Yes, doubtless a pretty one. Anthony Dexter delighted in the beauty of a woman in the same impersonal way that another man would regard a picture. And a son. A straight, tall young fellow, doubtless, with eyes like his father's--eyes that a woman would trust, not dreaming of the false heart and craven soul. Why had she been brought here to suffer this last insult, this last humiliation? Weakly, as many a woman before her, Miss Evelina groped in the maze of Life, searching for some clue to its blind mystery.

Was it possible that she had not suffered enough? If five-and-twenty years of sodden misery were not sufficient for one who had done no wrong, what punishment would be meted out to a sinner by a God who was always kind? Miss Evelina's lips curled scornfully. She had taken what he should have borne--Anthony Dexter had gone scot free.

"The man sins and the woman pays." The cynical saying, which, after all, is not wholly untrue, took shape in her thought and said itself--aloud. Yet it was not altogether impossible that he might yet be made to pay--could be--

Her cheeks burned and her hands closed tightly. What if she were the chosen instrument? What if she had been sent here, after all the dead, miserable years, for some purpose which hitherto she had not guessed?

What if she, herself, with her veiled face, were to be the tardy avenger of her own wrong? Her soul stirred in its despair as the dead might stir in the winding sheet. Out of her sodden grief, could she ever emerge--alive?

"The fire was kind," said Miss Evelina, in a whisper. "It showed me the truth. The fire was kind and God is kind. He has brought me here to pay my debt--in full."

She began to consider what she might do that would hurt Anthony Dexter and make him suffer as she had suffered for half a lifetime. If he had forgotten, she would make him remember--ah, yes, he must remember before he could be hurt. But what could she do? What had he given her aside from the misery that she hungered to give back to him?

The pearls! Miss Evelina lighted her candle and hurried upstairs.

In her dower chest, beneath the piles of heavy, yellowed linen, was a small jewel case. She knelt before the chest, gasping, and thrust her questioning fingers down through the linen to the solid oak. With a little cry, she rose to her feet, the jewel case in her hand.

The purple velvet was crushed, the satin was yellowed, but the string of pearls was there--yellowed, too, by the slow passage of the years. One or two of them were black. A slip of paper fluttered out as she opened the case, and she caught it as it fell. The paper was yellow and brittle and the ink had faded, but the words were still there, written in Anthony Dexter's clear, bold hand; "First from the depths of the sea, and then from the depths of my love."

"Depths!" muttered Miss Evelina, from between her clenched teeth.

Once the necklace had been beautiful--a single strand of large, perfectly matched pearls. The gold of the clasp was dull, but the diamond gleamed like the eye of some evil thing. She wound the necklace twice about her wrist, then shuddered, for it was cold and smooth and sinuous, like a snake.

She coiled the discoloured necklace carefully upon its yellowed satin bed, laid the folded slip of paper over it, and closed it with a snap. To-morrow--no, this very night, Anthony Dexter should have the pearls, that had come first from the depths of the sea, and then from the depths of his love.

No hand but hers should give them back, for she saw it written in the scheme of vengeance that she herself should, mutely, make him pay. She felt a new strength of body and a fresh clearness of mind as, with grim patience, she set herself to wait.

The clocks in the house were all still. Miss Evelina's watch had long ago been sold. There was no town clock in the village, but the train upon which she had come was due shortly after midnight. She knew every step of the way by dark as well as by daylight, but the night was clear and there would be the light of the dying moon,

Her own clouded skies were clearing. Dimly she began to perceive herself as a part of things, not set aside helplessly to suffer eternally, but in some sort of relation to the rest of the world.

On the Sunday before the catastrophe, Miss Evelina had been to church, and even yet, she remembered fragments of the sermon. "God often uses people to carry out His plans," the minister had said. At the time, it had not particularly impressed her, and she had never gone to church again. If she had listened further, she might have heard the minister say that the devil was wont to do the same thing.

Minute by minute, the hours passed. Miss Evelina's heart was beating painfully, but, all unknowingly, she had entered upon a new phase. She had turned in the winding sheet of her own weaving, and her hands were clutching at the binding fabric.

At last, the train came in. It did not stop, but thundered through the sleeping village, shrieking as it went. The sound died into a distant rumble, then merged into the stillness of the night. Miss Evelina rose from her chair, put on her wraps, slipped the jewel case into her bag, and went out, closely veiled.

The light of the waning moon was dim and, veiled as she was, she felt rather than saw the way. Steadfastly, she went down the steep road, avoiding the sidewalk, for she remembered that Miss Mehitable's ears were keen. Past the crossroads, to the right, down into the village, across the tracks, then sharply to the left--the way was the same, but the wayfarer was sadly changed.

She went unemotionally, seeing herself a divinely appointed instrument of vengeance. Something outside her obsession had its clutch upon her also, but it was new, and she did not guess that it was fully as hideous.

Doctor Dexter's house was near the corner on a shaded street. At the gate.

Miss Evelina paused and, with her veil lifted, carefully scrutinised the house for a possible light. She feared that some one might be stirring, late as it was, but the old housekeeper always went to bed promptly at nine, and on this particular night, Anthony Dexter had gone to his room at ten, making sleep sure by a drug.

With hushed steps, Miss Evelina went furtively up to the house on the bare earth beside the brick pavement. She was in a panic of fear, but something beyond her control urged her on. Reaching the steps, she hesitated, baffled for the moment, then sank to her knees. Slowly she crept to the threshold, placed the jewel case so that it would fall inward when the door was opened, and started back. Instinct bade her hurry, but reason made her cautious. She forced herself to walk slowly and to muffle the latch of the gate with her skirts as she had done when she came in.

It seemed an hour before she crossed the tracks again, at the deserted point she had chosen, but, in reality, it was only a few minutes. At last she reached home, utterly exhausted by the strain she had put upon herself. She had seen no one, heard no footstep save her own; she had gone and returned as mysteriously as the night itself.

When she slept, she dreamed of the poppy bed on the western slope of the garden. It was twilight, and she stood there with a vial of laudanum in one hand and a necklace of discoloured pearls in the other. She poured the laudanum upon the earth and a great black poppy with a deadly fragrance sprang up at her feet. Then Anthony Dexter drove up in a carriage and took the pearls away from her. She could not see him clearly, because his face was veiled, like her own.

The odour of the black poppy made her faint and she went into the house to escape from it, but the scent of it clung to her garments and hands and could not be washed away.

IV
"From the Depths of his Love"

At seven o'clock, precisely, Anthony Dexter's old housekeeper rang the rising bell. Drowsy with the soporific he had taken, the doctor did not at once respond to the summons. In fact, the breakfast bell had rung before he was fully awake.

He dressed leisurely, and was haunted by a vague feeling that something unpleasant had happened. At length he remembered that just before dusk, in the garden of Evelina Grey's old house, he had seen a ghost--a ghost who confronted him mutely with a thing he had long since forgotten.

"It was subjective, purely," mused Anthony Dexter. "I have been working too hard." His reason was fully satisfied with the plausible explanation, but he was not a man who was likely to have an hallucination of any sort.

He was strong and straight of body, finely muscular, and did not look over forty, though it was more than eight years ago that he had reached the fortieth milestone. His hair was thinning a little at the temples and the rest of it was touched generously with grey. His features were regular and his skin clear. A full beard, closely cropped, hid the weakness of his chin, but did not entirely conceal those fine lines about the mouth which mean cruelty.

Someway, in looking at him, one got the impression of a machine, well-nigh perfect of its kind. His dark eyes were sharp and penetrating. Once they had been sympathetic, but he had outgrown that. His hands were large, white, and well-kept, his fingers knotted, and blunt at the tips. He had, pre-eminently, the hand of the surgeon, capable of swiftness and strength, and yet of delicacy. It was not a hand that would tremble easily; it was powerful and, in a way, brutal.

He was thoroughly self-satisfied, as well he might be, for the entire countryside admitted his skill, and even in the operating rooms of the hospitals in the city not far distant. Doctor Dexter's name was well known. He had thought seriously, at times, of seeking a wider field, but he liked the country and the open air, and his practice would give Ralph the opportunity he needed. At his father's death, the young physician would fail heir to a practice which had taken many years of hard work to build up.

At the thought of Ralph, the man's face softened a trifle and his keen eyes became a little less keen. The boy's picture was before him upon his chiffonier. Ralph was twenty-three now and would finish in a few weeks at a famous medical school--Doctor Dexter's own alma mater. He had not been at home since he entered the school, having undertaken to do in three years the work which usually required four.

He wrote frequently, however, and Doctor Dexter invariably went to the post-office himself on the days Ralph's letters were expected. He had the entire correspondence on file and whiled away many a lonely evening by reading and re-reading the breezy epistles. The last one was in his pocket now.

"To think, Father," Ralph had written, "in three weeks more or less, I shall be at home with my sheepskin and a fine new shingle with 'Dr. Ralph Dexter' painted on it, all ready to hang up on the front of the house beside yours. I'll be glad to get out of the grind for a while, I can tell you that. I've worked as His Satanic Majesty undoubtedly does when he receives word that a fresh batch of Mormons has hit the trail for the good-intentions pavement. Decensus facilis Averni. That's about all the Latin I've got left.

"At first, I suppose, there won't be much for me to do. I'll have to win the confidence of the community by listening to the old ladies' symptoms three or four hours a day, regularly. Finally, they'll let me vaccinate the kids and the rest will be pitifully easy. Kids always like me, for some occult reason, and if the children cry for me, it won't be long till I've got your whole blooming job away from you. Never mind, though, dad--I'll be generous and whack up, as you've always done with me."

Remembering the boyishness of it, Anthony Dexter smiled a little and took another satisfying look at the pictured face before him. Ralph's eyes were as his father's had been--frank and friendly and clear, with no hint of suspicion. His chin was firm and his mouth determined, but the corners of it turned up decidedly, and the upper lip was short. The unprejudiced observer would have seen merely an honest, intelligent, manly young fellow, who looked as if he might be good company. Anthony Dexter saw all this--and a great deal more.

It was his pride that he was unemotional. By rigid self-discipline, he had wholly mastered himself. His detachment from his kind was at first spasmodic, then exceptionally complete. Excepting Ralph, his relation to the world was that of an unimpassioned critic. He was so sure of his own ground that he thought he considered Ralph impersonally, also.

Over a nature which, at the beginning, was warmly human, Doctor Dexter had laid this glacial mask. He did what he had to do with neatness and dispatch. If an operation was necessary, he said so at once, not troubling himself to approach the subject gradually. If there was doubt as to the outcome, he would cheerfully advise the patient to make a will first, but there was seldom doubt, for those white, blunt fingers were very sure. He believed in the clean-cut, sudden stroke, and conducted his life upon that basis.

Without so much as the quiver of an eyelash, Anthony Dexter could tell a man that within an hour his wife would be dead. He could predict the death of a child, almost to the minute, without a change in his mask-like expression, and feel a faint throb of professional pride when his prediction was precisely fulfilled. The people feared him, respected him, and admired his skill, but no one loved him except his son.

Among all his acquaintances, there was none who called him friend except Austin Thorpe, the old minister who had but lately come to town. This, in itself, was no distinction, for Thorpe was the friend of every man, woman, child, and animal in the village. No two men could have been more unlike, but friendship, like love, is often a matter of chemical affinity, wherein opposites rush together in obedience to a hidden law.

The broadly human creed of the minister included every living thing, and the man himself interested Doctor Dexter in much the same way that a new slide for his microscope might interest him. They exchanged visits frequently when the duties of both permitted, and the Doctor reflected that, when Ralph came, Thorpe would be lonely.

The Dexter house was an old one but it had been kept in good repair. From time to time, wings had been added to the original structure, until now it sprawled lazily in every direction. One wing, at the right of the house, contained the Doctor's medical library, office, reception room, and laboratory. Doors were arranged in metropolitan fashion, so that patients might go out of the office without meeting any one. The laboratory, at the back of the wing, was well fitted with modern appliances for original research, and had, too, its own outside door.

When Ralph came home, the other wing, at the left of the house, was to be arranged in like manner for him if he so desired. Doctor Dexter had some rough drawings under consideration, but wanted Ralph to order the plans in accordance with his own ideas.

The breakfast bell rang again, and Doctor Dexter went downstairs. The servant met him in the hall. "Breakfast is waiting, sir," she said.

"All right," returned the Doctor, absently. "I'll be there in a moment."

He opened the door for a breath of fresh air, and immediately perceived the small, purple velvet box at his feet. He picked it up, wonderingly, and opened it.

Inside were the discoloured pearls on their bed of yellowed satin, and the ivory-tinted slip of paper on which he had written, so long ago, in his clear, boyish hand: "First, from the depths of the sea, and then from the depths of my love."

Being unemotional, he experienced nothing at first, save natural surprise. He stood there, staring into vacancy, idly fingering the pearls. By some evil magic of the moment, the hour seemed set back a full quarter of a century. As though it were yesterday, he saw Evelina before him.

She had been a girl of extraordinary beauty and charm. He had travelled far and seen many, but there had been none like Evelina. How he had loved her, in those dead yesterdays, and how she had loved him! The poignant sweetness of it came back, changed by some fatal alchemy into bitterness.

Anthony Dexter had seen enough of the world to recognise cowardice when he saw it, even in himself. His books had taught him that the mind could hold but one thought at a time, and, persistently, he had displaced the unpleasant ones which constantly strove for the right of possession.

Hard work and new love and daily wearying of the body to the point of exhaustion had banished those phantoms of earlier years, save in his dreams. At night, the soul claims its own--its right to suffer for its secret sins, its shirking, its betrayals.

It is not pleasant for a man to be branded, in his own consciousness, a coward. Refusal to admit it by day does not change the hour of the night when life is at its lowest ebb, and, sleepless, man faces himself as he is.

The necklace slipped snakily over his hand--one of those white, firm hands which could guide the knife so well--and Anthony Dexter shuddered. He flung the box far from him into the shrubbery, went back into the house, and slammed the door.

He sat down at the table, but could not eat. The Past had come from its grave, veiled, like the ghost in the garden that he had seen yesterday.

It was not an hallucination, then. Only one person in the world could have laid those discoloured pearls at his door in the dead of night. The black figure in the garden, with the chiffon fluttering about its head, was Evelina Grey--or what was left of her.

"Why?" he questioned uneasily of himself. "Why?" He had repeatedly told himself that any other man, in his position, would do as he had done, yet it was as though some one had slipped a stiletto under his armour and found a vulnerable spot.

Before his mental vision hovered two women. One was a girl of twenty, laughing, exquisitely lovely. The other was a bent and broken woman in black, whose veil concealed the dreadful hideousness of her face.

"Pshaw!" grumbled Doctor Dexter, aloud. "I've overworked, that's all."

He determined to vanquish the spectre that had reared itself before him, not perceiving that Remorse incarnate, in the shape of Evelina, had come back to haunt him until his dying day.

V
Araminta

A raminta," said Miss Mehitable, "go and get your sewing and do your stent."

"Yes, Aunt Hitty," answered the girl, obediently.

Each year, Araminta made a new patchwork quilt. Seven were neatly folded and put away in an old trunk in the attic. The eighth was progressing well, but the young seamstress was becoming sated with quilts. She had never been to school, but Miss Mehitable had taught her all she knew. Unkind critics might have intimated that Araminta had not been taught much, but she could sew nicely, keep house neatly, and write a stilted letter in a queer, old-fashioned hand almost exactly like Miss Mehitable's.

That valiant dame saw no practical use in further knowledge. She was concerned with no books except the Bible and the ancient ledger in which, with painstaking exactness, she kept her household accounts. She deemed it wise, moreover, that Araminta should not know too much.

From a drawer in the high, black-walnut bureau in the upper hall, Araminta drew forth an assortment of red, white, and blue cotton squares and diamonds. This was to be a "patriotic" quilt, made after a famous old pattern which Miss Hitty had selfishly refused to give to any one else, though she had often been asked for it by contemporary ladies of similar interests.

The younger generation was inclined to scout at quilt-making, and needlework heresy was rampant in the neighbourhood. Tatting, crocheting, and knitting were on the wane. An "advanced" woman who had once spent a Summer in the village had spread abroad the delights of Battenberg and raised embroidery. At all of these, Miss Hitty sniffed contemptuously.

"Quilt makin' was good enough for their mas and their grandmas," she said scornfully, "and I reckon it's good enough for anybody else. I've no patience with such things."

Araminta knew that. She had never forgotten the vial of wrath which broke upon her luckless head the day she had timorously suggested making lace as a pleasing change from unending quilts.

She sat now, in a low rocker by the window, with one foot upon a wobbly stool. A marvellous cover, of Aunt Hitty's making, which dated back to her frivolous and girlish days, was underneath. Nobody ever saw it, however, and the gaudy woollen roses blushed unseen. A white linen cover, severely plain, was put upon the footstool every Wednesday and every Saturday, year in and year out.

Unlike most good housewives, Miss Mehitable used her parlour every day in the week. She was obliged to, in fact, for it was the only room in her house, except Mr. Thorpe's, which commanded an unobstructed view of the crossroads. A cover of brown denim protected the carpet, and the chairs were shrouded in shapeless habiliments of cambric and calico. For the rest, however, the room was mildly cheerful, and had a habitable look which was distinctly uncommon in village parlours.

There was a fireplace, which was dusted and scrubbed at intervals, but never, under any circumstances, profaned by a fire. It was curtained by a gay remnant of figured plush, however, so nobody missed the fire. White and gold china vases stood on the mantel, and a little china dog, who would never have dared to bark had he been alive, so chaste and humble of countenance was he, sat forever between the two vases, keeping faithful guard over Miss Mehitable's treasures.

The silver coffin plates of the Smiths, matted with black, and deeply framed, occupied the place of honour over the mantel. On the marble-topped table in the exact centre of the room was a basket of wax flowers and fruit, covered by a bell-shaped glass shade. Miss Hitty's album and her Bible were placed near it with mathematical precision. On the opposite wall was a hair wreath, made from the shorn locks of departed Smiths by Miss Hitty's mother. The proud possessor felt a covert reproach in the fact that she herself was unable to make hair wreaths. It was a talent for which she had great admiration.

Araminta rocked back and forth in her low chair by the window. She hummed a bit of "Sweet Bye and Bye" to herself, for hymns were the only songs she knew.

She could play some of them, with one hand, on the melodeon in the corner, but she dared not touch the yellow keys of the venerated instrument except when Miss Hitty was out.

The sunlight shone lovingly on Araminta's brown hair, tightly combed back, braided, and pinned up, but rippling riotously, none the less. Her deep, thoughtful eyes were grey and her nose turned up coquettishly. To a guardian of greater penetration, Araminta's mouth would have given deep concern. It was a demure, rosy mouth, warning and tantalising by turns. Mischievous little dimples lurked in the corners of it, and even Aunt Hitty was not proof against the magic of Araminta's smile. The girl's face had the creamy softness of a white rose petal, but her cheeks bloomed with the flush of health and she had a most disconcerting trick of blushing. With Spartan thoroughness, Miss Mehitable constantly strove to cure Araminta of this distressing fault, but as yet she had not succeeded.

The pretty child had grown into an exquisitely lovely woman, to her stern guardian's secret uneasiness. "It's goin' to be harder to keep Minty right than 't would be if she was plain," mused Miss Hitty, "but t guess I'll be given strength to do it. I've done well by her so far."

"In the Sweet Bye and Bye," sang Araminta, in a piping, girlish soprano, "we shall meet on that beautiful shore."

"Maybe we shall and maybe we sha'n't," said Miss Hitty, grimly. "Some folks 'll never see the beautiful shore. They'll go to the bad place."

Araminta lifted her great, grey, questioning eyes. "Why?" she asked, simply.

"Because they've been bad," answered Miss Hitty, defiantly.

"But if they didn't know any better?" queried Araminta, threading her needle. "Would they go to the bad place just because they didn't know?"

Miss Mehitable squirmed in her chair, for never before had Araminta spoken thus. "There's no excuse for their not knowin'," she said, sharply.

"Perhaps not," sighed Araminta, "but it seems dreadful to think of people being burned up just for ignorance. Do you think I'll be burned up, Aunt Hitty?" she continued, anxiously. "There's so many things I don't know!"

Miss Mehitable set herself firmly to her task. "Araminta Lee," she said, harshly, "don't get to bothering about what you don't know. That's the sure way to perdition. I've told you time and time again what's right for you to believe and what's right for you to do. You walk in that path and turn neither to the right nor the left, and you won't have no trouble--here or anywheres else."

"Yes, Aunt Hitty," said the girl, dutifully. "It must be awful to be burned."

Miss Mehitable looked about her furtively, then drew her chair closer to Araminta's. "That brings to my mind something I wanted to speak to you about, and I don't know but what this is as good a chance as any. You know where I told you to go the other day with the tray, and to set it down at the back door, and rap, and run?"

"Yes." Araminta's eyes were wide open now. She had wondered much at her mysterious errand, but had not dared to ask questions.

"Well," continued Aunt Hitty, after an aggravating pause, "the woman that lives in that house has been burnt."

Araminta gasped. "Oh, Aunt Hitty, was she bad? What did she do and how did she get burned before she was dead?"

Miss Mehitable brushed aside the question as though it were an annoying fly. "I don't want it talked of," she said, severely. "Evelina Grey was a friend of mine, and she is yet. If there's anything on earth I despise, it's a gossip. People who haven't anything better to do than to go around prying into other folks's affairs are better off dead, I take it. My mother never permitted me to gossip, and I've held true to her teachin'." Aunt Hitty smoothed her skirts with superior virtue and tied a knot in her thread.

"How did she get burned?" asked Araminta, eagerly.

"Gossip," said Miss Mehitable, sententiously, "does a lot of harm and makes a lot of folks miserable. It's a good thing to keep away from, and if I ever hear of your gossiping about anybody, I'll shut you up in your room for two weeks and keep you on bread and water."

Araminta trembled. "What is gossiping, Aunt Hitty?" she asked in a timid, awe-struck tone.

"Talking about folks," explained Miss Hitty. "Tellin' things about 'em they wouldn't tell themselves."

It occurred to Araminta that much of the conversation at the crossroads might appropriately be classed under that head, but, of course, Aunt Hitty knew what she was talking about. She remembered the last quilting Aunt Hitty had given, when the Ladies' Aid Society had been invited, en masse, to finish off the quilt Araminta's rebellious fingers had just completed. One of the ladies had been obliged to leave earlier than the rest, and----

"I don't believe," thought Araminta, "that Mrs. Gardner would have told how her son ran away from home, nor that she didn't dust her bed slats except at house-cleaning time, nor that they ate things other people would give to the pigs."

"I expect there'll be a lot of questions asked about Evelina," observed Miss Mehitable, breaking in rudely upon Araminta's train of thought, "as soon 's folks finds out she's come back to live here, and that she has to wear a veil all the time, even when she doesn't wear her hat. What I'm telling you for is to show you what happens to women that haven't sense enough to keep away from men. If Evelina 'd kept away from Doctor Dexter, she wouldn't have got burnt."

"Did Doctor Dexter burn her?" asked Araminta, breathlessly. "I thought it was God."

At the psychological moment, Doctor Dexter drove by, bowing to Miss Mehitable as he passed. Araminta had observed that this particular event always flustered her aunt.

"Maybe, it was God and maybe it was Doctor Dexter," answered Miss Mehitable, quickly. "That's something there don't nobody know except Evelina and Doctor Dexter, and it's not for me to ask either one of 'em, though I don't doubt some of the sewin' society 'll make an errand to Evelina's to find out. I've got to keep 'em off 'n her, if I can, and that's a big job for one woman to tackle.

"Anyhow, she got burnt and got burnt awful, and it was at his house that it happened. It was shameless, the way Evelina carried on. Why, if you'll believe me, she'd actually go to his house when there wa'n't no need of it--nobody sick, nor no medicine to be bought, nor anything. Some said they was goin' to be married."

The scorn which Miss Mehitable managed to throw into the word "married" indicated that the state was the crowning ignominy of the race. The girl's cheek flamed into crimson, for her own mother had been married, and everybody knew it. Sometimes the deep disgrace seemed almost too much for Araminta to endure.

"That's what comes of it," explained Miss Hitty, patiently, as a teacher might point to a demonstration clearly made out on a blackboard for an eager class. "If she'd stayed at home as a girl should stay, and hadn't gone to Doctor Dexter's, she wouldn't have got burnt. Anybody can see that.

"There was so much goin' on at the time that I sorter lost track of everything, otherwise I'd have known more about it, but I guess I know as much as anybody ever knew. Evelina was to Doctor Dexter's--shameless hussy that she was--and she got burnt. She was there all the afternoon and they took her to the hospital in the city on the night train and she stayed there until she was well, but she never came back here until just now. Her mother went with her to take care of her and before Evelina came out of the hospital, her mother keeled over and died. Sarah Grey always had a weak heart and a weak head to match it. If she hadn't have had, she'd have brought up Evelina different,

"Neither of 'em was ever in the house again. Neither one ever came back, even for their clothes. They had plenty of money, then, and they just bought new ones. When the word come that Evelina was burnt, Sarah Grey just put on her hat and locked her doors and run up to Doctor Dexter's. Nobody ever heard from them again until Jim Gardner's second cousin on his father's side sent a paper with Sarah Grey's obituary in it. And now, after twenty-five years, Evelina's come back.

"The poor soul's just sittin' there, in all the dust and cobwebs. When I get time, I aim to go over there and clean up the house for her--'t ain't decent for a body to live like that. I'll take you with me, to help scrub, and what I'm telling you all this for is so 's you won't ask any questions, nor act as if you thought it was queer for a woman to wear a white veil all the time. You'll have to act as if nothing was out of the way at all, and not look at her any more than you can help. Just pretend it's the style to wear a veil pinned to your hair all the time, and you've been wearin' one right along and have forgot and left it to home. Do you understand me?"

"Yes, Aunt Hitty."

"And when people come here to find out about it, you're not to say anything. Leave it all to me. 'T ain't necessary for you to lie, but you can keep your mouth shut. And I hope you see now what it means to a woman to walk straight on her own path that the Lord has laid out for her, and to let men alone. They're pizen, every one of 'em."

Nun-like, Araminta sat in her chair and sewed steadily at her dainty seam, but, none the less, she was deeply stirred with pity for women who so forgot themselves--who had not Aunt Hitty's superior wisdom. At the end of the prayer which Miss

Mehitable had taught the child, and which the woman still repeated in her nightly devotions, was this eloquent passage:

"And, Oh Lord, keep me from the contamination of marriage. For Thy sake. Amen."

"Araminta," said Aunt Hitty, severely, "cover up your foot!" Modestly, Araminta drew down her skirt. One foot was on the immaculate footstool and her ankle was exposed to view--a lovely ankle, in spite of the broad-soled, common-sense shoes which she always wore.

"How often have I told you to keep your ankles covered ?" demanded Miss Mehitable. "Suppose the minister had come in suddenly! Suppose--upon my word! Speakin' of angels--if there ain't the minister now!"

The Reverend Austin Thorpe came slowly up the brick-bordered path, his head bowed in thought. He was painfully near-sighted, but he refused to wear glasses. On the doorstep he paused and wiped his feet upon the corn-husk mat until even Miss Mehitable, beaming at him through the window, thought he was overdoing it. Unconsciously, she took credit to herself for the minister's neatness.

Stepping carefully, lest he profane the hall carpet by wandering off the rug, the minister entered the parlour, having first taken off his coat and hat and hung them upon their appointed hooks in the hall. It was cold, and the cheery warmth of the room beckoned him in. He did not know that he tried Miss Hitty by trespassing, so to speak, upon her preserves. She would have been better pleased if he remained in his room when he was not at the table or out, but, to do him justice, the reverend gentleman did not often offend her thus.

Araminta, blushing, took her foot from the footstool and pulled feverishly at her skirts. As Mr. Thorpe entered the room, she did not look up, but kept her eyes modestly upon her work.

"There ain't no need to tear out the gathers," Miss Hitty said, in a warning undertone, referring to Aramlnta's skirts. "Why, Mr. Thorpe! How you surprised me! Come in and set a spell," she added, grudgingly.

Steering well away from the centre-table with its highly prized ornament, Thorpe gained the chair in which, if he did not lean against the tidy, he was permitted to sit. He held himself bolt upright and warmed his hands at the stove. "It is good to be out," he said, cheerfully, "and good to come in again. A day like this makes one appreciate the blessing of a home."

Miss Hitty watched the white-haired, inoffensive old man with the keen scrutiny of an eagle guarding its nest. He did not lean upon the tidy, nor rest his elbows upon the crocheted mats which protected the arms of the chair. In short, he conducted himself as a gentleman should when in the parlour of a lady.

His blue, near-sighted eyes rested approvingly upon Araminta. "How the child grows!" he said, with a friendly smile upon his kindly old face. "Soon we shall have a young lady on our hands."

Araminta coloured and bent more closely to her sewing.

"I hope I'm not annoying you?" questioned the minister, after an interval.

"Not at all," said Miss Mehitable, politely.

"I wanted to ask about some one," pursued the Reverend Mr. Thorpe. "It seems that there is a new tenant in the old house on the hill that has been empty for so long--the one the village people say is haunted. It seems a woman is living there, quite alone; and she always wears a veil, on account of some--some disfigurement."

Miss Hitty's false teeth clicked, sharply, but there was no other sound except the clock, which, in the pause, struck four. "I thought--" continued the minister, with a rising inflection.

Hitherto, he had found his hostess of invaluable assistance in his parish work. It had been necessary to mention only the name. As upon the turning of a faucet a stream of information gushed forth from the fountain of her knowledge. Age, date and place of birth, ancestry on both sides three generations back, with complete and illuminating biographical details of ancestry and individual; education, financial standing, manner of living, illnesses in the family, including dates and durations of said illnesses, accidents, if any, medical attendance, marriages, births, deaths, opinions, reverses, present locations and various careers of descendants, list of misfortunes, festivities, entertainments, church affiliation past and present, political leanings, and a vast amount of other personal data had been immediately forthcoming. Tagged to it, like the postscript of a woman's letter, was Miss Hitty's own concise, permanent, neatly labelled opinion of the family or individual, the latter thrown in without extra charge.

"Perhaps you didn't know," remarked the minister, "that such a woman had come." His tone was inquiring. It seemed to him that something must be wrong if she did not know.

"Minty," said Miss Hitty, abruptly, "leave the room!"

Araminta rose, gathered up her patchwork, and went out, carefully closing the door. It was only in moments of great tenderness that her aunt called her "Minty."

The light footsteps died away upon the stairs. Tactlessly, the minister persisted. "Don't you know?" he asked.

Miss Mehitable turned upon him. "If I did," she replied, hotly, "I wouldn't tell any prying, gossiping man. I never knew before it was part of a minister's business to meddle in folks' private affairs. You'd better be writing your sermon and studyin' up on hell."

"I--I--" stammered the minister, taken wholly by surprise, "I only hoped to give her the consolation of the church."

"Consolation nothing!" snorted Miss Hitty. "Let her alone!" She went out of the room and slammed the door furiously, leaving the Reverend Austin Thorpe overcome with deep and lasting amazement.

VI
Pipes o' Pan

Sleet had fallen in the night, but at sunrise, the storm ceased. Miss Evelina had gone to sleep, lulled into a sense of security by the icy fingers tapping at her cobwebbed window pane. She awoke in a transfigured world. Every branch and twig was encased in crystal, upon which the sun was dazzling. Jewels, poised in midair, twinkled with the colours of the rainbow. On the tip of the cypress at the gate was a ruby, a sapphire gleamed from the rose-bush, and everywhere were diamonds and pearls.

Frosty vapour veiled the spaces between the trees and javelins of sunlight pierced it here and there. Beyond, there were glimpses of blue sky, and drops of water, falling from the trees, made a musical, cadence upon the earth beneath.

Miss Evelina opened her window still more. The air was peculiarly soft and sweet. It had the fragrance of opening buds and growing things and still had not lost the tang of the frost.

She drew a long breath of it and straightway was uplifted, though seemingly against her will. Spring was stirring at the heart of the world, sending new currents of sap into the veins of the trees, new aspirations into dead roots and fibres, fresh hopes of bloom into every sleeping rose. Life incarnate knocked at the wintry tomb; eager, unseen hands were rolling away the stone. The tide of the year was rising, soon to break into the wonder of green boughs and violets, shimmering wings and singing winds.

The cold hand that clutched her heart took a firmer hold. With acute self-pity, she perceived her isolation. Of all the world, she alone was set apart; branded, scarred, locked in a prison house that had no door. The one release was denied her until she could get away.

Poverty had driven her back. Circumstances outside her control had pushed her through the door she had thought never to enter again. Through all the five-and-twenty years, she had thought of the house with a shudder, peopling it with a thousand terrors, not knowing that there was no terror save her own fear.

Sorrow had put its chains upon her suddenly, at a time when she had not the strength to break the bond. At first she had struggled; then ceased. Since then, her faculties had been in suspense, as it were. She had forgotten laughter, veiled herself from joy, and walked hand in hand with the grisly phantom of her own conjuring.

Behind the shelter of her veil she had mutely prayed for peace--she dared not ask for more. And peace had never come. Her crowning humiliation would be to meet Anthony Dexter face to face--to know him, and to have him know her. Not knowing where he was, she had travelled far to avoid him. Now, seeking the last refuge, the one place on earth where he could not be, she found herself separated from him by less than a mile. More than that, she had gone to his house, as she had gone on the fateful day a quarter of a century ago. She had taken back the pearls, and had not died in doing it. Strangely enough, it had given her a vague relief.

Miss Evelina's mind had paused at twenty; she had not grown. The acute suffering of Youth was still upon her, a woman of forty-five. It was as though a clock had gone on ticking and the hands had never moved; the dial of her being was held at that dread hour, while her broken heart beat on.

She had not discovered that secret compensation which clings to the commonest affairs of life. One sees before him a mountain of toil, an apparently endless drudgery from which there is no escape. Having once begun it, an interest appears unexpectedly; new forces ally themselves with the fumbling hands. Misfortunes come, "not singly, but in battalions." After the first shock of realisation, one perceives through the darkness that the strength to bear them has come also, like some good angel.

A lover shudders at the thought of Death, yet knows that some day, on the road they walk together, the Grey Angel with the white poppies will surely take one of them by the hand. The road winds through shadows, past many strange and difficult places, and wrecks are strewn all along the way. They laugh at the storms that beat upon them, take no reck of bruised feet nor stumbling, for, behold, they are together, and in that one word lies all.

Sometimes, in the mist ahead, which, as they enter it, is seen to be wholly of tears, the road forks blindly, and there is nothing but night ahead for each. The Grey Angel with the unfathomable eyes approaches slowly, with no sound save the hushed murmur of wings. The dread white poppies are in his outstretched hand-- the great, nodding white poppies which have come from the dank places and have never known the sun.

There is no possible denial. At first, one knows only that the faithful hand has grown cold, then, that it has unclasped. In the intolerable darkness, one fares forth alone on the other fork of the road, too stricken for tears.

At length there is a change. Memories troop from the shadow to whisper consolation, to say that Death himself is powerless against Love, when a heart is deep enough to hold a grave. The clouds lift, and through the night comes some stray gleam of dawn. No longer cold, the dear hand nestles once more into the one that held it so long. Not as an uncertain presence but as a loved reality, that other abides with him still.

Shut out forever from the possibility of estrangement, for there is always that drop of bitterness in the cup of Life and Love; eternally beyond the reach of misunderstanding or change, spared the pitfalls and disasters of the way ahead, blinded no longer by the mists of earth, but immortally and unchangeably his, that other fares with him, though unseen, upon the selfsame road.

From the broken night comes singing, for the white poppies have also brought balm. Step by step, his Sorrow has become his friend, and at the last, when the old feet are weary and the steep road has grown still more steep, the Grey Angel comes once more.

Past the mist of tears in which he once was shrouded, the face of the Grey Angel is seen to be wondrously kind. By his mysterious alchemy, he has crystallised the doubtful waters, which once were in the cup of Life and Love, into a jewel which has no flaw. He has kept the child forever a child, caught the maiden at the noon of her beauty to enshrine her thus for always in the heart that loved her most; made the true and loving comrade a comrade always, though on the highways of the vast Unknown.

It is seen now that the road has many windings and that, unconsciously, the wayfarer has turned back. Eagerly the trembling hands reach forward to take the

white poppies, and the tired eyes close as though the silken petals had already fluttered downward on the lids, for, radiant past all believing, the Grey Angel still holds
the Best Beloved by the hand, and the roads that long ago had forked in darkness,
have come together, in more than mortal dawn, at the selfsame place.

Upon the beauty of the crystalline March morning, the memory of the Winter
sorrow still lay. The bare, brown earth was not wholly hidden by the mantle of
sleet and snow, yet there was some intangible Easter close at hand. Miss Evelina
felt it, stricken though she was.

From a distant thicket came a robin's cheery call, a glimmer of blue wings
flashed across the desolate garden, a south wind stirred the bending, icy branches
to a tinkling music, and she knew that Spring had come to all but her.

Some indefinite impulse sent her outdoors. Closely veiled, she started off down
the road, looking neither to the right nor the left. Miss Hitty saw her pass, but gra-
ciously forbore to call to her; Araminta looked up enquiringly from her sewing, but
the question died on her lips.

Down through the village she went, across the tracks, and up to the river road.
It had been a favourite walk of hers in her girlhood. Then she had gone with a
quick, light step; now she went slowly, like one grown old.

Yet, all unconsciously, life was quickening in her pulses; the old magic of Spring
was stirring in her, too. Dark and deep, the waters of the river rolled dreamily by,
waiting for the impulse which should send the shallows singing to the sea, and stir
the depths to a low, murmurous symphony.

Upon the left, as she walked, the road was bordered with elms and maples,
stretching far back to the hills. The woods were full of unsuspected ravines and
hollows, queer winding paths, great rocks, and tiny streams. The children had
called it the enchanted forest, and played that a fairy prince and princess dwelt
therein.

The childhood memories came back to Evelina with a pang. She stopped to
wipe away the tears beneath her veil, to choke back a sob that tightened her throat.
Suddenly, she felt a presentiment of oncoming evil, a rushing destiny that could not
be swerved aside. Frightened, she turned to go back; then stopped again.

From above, on the upper part of the road, came the tread of horse's feet and
the murmur of wheels. Her face paled to marble, her feet refused to move. The

heart within her stood portentously still. With downcast eyes she stood there, petrified, motionless, like a woman carved in stone and clothed in black, veiled impenetrably in chiffon.

At a furious pace, Anthony Dexter dashed by, his face as white as her chiffon. She had known unerringly who was coming; and had felt the searing consciousness of his single glance before, with a muttered oath, he had lashed his horse to a gallop. This, then, was the last; there was nothing more.

The sound of the wheels died away in the distance. He had the pearls, he had seen her, he knew that she had come back. And still she lived.

Clear and high, like a bugle call, a strain of wild music came from the enchanted forest. Evelina threw back her head, gasping for breath; her sluggish feet stirred forward. Some forgotten valour of her spirit leaped to answer the summons, as a soldier, wounded unto death, turns to follow the singing trumpets that lead the charge.

Strangely soft and tender, the strain came again, less militant, less challenging. Swiftly upon its echo breathed another, hinting of peace. Shaken to her inmost soul by agony, she took heed of the music with the precise consciousness one gives to trifles at moments of unendurable stress. Blindly she turned into the forest.

"What was it?" she asked herself, repeatedly, wondering that she could even hear at a time like this. A bird? No, there was never a bird to sing like that. Almost it might be Pan himself with his syrinx, walking abroad on the first day of Spring.

The fancy appealed to her strongly, her swirling senses having become exquisitely acute. "Pipes o' Pan," she whispered, "I will find and follow you." To see the face of Pan meant death, according to the old Greek legend, but death was something of which she was not afraid.

Lyric, tremulous, softly appealing, the music came again. The bare boughs bent with their chiming crystal, and a twig fell at her feet, Sunlight starred the misty distance with pearl; shining branches swayed to meet her as she passed.

Farther in the wood, she turned, unconsciously in pursuit of that will-o'-the-wisp of sound. Here and there out of the silence, it came to startle her; to fill her with strange forebodings which were not wholly of pain.

Some subliminal self guided her, for heart and soul were merged in a quivering ecstasy of torture which throbbed and thundered and overflowed. "He saw me! He saw me! He saw me! He knew me! He knew me! He knew me!" In a triple rhythm the words vibrated back and forth unceasingly, as though upon a weaver's shuttle.

For nearly an hour she went blindly in search of the music, pausing now and then to listen intently, at times disheartened enough to turn back. She had a mad fancy that Death was calling her, from some far height, because Anthony Dexter had passed her on the road.

Now trumpet-like and commanding, now tender and appealing, the mystic music danced about her capriciously. Her feet grew weary, but the blood and the love of life had begun to move in her, too, when her whole nature was unspeakably stirred. She paused and leaned against a tree, to listen for the pipes o' Pan. But all was silent; the white stillness of the enchanted forest was like that of another world. With a sigh, she turned to the left, reflecting that a long walk straight through the woods would bring her out on the other road at a point near her own home.

Exquisitely faint and tender, the call rang out again. It was like some far flute of April blown in a March dawn. "Oh, pipes o' Pan," breathed Evelina, behind her shielding veil; "I pray you find me! I pray you, give me joy--or death!"

Swiftly the music answered, like a trumpet chanting from a height. Scarcely knowing what she did, she began to climb the hill. It was a more difficult way, but a nearer one, for just beyond the hill was her house.

Half-way up the ascent, the hill sloped back. There was a small level place where one might rest before going on to the summit. It was not more than a little nook, surrounded by pines. As she came to it, there was a frightened chirp, and a flock of birds fluttered up from her feet, leaving a generous supply of crumbs and grain spread upon the earth.

Against a great tree leaned a man, so brown and shaggy in his short coat that he seemed like part of the tree trunk. He was of medium height, wore high leather gaiters, and a grey felt hat with a long red quill thrust rakishly through the band. His face was round and rosy and the kindest eyes in the world twinkled at Evelina from beneath his bushy eyebrows. At his feet, quietly happy, was a bright-eyed, yellow mongrel with a stubby tail which wagged violently as Evelina approached. Slung over the man's shoulder by a cord was a silver-mounted flute.

From his elevated position, he must have seen her when she entered the wood, and had glimpses of her at intervals ever since. It was evident that he thoroughly enjoyed the musical hide-and-seek he had forced her to play while he was feeding the birds. His eyes laughed and there were mischievous dimples in his round, rosy cheeks.

"Oh," cried Evelina, in a tone of dull disappointment.

"I called you," said the Piper, gently, "and you came."

She turned on her heel and walked swiftly away. She went downhill with more haste than dignity, turned to her right, and struck out through the woods for the main road.

The Piper watched her until she was lost among the trees. The birds came back for their crumbs and grain and he stood patiently until his feathered pensioners had finished and flown away, chirping with satisfaction. Then he stooped to pat the yellow mongrel.

"Laddie," he said, "I'm thinking there's no more gypsying for us just now. To-morrow, we will not pack our shop upon our back and march on, as we had thought to do. Some one needs us here, eh, Laddie?"

The dog capered about his master's feet as if he understood and fully agreed. He was a pitiful sort, even for a mongrel. One of his legs had been broken and unskilfully set, so he did not run quite like other dogs.

"'T isn't a very good leg, Laddie," the Piper observed, "but I'm thinking 't is better than none. Anyway, I did my best with it, and now we'll push on a bit. It's our turn to follow, and we 're fain, Laddie, you and I, to see where she lives."

Bidding the dog stay at heel, the Piper followed Miss Evelina's track. By dint of rapid walking, he reached the main road shortly after she did. Keeping a respectful distance, and walking at the side of the road, he watched her as she went home. From the safe shelter of a clump of alders just below Miss Mehitable's he saw the veiled figure enter the broken gate.

"'T is the old house, Laddie," he said to the dog; "the very one we were thinking of taking ourselves. Come on, now; we'll be going. Down, sir! Home!"

VII
"The Honour of the Spoken Word"

Anthony Dexter sat in his library, alone, as usual. Under the lamp, Ralph's letters were spread out before him, but he was not reading. Indeed, he knew every line of them by heart, but he could not keep his mind upon the letters.

Between his eyes and the written pages there came persistently a veiled figure, clothed shabbily in sombre black. Continually he fancied the horror the veil concealed; continually, out of the past, his cowardice and his shirking arose to confront him.

A photograph of his wife, who had died soon after Ralph was born, had been taken from the drawer. "A pretty, sweet woman," he mused. "A good wife and a good mother." He told himself again that he had loved her--that he loved her still.

Yet behind his thought was sure knowledge. The woman who had entered the secret fastnesses of his soul, and before whom he had trembled, was the one whom he had seen in the dead garden, frail as a ghost, and again on the road that morning.

Dimly, and now for the first time, there came to his perception that recognition of his mate which each man carries in his secret heart when he has found his mate at all. Past the anguish that lay between them like a two-edged sword, and through the mists of the estranging years, Evelina had come back to claim her own.

He saw that they were bound together, scarred in body or scarred in soul; crippled, mutilated, or maimed though either or both might be, the one significant fact was not altered.

He knew now that his wife and the mother of his child had stood outside, as all women but the one must ever stand. Nor did he guess that she had known it from the first and that heart-hunger had hastened her death.

Aside from a very deep-seated gratitude to her for his son, Anthony Dexter cherished no emotion for the sake of his dead wife. She had come and gone across his existence as a butterfly crosses a field, touching lightly here and there, but lingering not at all. Except for Ralph, it was as though she had never been, so little did she now exist for him.

Yet Evelina was vital, alive, and out of the horror she had come back. To him? He did not believe that she had come definitely to seek him--he knew her pride too well for that. His mind strove to grasp the reason of her coming, but it eluded him; evaded him at every point. She had not forgotten; if she had, she would not have given back that sinuous necklace of discoloured pearls.

By the way, what had he done with the necklace? He remembered now. He had thrown it far into the shrubbery, for the pearls were dead and the love was dead.

"First from the depths of the sea and then from the depths of my love." The mocking words, written in faded ink on the yellowed slip of paper, danced impishly across the pages of Ralph's letters. He had a curious fancy that if his love had been deep enough the pearls would not have turned black.

Impatiently, he rose from the table and paced back and forth restlessly across the library. "I'm a fool," he growled; "a doddering old fool. No, that's not it--I've worked too hard."

Valiantly he strove to dispel the phantoms that clustered about him. A light step behind him chimed in with his as he walked and he feared to look around, not knowing it was but the echo of his own.

He went to a desk in the corner of the room and opened a secret drawer that had not been opened for a long time. He took out a photograph, wrapped in yellowed tissue paper, and went back to the table. He unwrapped it, his blunt white fingers trembling ever so slightly, and sat down.

A face of surpassing loveliness looked back at him. It was Evelina, at the noon of her girlish beauty, her face alight with love. Anthony Dexter looked long at the perfect features, the warm, sweet, tempting mouth, the great, trusting eyes, and the brown hair that waved so softly back from her face; the all-pervading and abiding womanliness. There was strength as well as beauty; tenderness, courage, charm.

"Mate for a man," said Dexter, aloud. For such women as Evelina, the knights of old did battle, and men of other centuries fought with their own temptations and weaknesses. It was such as she who led men to the heights, and pointed them to heights yet farther on.

Insensibly, he compared Ralph's mother with Evelina. The two women stood as far apart as a little, meaningless song stands from a great symphony. One would fire a man with high ambition, exalt him with noble striving--ah, but had she? Was it Evelina's fault that Anthony Dexter was a coward and a shirk? Cravenly, he began to blame the woman, to lay the burden of his own shortcomings at Evelina's door.

Yet still the face stirred him. There was life in those walled fastnesses of his nature which long ago he had denied. Self-knowledge at last confronted him, and would not be put away.

"And so, Evelina," he said aloud, "you have come back. And what do you want? What can I do for you?"

The bell rang sharply, as if answering his question. He started from his chair, having heard no approaching footsteps. He covered the photograph of Evelina with Ralph's letters, but the sweet face of the boy's mother still looked out at him from its gilt frame.

The old housekeeper went to the door with the utmost leisure. It seemed to him an eternity before the door was opened. He stood there, waiting, summoning his faculties of calmness and his powers of control, to meet Evelina--to have out, at last, all the shame of the years.

But it was not Evelina. The Reverend Austin Thorpe was wiping his feet carefully upon the door-mat, and asking in deep, vibrant tones: "Is the Doctor in?"

Anthony Dexter could have cried out from relief. When the white-haired old man came in, floundering helplessly among the furniture, as a near-sighted person does, he greeted him with a cordiality that warmed his heart.

"I am glad," said the minister, "to find you in. Sometimes I am not so fortunate. I came late, for that reason."

"I've been busy," returned the Doctor. "Sit down."

The minister sank into an easy chair and leaned toward the light. "I wish I could have a lamp like this in my room," he remarked. "It gives a good light."

"You can have this one," returned Dexter, with an hysterical laugh,

"I was not begging," said Mr. Thorpe, with dignity. "Miss Mehitable's lamps are all small. Some of them give no more light than a candle."

"'How far that little candle throws its beams,'" quoted Dexter. "'So shines a good deed in a naughty world.'"

There was a long interval of silence. Sometimes Thorpe and Doctor Dexter would sit for an entire evening with less than a dozen words spoken on either side, yet feeling the comfort of human companionship.

"I was thinking," said, Thorpe, finally, "of the supreme isolation of the human soul. You and I sit here, talking or not, as the mood strikes us, and yet, what does speech matter? You know no more of me than I choose to give you, nor I of you."

"No," responded Dexter, "that is quite true." He did not realise what Thorpe had just said, but he felt that it was safe to agree.

"One grows morbid in thinking of it," pursued Thorpe, screening his blue eyes from the light with his hand. "We are like a vast plain of mountain peaks. Some of us have our heads in the clouds always, up among the eternal snows. Thunders boom about us, lightning rives us, storm and sleet beat upon us. There is a rumbling on some distant peak and we know that it rains there, too. That is all we ever know. We are not quite sure when our neighbours are happy or when they are troubled; when there is sun and when there is storm. The secret forces in the interior of the mountain work on unceasingly. The distance hides it all. We never get near enough to another peak to see the scars upon its surface, to know of the dead timber and the dried streams, the marks of avalanches and glacial drift, the precipices and pitfalls, the barren wastes. In blue, shimmering distance, the peaks are veiled and all seem fair but our own."

At the word "veiled," Dexter shuddered. "Very pretty," he said, with a forced laugh which sounded flat. "Why don't you put it into a sermon?"

Thorpe's face became troubled. "My sermons do not please," he answered, with touching simplicity. "They say there is not enough of hell."

"I'm satisfied," commented the Doctor, in a grating voice. "I think there's plenty of hell."

"You never come to church," remarked the minister, not seeing the point.

"There's hell enough outside--for any reasonable mortal," returned Dexter. He was keyed to a high pitch. He felt that, at any instant, something might snap and leave him inert.

Thorpe sighed. His wrinkled old hand strayed out across the papers and turned the face of Ralph's mother toward him. He studied it closely, not having seen it before. Then he looked up at the Doctor, whose face was again like a mask.

"Your--?" A lift of the eyebrows finished the question.

Dexter nodded, with assumed carelessness. There was another long pause.

"Sometimes I envy you," said Thorpe, laying the picture down carefully, "you have had so much of life and joy. I think it is better for you to have had her and lost her than not to have had her at all," he continued, unconsciously paraphrasing. "Even in your loneliness, you have the comfort of memory, and your boy--I have wondered what a son might mean to me, now, in my old age. Dead though she is, you know she still loves you; that somewhere she is waiting to take your hand in hers."

"Don't!" cried Dexter. The strain was well-nigh insupportable.

"Forgive me, my friend," returned Thorpe, quickly. "I--" Then he paused. "As I was saying," he went on, after a little, "I have often envied you."

"Don't," said Dexter, again. "As you were also saying, distance hides the peak and you do not see the scars."

Thorpe's eyes sought the picture of Dexter's wife with an evident tenderness, mingled with yearning. "I often think," he sighed, "that in Heaven we may have a chance to pay our debt to woman. Through woman's agony we come into the world, by woman's care we are nourished, by woman's wisdom we are taught, by woman's love we are sheltered, and, at the last, it is a woman who closes our eyes. At every crisis of a man's life, a woman is always waiting, to help him if she may, and I have seen that at any crisis in a woman's life, we are apt to draw back and shirk. She helps us bear our difficulties; she faces hers alone."

Dexter turned uneasily in his chair. His face was inscrutable. The silent moment cried out for speech--for anything to relieve the tension. Through Ralph's letters Evelina's eyes seemed to be upon him, beseeching him to speak.

"I knew a man,", said Anthony Dexter, hoarsely, "who unintentionally contracted quite an unusual debt to a woman."

"Yes?" returned, Thorpe, inquiringly. He was interested.

"He was a friend of mine," the Doctor continued, with difficulty, "or rather a classmate. I knew him best at college and afterward--only slightly."

"The debt," Thorpe reminded him, after a pause. "You were speaking, of his debt to a woman."

Dexter turned his face away from Thorpe and from the accusing eyes beneath Ralph's letters. "She was a very beautiful girl," he went on, carefully choosing his words, "and they loved each other as people love but once. My--my friend was much absorbed in chemistry and had a fondness for original experiment. She--the girl, you know--used to study with him. He was teaching her and she often helped him in the laboratory.

"They were to be married," continued Dexter. "The day before they were to be married, he went to her house and invited her to come to the laboratory to see an experiment which he was trying for the first time and which promised to be unusually interesting. I need not explain the experiment--you would not understand.

"On the way to the laboratory, they were talking, as lovers will. She asked him if he loved her because she was herself; because, of all the women in the world, she was the one God meant for him, or if he loved her because he thought her beautiful.

"He said that he loved her because she was herself, and, most of all, because she was his. 'Then,' she asked, timidly, 'when I am old and all the beauty has gone, you will love me still? It will be the same, even when I am no longer lovely?'

"He answered her as any man would, never dreaming how soon he was to be tested.

"In the laboratory, they were quite alone. He began the experiment, explaining as he went, and she watched it as eagerly as he. He turned away for a moment, to get another chemical. As he leaned over the retort to put it in, he heard it seethe. With all her strength, she pushed him away instantly. There was an explosion which shook the walls of the laboratory, a quantity of deadly gas was released, and, in the fumes, they both fainted.

"When he came to his senses, he learned that she had been terribly burned, and had been taken on the train to the hospital. He was the one physician in the place and it was the only thing to be done.

"As soon as he could, he went to the hospital. They told him there that her life would be saved and they hoped for her eyesight, but that she would be permanently and horribly disfigured. All of her features were destroyed, they said--she would be only a pitiful wreck of a woman."

Thorpe was silent. His blue eyes were dim with pity. Dexter rose and stood in front of him. "Do you understand?" he asked, in a voice that was almost unrecognisable. "His face was close to the retort when she pushed him away. She saved his life and he went away--he never saw her again. He left her without so much as a word."

"He went away?" asked the minister, incredulously. "Went away and left her when she had so much to bear? Deserted her when she needed him to help her bear it, and when she had saved him from death, or worse?"

"You would not believe it possible?" queried Dexter, endeavouring to make his voice even.

"Of a cur, yes," said the minister, his voice trembling with indignation, "but of a man, no."

Anthony Dexter shrank back within himself. He was breathing heavily, but his companion did not notice.

"It was long ago," the Doctor continued, when he had partially regained his composure. He dared not tell Thorpe that the man had married in the meantime, lest he should guess too much. "The woman still lives, and my--friend lives also. He has never felt right about it. What should he do?"

"The honour of the spoken word still holds him," said Thorpe, evenly. "As I understand, he asked her to marry him and she consented. He was never released from his promise--did not even ask for it. He slunk away like a cur. In the sight of God he is bound to her by his own word still. He should go to her and either fulfil his promise or ask for release. The tardy fulfilment of his promise would be the only atonement he could make."

The midnight train came in and stopped, but neither heard it.

"It would be very difficult," Thorpe was saying, "to retain any shred of respect for a man like that. It shows your broad charity when you call him 'friend.' I myself have not so much grace."

Anthony Dexter's breath came painfully. He tightened his fingers on the arm of the chair and said nothing.

"It is a peculiar coincidence," mused Thorpe, He was thinking aloud now. "In the old house just beyond Miss Mehitable's, farther up, you know, a woman has just come to live who seems to have passed through something like that. It would be strange, would it not, if she were the one whom your--friend--had wronged?"

"Very," answered Dexter, in a voice the other scarcely heard.

"Perhaps, in this way, we may bring them together again. If the woman is here, and you can find your friend, we may help him to wash the stain of cowardice off his soul. Sometimes," cried Thorpe passionately, "I think there is no sin but shirking. I can excuse a liar, I can pardon a thief, I can pity a murderer, but a shirk--no!" His voice broke and his wrinkled old hands trembled.

"My--my friend," lied Anthony Dexter, wiping the cold sweat from his forehead, "lives abroad. I have no way of finding him."

"It is a pity," returned Thorpe. "Think of a man meeting his God like that! It tempts one to believe in a veritable hell!"

"I think there is a veritable hell," said Dexter, with a laugh which was not good to hear. "I think, by this time, my friend must believe in it as well. I remember that he did not, before the--it, I mean, happened."

Far from feeling relief, Anthony Dexter was scourged anew. A thousand demons leaped from the silence to mock him; the earth rolled beneath his feet. The impulse of confession was strong upon him, even in the face of Thorpe's scorn. He wondered why only one church saw the need of the confessional, why he could not go, even to Thorpe, and share the burden that oppressed his guilty soul.

The silence was not to be borne. The walls of the room swayed back and forth, as though they were of fabric and stirred by all the winds of hell. The floor undulated; his chair sank dizzily beneath him.

Dexter struggled to his feet, clutching convulsively at the table. His lips were parched and his tongue clung to the roof of his mouth. "Thorpe," he said, in a hoarse whisper, "I----"

The minister raised his hand. "Listen! I thought I heard----"

A whistle sounded outside, the gate clanged shut. A quick, light step ran up the walk, the door opened noisily, and a man rushed in. He seemed to bring into that hopeless place all the freshness of immortal Youth.

Blinded, Dexter moved forward, his hands outstretched to meet that eager clasp.

"Father! Father!" cried Ralph, joyously; "I've come home!"

VIII
Piper Tom

L addie," said the Piper to the yellow mongrel, "we'll be having breakfast now."

The dog answered with a joyous yelp. "You talk too much," observed his master, in affectionate reproof; "'t is fitting that small yellow dogs should be seen and not heard."

It was scarcely sunrise, but the Piper's day began--and ended--early. He had a roaring fire in the tiny stove which warmed his shop, and the tea-kettle hummed cheerily. All about him was the atmosphere of immaculate neatness. It was not merely the lack of dust and dirt, but a positive cleanliness.

His beardless face was youthful, but the Piper's hair was tinged with grey at the temples. One judged him to be well past forty, yet fully to have retained his youth. His round, rosy mouth was puckered in a whistle as he moved about the shop and spread the tiny table with a clean cloth.

Ranged about him in orderly rows was his merchandise. Tom Barnaby never bothered with fixtures and showcases. Chairs, drygoods boxes, rough shelves of his own making, and a few baskets sufficed him.

In the waterproof pedler's pack which he carried on his back when his shop was in transit, he had only the smaller articles which women continually need. Calico, mosquito netting, buttons, needles, thread, tape, ribbons, stationery, hooks and eyes, elastic, shoe laces, sewing silk, darning cotton, pins, skirt binding, and a few small frivolities in the way of neckwear, veils, and belts--these formed Piper Tom's stock in trade. By dint of close packing, he wedged an astonishing number of things into a small space, and was not too heavily laden when, with his dog and his flute, he set forth upon the highway to establish his shop in the next place that seemed promising.

"All unknowing, Laddie," he said to the dog, as he sat down to his simple breakfast, "we've come into competition with a woman who keeps a shop like ours, which we didn't mean to do. It's for this that we were making a new set of price tags all day of yesterday, which happened to be the Sabbath. It wouldn't be becoming of us to charge less than she and take her trade away from her, so we've started out on an even basis.

"Poor lady," laughed the Piper, "she was not willing for us to know her prices, thinking we were going to sell cheaper than she. 'T is a hard world for women, Laddie. I'm thinking 'tis no wonder they grow suspicious at times."

The dog sat patiently till Piper Tom finished his breakfast, well knowing that a generous share would be given him outside. While the dog ate, his master put the shop into the most perfect order, removing every particle of dust, and whistling meanwhile.

When the weather permitted, the shop was often left to keep itself, the door being hospitably propped open with a brick, while the dog and his master went gypsying. With a ragged, well-worn book in one pocket, a parcel of bread and cheese in another, and his flute slung over his shoulder, the Piper was prepared to spend the day abroad. He carried, too, a bone for the dog, well wrapped in newspaper, and an old silver cup to drink from.

Having finished his breakfast, the dog scampered about eagerly, indicating, by many leaps and barks, that it was time to travel, but the Piper raised his hand.

"Not to-day, Laddie," he said. "If we travel to-day, we'll not be going far. Have you forgotten that 't was only day before yesterday we found our work? Come here."

The dog seated himself before the Piper, his stubby tail wagging impatiently.

"She's a poor soul, Laddie," sighed the Piper, at length. "I'm thinking she's seen Sorrow face to face and has never had the courage to turn away. She was walking in the woods, trying to find the strange music, and was disappointed when she saw 't was only us. We must make her glad 't was us."

After a long time, the Piper spoke again, with a lingering tenderness. "She must be very beautiful, I'm thinking, Laddie; else she would not hide her face. Very beautiful and very sad."

When the sun was high, Piper Tom climbed the hill, followed by his faithful dog. On his shoulder he bore a scythe and under the other arm was a spade. He entered Miss Evelina's gate without ceremony and made a wry face as he looked about him. He scarcely knew where to begin.

The sound of the wide, even strokes roused Miss Evelina from her lethargy, and she went to the window, veiled. At first she was frightened when she saw the queer man whom she had met in the woods hard at work in her garden.

The red feather in his hat bobbed cheerfully up and down, the little yellow dog ran about busily, and the Piper was whistling lustily an old, half-forgotten tune.

She watched him for some time, then a new thought frightened her again. She had no money with which to pay him for clearing out her garden, and he would undoubtedly expect payment. She must go out and tell him not to work any more; that she did not wish to have the weeds removed.

Cringing before the necessity, she went out. The Piper did not see her until she was very near him, then, startled in his turn, he said, "Oh!" and took off his hat.

"Good-morning, madam," he went on, making a low bow. She noted that the tip of his red feather brushed the ground. "What can I do for you, more than I'm doing now?"

"It is about that," stammered Evelina, "that I came. You must not work in my garden."

"Surely," said the Piper, "you don't mean that! Would you have it all weeds? And 't is hard work for such as you."

"I--I--" answered Miss Evelina, almost in a whisper; "I have no money."

The Piper laughed heartily and put on his hat again. "Neither have I," he said, between bursts of seemingly uncalled-for merriment, "and probably I'm the only man in these parts who's not looking for it. Did you think I'd ask for pay for working in the garden?"

His tone made her feel that she had misjudged him and she did not know what to say in reply.

"Laddie and I have no garden of our own," he explained, "and so we're digging in yours. The place wants cleaning, for 't is a long time since any one cared enough for it to dig. I was passing, and I saw a place I thought I could make more pleasant. Have I your leave to try?"

"Why--why, yes," returned Miss Evelina, slowly. "If you'd like to, I don't mind."

He dismissed her airily, with a wave of his hand, and she went back into the house, never once turning her head.

"She's our work, Laddie," said the Piper, "and I'm thinking we've begun in the right way. All the old sadness is piled up in the garden, and I'm thinking there's weeds in her life, too, that it's our business to take out. At any rate, we'll begin here and do this first. One step at a time, Laddie--one step at a time. That's all we have to take, fortunately. When we can't see ahead, it's because we can't look around a corner."

All that day from behind her cobwebbed windows, Miss Evelina watched the Piper and his dog. Weeds and thistles fell like magic before his strong, sure strokes. He carried out armful after armful of rubbish and made a small-sized mountain in the road, confining it with stray boards and broken branches, as it was too wet to be burned.

Wherever she went, in the empty house, she heard that cheery, persistent whistle. As usual, Miss Hitty left a tray on her doorstep, laden with warm, whole-some food. Since that first day, she had made no attempt to see Miss Evelina. She brought her tray, rapped, and went away quietly, exchanging it for another when it was time for the next meal.

Meanwhile, Miss Evelina's starved body was responding, slowly but surely, to the simple, well-cooked food. Hitherto, she had not cared to eat and scarcely knew what she was eating. Now she had learned to discriminate between hot rolls and baking-powder biscuit, between thick soups and thin broths, custards and jellies.

Miss Evelina had wound one of the clocks, setting it by the midnight train, and loosening the machinery by a few drops of oil which she had found in an old bottle, securely corked. At eight, at one, and at six, Miss Hitty's tray was left at her back door--there had not been the variation of a minute since the first day. Preoccupied though she was, Evelina was not insensible of the kindness, nor of the fact that she was stronger, physically, than she had been for years.

And now in the desolate garden, there was visible evidence of more kindness. Perhaps the world was not wholly a place of grief and tears. Out there among the weeds a man laboured cheerfully--a man of whom she had no knowledge and upon whom she had no claim.

He sang and whistled as he strove mightily with the weeds. Now and then, he sharpened his scythe with his whetstone and attacked the dense undergrowth with yet more vigour. The little yellow mongrel capered joyfully and unceasingly, affecting to hide amidst the mass of rubbish, scrambling out with sharp, eager barks when his master playfully buried him, and retreating hastily before the oncoming scythe.

Miss Evelina could not hear, but she knew that the man was talking to the dog in the pauses of his whistling. She knew also that the dog liked it, even if he did not understand. She observed that the dog was not beautiful--could not be called so by any stretch of the imagination--and yet the man talked to him, made a friend of him, loved him.

At noon, the Piper laid down his scythe, clambered up on the crumbling stone wall, and ate his bread and cheese, while the dog nibbled at his bone. From behind a shutter in an upper room, Miss Evelina noted that the dog also had bread and cheese, sharing equally with his master.

The Piper went to the well, near the kitchen door, and drank copiously of the cool, clear water from his silver cup. Then he went back to work again.

Out in the road, the rubbish accumulated. When the Piper stood behind it. Miss Evelina could barely see the tip of the red feather that bobbed rakishly in his hat. Once he disappeared, leaving the dog to keep a reluctant guard over the spade and scythe. When he came back, he had a rake and a large basket, which made the collection of rubbish easier.

Safe in her house, Miss Evelina watched him idly. Her thought was taken from herself for the first time in all the five-and-twenty years. She contemplated anew the willing service of Miss Mehitable, who asked nothing of her except the privilege of leaving daily sustenance at her barred and forbidding door. "Truly," said Miss Evelina to herself, "it is a strange world."

The personality of the Piper affected her in a way she could not analyse. He did not attract her, neither was he wholly repellent. She did not feel friendly toward him, yet she could not turn wholly aside. There had been something strangely alluring in his music, which haunted her even now, though she resented his making game of her and leading her through the woods as he had.

Over and above and beyond all, she remembered the encounter upon the road, always with a keen, remorseless pain which cut at her heart like a knife. Miss Evelina thought she was familiar with knives, but this one hurt in a new way and cut, seemingly, at a place which had not been touched before.

Since the "white night" which had turned her hair to lustreless snow, nothing had hurt her so much. Her coming to the empty house, driven, as she was, by poverty--entering alone into a tomb of memories and dead happiness,--had not stabbed so deeply or so surely. She saw herself first on one peak and then on another, a valley of humiliation and suffering between which it had taken twenty-five years to cross. From the greatest hurt at the beginning to the greatest hurt--at the end? Miss Evelina started from her chair, her hands upon her leaping heart. The end? Ah, dear God, no! There was no end to grief like hers!

Insistently, through her memory, sounded the pipes o' Pan--the wild, sweet, tremulous strain which had led her away from the road where she had been splashed with the mud from Anthony Dexter's carriage wheels. The man with the red feather in his hat had called her, and she had come. Now he was digging in her garden, making the desolate place clean, if not cheerful.

Conscious of an unfamiliar detachment, Miss Evelina settled herself to think. The first hurt and the long pain which followed it, the blurred agony of remembrance when she had come back to the empty house, then the sharp, clean-cut stroke when she stood on the road, her eyes downcast, and heard the wheels rush by, then clear and challenging, the pipes o' Pan.

"'There is a divinity that shapes our ends,'" she thought, "'rough-hew them how we may.'" Where had she heard that before? She remembered, now--it was a favourite quotation of Anthony Dexter's.

Her lip curled scornfully. Was she never to be free from Anthony Dexter? Was she always to be confronted with his cowardice, his shirking, his spoken and written thoughts? Was she always to see his face as she had seen it last, his great love for her shining in his eyes for all the world to read? Was she to see forever his pearl necklace, discoloured, snaky, and cold, as meaningless as the yellow slip of paper that had come with it?

Where was the divinity that had shaped her course hither? Why had she been driven back to the place of her crucifixion, to stand veiled in the road while he drove by and splashed her with mud from his wheels?

Out in the garden, the Piper still strove with the weeds. He had the place nearly half cleared now. The space on the other side of the house was, as yet, untouched, and the trees and shrubbery all needed trimming. The wall was broken in places, earth had drifted upon it, and grass and weeds had taken root in the crevices.

Upon one side of the house, nearly all of the bare earth had been raked clean. He was on the western slope, now, where the splendid poppies had once grown. Pausing in his whistling, the Piper stooped and picked up some small object. Miss Evelina cowered behind her shielding shutters, for she guessed that he had found the empty vial which had contained laudanum.

The Piper sniffed twice at the bottle. His scent was as keen as a hunting dog's. Then he glanced quickly toward the house where Miss Evelina, unveiled, shrank back into the farthest corner of an upper room.

He walked to the gate, no longer whistling, and slowly, thoughtfully, buried it deep in the rubbish. Could Miss Evelina have seen his face, she would have marvelled at the tenderness which transfigured it and wondered at the mist that veiled his eyes.

He stood at the gate for a long time, leaning on his scythe, his back to the house. In sympathy with his master's mood, the dog was quiet, and merely nosed about among the rubbish. By a flash of intuition, Miss Evelina knew that the finding of the bottle had made clear to the Piper much that he had not known before.

She felt herself an open book before those kind, keen eyes, which neither sought nor avoided her veiled face. All the sorrow and the secret suffering would be his, if he chose to read it. Miss Evelina knew that she must keep away.

The sun set without splendour. Still the Piper stood there, leaning on his scythe, thinking. All the rubbish in the garden was old, except the empty laudanum bottle. The label was still legible, and also the warning word, "Poison." She had put it there herself--he had no doubt of that.

The dog whined and licked his master's hand, as though to say it was time to go home. At length the Piper roused himself and gathered up his tools. He carried them to a shed at the back of the house, and Miss Evelina, watching, knew that he was coming back to finish his self-appointed task.

"Yes," said the Piper, "we'll be going. 'T is not needful to bark."

He went down-hill slowly, the little dog trotting beside him and occasionally licking his hand. They went into the shop, the door of which was still propped open. The Piper built a fire, removed his coat and hat, took off his leggings, cleaned his boots, and washed his hands.

Then, unmindful of the fact that it was supper-time, he sat down. The dog sat down, too, pressing hard against him. The Piper took the dog's head between his hands and looked long into the loving, eager eyes.

"She will be very beautiful, Laddie," he sighed, at length, "very beautiful and very brave."

IX
Housecleaning

The brisk, steady tap sounded at Miss Evelina's door. It was a little after eight, and she opened it, expecting to find her breakfast, as usual. Much to her surprise, Miss Mehitable stood there, armed with a pail, mop, and broom. Behind her, shy and frightened, was Araminta, similarly equipped.

The Reverend Austin Thorpe, having carried a step-ladder to the back door, had then been abruptly dismissed. Under the handle of her scrubbing pail, the ministering angel had slipped the tray containing Miss Evelina's breakfast.

"I've slopped it over some," she said, in explanation, "but you won't mind that. Someway, I've never had hands enough to do what I've had to do. Most of the work in the world is slid onto women, and then, as if that wasn't enough, they're given skirts to hold up, too. Seems me that if the Almighty had meant for women to be carrying skirts all their lives, He'd have give us another hand and elbow in our backs, like a jinted stove-pipe, for the purpose. Not having the extra hand, I go short on skirts when I'm cleaning."

Miss Mehitable's clean, crisp, calico gown ceased abruptly at her ankles. Araminta's blue and white gingham was of a similar length, and her sleeves, guiltless of ruffles, came only to her dimpled elbows. Araminta was trying hard not to stare at Miss Evelina's veil while Aunt Hitty talked.

"We've come," asserted Miss Mehitable, "to clean your house. We've cleaned our own and we ain't tired yet, so we're going to do some scrubbing here. I guess it needs it."

Miss Evelina was reminded of the Piper, who was digging in her garden because he had no garden of his own. "I can't let you," she said, hesitating over the words. "You're too kind to me, and I'm going to do my cleaning myself."

"Fiddlesticks!" snorted Miss Hitty, brushing Miss Evelina from her path and marching triumphantly in. "You ain't strong enough to do cleaning. You just set down and eat your breakfast. Me and Minty will begin upstairs."

In obedience to a gesture from her aunt, Araminta crept upstairs. The house had not yet taken on a habitable look, and as she stood in the large front room, deep in dust and draped with cobwebs, she was afraid.

Meanwhile Miss Mehitable had built a fire in the kitchen stove, put kettles of water on to heat, stretched a line across the yard, and brought in the step-ladder. Miss Evelina sat quietly, and apparently took no notice of the stir that was going on about her. She had not touched her breakfast.

"Why don't you eat?" inquired Miss Hitty, not unkindly.

"I'm not hungry," returned Miss Evelina, timidly.

"Well," answered Miss Mehitable, her perception having acted in the interval, "I don't wonder you ain't, with all this racket goin' on. I'll be out of here in a minute and then you can set here, nice and quiet, and eat. I never like to eat when there's anything else going on around me. It drives me crazy."

True to her word, she soon ascended the stairs, where the quaking Araminta awaited her. "It'll take some time for the water to heat," observed Miss Hitty, "but there's plenty to do before we get to scrubbing. Remember what I've told you, Minty. The first step in cleaning a room is to take out of it everything that ain't nailed to it."

Every window was opened to its highest point. Some were difficult to move, but with the aid of Araminta's strong young arms, they eventually went up as desired. From the windows descended torrents of bedding, rugs, and curtains, a veritable dust storm being raised in the process.

"When I go down after the hot water, I'll hang these things on the line," said Miss Mehitable, briskly. "They can't get any dustier on the ground than they are now."

The curtains were so frail that they fell apart in Miss Hitty's hands. "You can make her some new ones, Minty," she said. "She can get some muslin at Mis' Allen's, and you can sew on curtains for a while instead of quilts. It'll be a change."

None too carefully, Miss Mehitable tore up the rag carpet and threw it out of the window, sneezing violently. "There's considerable less dirt here already than there was when we come," she continued, "though we ain't done any real cleaning yet. She can't never put that carpet down again, it's too weak. We'll get a bucket of paint and paint the floors. I guess Sarah Grey had plenty of rugs. She's got a lot of rag carpeting put away in the attic if the moths ain't ate it, and, now that I think of it, I believe she packed it into the cedar chest. Anyway I advised her to. 'It'll come handy,' I told her, 'for Evelina, if you don't live to use it yourself.' So if the moths ain't got the good of it, there's carpet that can be made into rugs with some fringe on the ends. I always did like the smell of fresh paint, anyhow. There's nothin' you can put into a house that'll make it smell as fresh and clean as paint. Varnish is good, too, but it's more expensive. I'll go down now, and get the hot water and the ladder. I reckon she's through with her breakfast by this time."

Miss Evelina had finished her breakfast, as the empty tray proved. She sat listlessly in her chair and the water on the stove was boiling over.

"My sakes, Evelina," cried Miss Hitty, sharply, "I should think you'd--I should think you'd hear the water fallin' on the stove," she concluded, lamely. It was impossible to scold her as she would have scolded Araminta.

"I'm goin' out now to put things on the line," continued Miss Hitty. "When I get Minty started to cleanin', I'll come down and beat."

Miss Evelina made no response. She watched her brisk neighbour wearily, without interest, as she hurried about the yard, dragging mattresses into the sunlight, hanging musty bedding on the line, and carrying the worn curtains to the mountain of rubbish which the Piper had reared in front of the house.

"That creeter with the red feather can clean the yard if he's a mind to," mused Miss Hitty, who was fully conversant with the Piper's work, "but he can't clean the house. I'm going to do that myself."

She went in and was presently in her element. The smell of yellow soap was as sweet incense in the nostrils of Miss Hitty, and the sound of the scrubbing brush was melodious in her ears. She brushed down the walls with a flannel cloth tied over a broom, washed the windows, scrubbed every inch of the woodwork, and prepared the floor for its destined coat of paint.

Then she sent Araminta into the next room with the ladder, and began on the furniture. This, too, was thoroughly scrubbed, and as much paint and varnish as would come off was allowed to come. "It'll have to be painted," thought Miss Hitty, scrubbing happily, "but when it is painted, it'll be clean underneath, and that's more than it has been. Evelina 'll sleep clean to-night for the first time since she come here. There's a year's washin' to be done in this house and before I get round to that, I'll lend her some of my clean sheets and a quilt or two of Minty's."

Adjourning to the back yard, Miss Mehitable energetically beat a mattress until no more dust rose from it. With Araminta's aid she carried it upstairs and put it in place. "I'm goin' home now after my dinner and Evelina's," said Miss Hitty, "and when I come back I'll bring sheets and quilts for this. You clean till I come back, and then you can go home for your own lunch."

Araminta assented and continued her work. She never questioned her aunt's dictates, and this was why there was no friction between the two.

When Miss Mehitable came back, however, half buried under the mountain of bedding, she was greeted by a portentous silence. Hurrying upstairs, she discovered that Araminta had fallen from the ladder and was in a white and helpless heap on the floor, while Miss Evelina chafed her hands and sprinkled her face with water.

"For the land's sake!" cried Miss Hitty. "What possessed Minty to go and fall off the ladder! Help me pick her up, Evelina, and we'll lay her on the bed in the room we've just cleaned. She'll come to presently. She ain't hurt."

But Araminta did not "come to." Miss Mehitable tried everything she could think of, and fairly drenched the girl with cold water, without avail.

"What did it?" she demanded with some asperity. "Did she see anything that scared her?"

"No," answered Miss Evelina, shrinking farther back into her veil. "I was downstairs and heard her scream, then she fell and I ran up. It was just a minute or two before you came in."

"Well," sighed Miss Hitty, "I suppose we'll have to have a doctor. You fix that bed with the clean things I brought. It's easy to do it without movin' her after the under sheet is on and I'll help you with that. Don't pour any more cold water on her. If water would have brung her to she'd be settin' up by now. And don't get scared. Minty ain't hurt."

With this comforting assurance, Miss Hitty sped down-stairs, but her mind was far from at rest. At the gate she stopped, suddenly confronted by the fact that she could not bring Anthony Dexter to Evelina's house.

"What'll I do!" moaned Miss Hitty. "What'll I do! Minty'll die if she ain't dead now!"

The tears rolled down her wrinkled cheeks, but she ran on, as fast as her feet would carry her, toward Doctor Dexter's. "The way'll be opened," she thought--"I'm sure it will."

The way was opened in an unexpected fashion, for Doctor Ralph Dexter answered Miss Hitty's frantic ring at his door.

"I'd clean forgotten you," she stammered, wholly taken aback. "I don't believe you're anything but a play doctor, but, as things is, I reckon you'll have to do."

Doctor Ralph Dexter threw back his head and laughed--a clear, ringing boyish laugh which was very good to hear.

"'Play doctor' is good," he said, "when anybody's worked as much like a yellow dog as I have. Anyhow, I'll have to do, for father's not at home. Who's dead?"

"It's Araminta," explained Miss Hitty, already greatly relieved. "She fell off a step-ladder and ain't come to yet."

Doctor Ralph's face grew grave. "Wait a minute." He went into the office and returned almost immediately. As luck would have it, the doctor's carriage was at the door, waiting for a hurry call.

"Jump in," commanded Doctor Ralph. "You can tell me about it on the way. Where do we go?"

Miss Hitty issued directions to the driver and climbed in. In spite of her trouble, she was not insensible of the comfort of the cushions nor the comparative luxury of the conveyance. She was also mindful of the excitement her presence in the doctor's carriage produced in her acquaintances as they rushed past.

By dint of much questioning, Doctor Ralph obtained a full account of the accident, all immaterial circumstances being brutally eliminated as they cropped up in the course of her speech. "It's God's own mercy," said Miss Hitty, as they stopped at the gate, "that we'd cleaned that room. We couldn't have got it any cleaner if 't was for a layin' out instead of a sickness. Oh, Ralph," she pleaded, "don't let Minty die!"

"Hush!" said Doctor Ralph, sternly. He spoke with an authority new to Miss Hitty, who, in earlier days, had been wont to drive Ralph out of her incipient orchard with a bed slat, sharpened at one end into a formidable weapon of offence.

Araminta was still unconscious, but she was undressed, and in bed, clad in one of Miss Evelina's dainty but yellowed nightgowns. Doctor Ralph worked with incredible quickness and Miss Hitty watched him, wondering, frightened, yet with a certain sneaking confidence in him.

"Fracture of the ankle," he announced, briefly, "and one or two bad bruises. Plaster cast and no moving."

When Araminta returned to consciousness, she thought she was dead and had gone to Heaven. The room was heavy with soothing antiseptic odours, and she seemed to be suspended in a vapoury cloud. On the edge of the cloud hovered Miss Evelina, veiled, and Aunt Hitty, who was most assuredly crying. There was a stranger, too, and Araminta gazed at him questioningly.

Doctor Ralph's hand, firm and cool, closed over hers. "Don't you remember me, Araminta?" he asked, much as one would speak to a child. "The last time I saw you, you were hanging out a basket of clothes. The grass was very green and the sky was a bright blue, and the petals of apple blossoms were drifting all round your feet. I called to you, and you ran into the house. Now I've got you where you can't get away."

Araminta's pale cheeks flushed. She looked pleadingly at Aunt Hitty, who had always valiantly defended her from the encroachments of boys and men.

"You come downstairs with me, Ralph Dexter," commanded Aunt Hitty. "I've got some talking to do to you. Evelina, you set here with Araminta till I get back."

Miss Evelina drew a damp, freshly scrubbed chair to the bedside. "I fell off the step-ladder, didn't I?" asked Araminta, vaguely.

"Yes, dear." Miss Evelina's voice was very low and sweet. "You fell, but you're all right now. You're going to stay here until you get well. Aunt Hitty and I are going to take care of you."

In the cobwebbed parlour, meanwhile, Doctor Ralph was in the hands of the attorney for the prosecution, who questioned him ceaselessly.

"What's wrong with Minty?"

"Broken ankle."

"How did it happen to get broke?" demanded Miss Hitty, with harshness. "I never knew an ankle to get broke by falling off a ladder."

"Any ankle will break," temporised Dr. Ralph, "if it is hurt at the right point."

"I wish I could have had your father."

"Father wasn't there," returned Ralph, secretly amused. "You had to take me."

Miss Hitty's face softened. There were other reasons why she could not have had Ralph's father.

"When can Minty go home?"

"Minty can't go home until she's well. She's got to stay right here."

"If she'd fell in the yard," asked Miss Hitty, peering keenly at him over her spectacles, "would she have had to stay in the yard till she got well?"

The merest suspicion of a dimple crept into the corner of Doctor Ralph's mouth. His eyes danced, but otherwise his face was very grave. "She would," he said, in his best professional manner. "A shed would have had to be built over her." He fancied that Miss Hitty's constant presence might prove disastrous to a nervous patient. He liked the quiet, veiled woman, who obeyed his orders without question.

"How much," demanded Miss Mehitable, "is it going to cost?"

"I don't know," answered Ralph, honestly. "I'll have to come every day for a long time--perhaps twice a day," he added, remembering the curve of Araminta's cheek and her long, dark lashes.

Miss Hitty made an indescribable sound. Pain, fear, disbelief, and contempt were all mingled in it.

"Don't worry," said Ralph, kindly. "You know doctoring sometimes comes by wholesale."

Miss Hitty's relief was instantaneous and evident. "There's regular prices, I suppose," she said. "Broken toe, broken ankle, broken leg--each one so much. Is that it?"

Doctor Ralph was seized with a violent fit of coughing.

"How much is ankles?" demanded his inquisitor.

"I'll leave that all to you, Miss Hitty," said Ralph, when he recovered his composure. "You can pay me whatever you think is right."

"I shouldn't pay you anything I didn't think was right," she returned, sharply, "unless I was made to by law. As long as you've got to come every day for a spell, and mebbe twice, I'll give you five dollars the day Minty walks again. If that won't do, I'll get the doctor over to the Ridge."

Doctor Ralph coughed so hard that he was obliged to cover his face with his handkerchief. "I should think," said Miss Mehitable, "that if you were as good a doctor as you pretend to be, you'd cure your own coughin' spells. First thing you know, you'll be running into quick consumption. Will five dollars do?"

Ralph bowed, but his face was very red and he appeared to be struggling with some secret emotion. "I couldn't think of taking as much as five dollars, Miss Hitty," he said, gallantly. "I should not have ventured to suggest over four and a half."

"He's cheaper than his father," thought Miss Hitty, quickly suspicious. "That's because he ain't as good a doctor."

"Four and a half, then," she said aloud. "Is it a bargain?"

"It is," said Ralph, "and I'll take the best possible care of Araminta. Shake hands on it." He went out, his shoulders shaking with suppressed merriment, and Miss Hitty watched him through the grimy front window.

"Seems sort of decent," she thought, "and not too grasping. He might be real nice if he wasn't a man."

X
Ralph's First Case

Father," said Ralph at breakfast, "I got my first case yesterday."

Anthony Dexter smiled at the tall, straight young fellow who sat opposite him. He did not care about the case but he found endless satisfaction in Ralph.

"What was it?" he asked, idly.

"Broken ankle. I only happened to get it because you were out. I was accused of being a 'play doctor,' but, under the circumstances, I had to do."

"Miss Mehitable?" queried Doctor Dexter, with lifted brows. "I wouldn't have thought her ankles could be broken by anything short of machinery."

"Guess they couldn't," laughed Ralph. "Anyhow, they were all right at last accounts. It's Araminta--the pretty little thing who lives with the dragon."

"Oh!" There was the merest shade of tenderness in the exclamation. "How did it happen?"

"Divesting the circumstance of all irrelevant material," returned Ralph, reaching for another crisp roll, "it was like this. With true missionary spirit and in the belief that cleanliness is closely related to godliness, Miss Mehitable determined to clean the old house on the hill. The shack has been empty a long time; but now has a tenant--of whom more anon.

"Miss Mehitable's own mansion, it seems, has been scrubbed inside and out, and painted and varnished and generally torn up, even though it is early in the year for such unholy doings. Having finished her own premises, and still having strength in her elbow, and the housecleaning microbe being yet on an unchecked rampage through her virtuous system, and there being some soap left, Miss Mehitable wanders up to the house with her pail.

"Shackled to her, also with a pail, is the helpless Araminta. Among the impedimenta are the Reverend Austin Thorpe and the step-ladder, the Reverend Thorpe being, dismissed at the door and allowed to run amuck for the day.

"The Penates are duly thrown out of the windows, the veiled chatelaine sitting by mute and helpless. One room is scrubbed till it's so clean a fly would fall down in it, and the ministering angel goes back to her own spotless residence after bedding. I believe I didn't understand exactly why she went after the bedding, but I can doubtless find out the next time I see Miss Mehitable.

"In the absence of the superintendent, Araminta seizes the opportunity to fall off the top of the ladder, lighting on her ankle, and fainting most completely on the way down. The rest is history.

"Doctor Dexter being out, his son, perforce, has to serve. The ankle being duly set and the excitement allayed, terms are made in private with the 'play doctor.' How much, Father, do you suppose I am to be paid the day Araminta walks again?"

Doctor Dexter dismissed the question. "Couldn't guess," he grunted.

"Four and a half," said Ralph, proudly.

"Hundred?" asked Doctor Dexter, with a gleam of interest. "You must have imbibed high notions at college."

"Hundred!" shouted Ralph, "Heavens, no! Four dollars and a half! Four dollars and fifty cents, marked down from five for this day only. Special remnant sale of repaired ankles!" The boy literally doubled himself in his merriment.

"You bloated bondholder," said his father, fondly. "Don't be extravagant with it."

"I won't," returned Ralph, between gasps. "I thought I'd put some of it into unincumbered real estate and loan the rest on good security at five per cent."

Into the lonely house Ralph's laughter came like the embodied spirit of Youth. It searched out the hidden corners, illuminated the shadows, stirred the silences to music. A sunbeam danced on the stair, where, according to Doctor Dexter's recollection, no sunbeam had ever dared to dance before. Ah, it, was good to have the boy at home!

"Miss Mehitable," observed Doctor Dexter, after a pause, "is like the poor-- always with us. I seldom get to a patient who is really in danger before she does.

She seems to have secret wires stretched all over the country and she has the clinical history of the neighbourhood at her tongue's end. What's more, she distributes it, continually, painstakingly, untiringly. Every detail of every case I have charge of is spread broadcast, by Miss Mehitable. I'd have a bad reputation, professionally, if so much about my patients was generally known anywhere else."

"Is she a good nurse?" asked Ralph.

"According to her light, yes; but she isn't willing to work on recognised lines. She'll dose my patients with roots and herbs of her own concocting if she gets a chance, and proudly claim credit for the cure. If the patient dies, everybody blames me. I can't sit by a case of measles and keep Miss Mehitable from throwing sassafras tea into it more than ten hours at a stretch."

"Why don't you talk to her?" queried Ralph.

"Talk to her!" snorted Doctor Dexter. "Do you suppose I haven't ruptured my vocal cords more than once? I might just as well put my head out of the front window and whisper it as to talk to her."

"She won't monkey with my case," said Ralph. His mouth was firmly set.

"Won't she?" parried Doctor Dexter, sarcastically. "You go up there and see if the cast isn't off and the fracture being fomented with pennyroyal tea or some such mess."

"I always had an impression," said Ralph, thoughtfully, "that people were afraid of you."

"They are," grunted Doctor Dexter, "but Miss Mehitable isn't 'people.' She goes by herself, and isn't afraid of man or devil. If I had horns and a barbed tail and breathed smoke, I couldn't scare her. The patient's family, being more afraid of her than of me, invariably give her free access to the sick-room."

"I don't want her to worry Araminta," said Ralph.

"If you don't want Araminta worried," replied Doctor Dexter, conclusively, "you'd better put a few things into your suit case, and move up there until she walks."

"All right," said Ralph. "I'm here to rout your malign influence. It's me to sit by Araminta's crib and scare the old girl off. I'll bet I can fix her."

"If you can," returned Doctor Dexter, "you are considerably more intelligent than I take you to be."

With the welfare of his young patient very earnestly at heart, Ralph went up the hill. Miss Evelina admitted him, and Ralph drew her into the dusty parlour. "Can you take care of anybody?" he inquired, without preliminary. "Can you follow directions?"

"I--think so."

"Then," Ralph went on, "I turn Araminta over to you. Miss Mehitable has nothing to do with the case from this moment. Araminta is in your care and mine. You take directions from me and from nobody else. Do you understand?"

"Yes," whispered Miss Evelina, "but Mehitable won't--won't let me."

"Won't let you nothing," said Ralph, scornfully. "She's to be kept out."

"She--she--" stammered Miss Evelina, "she's up there now."

Ralph started upstairs. Half-way up, he heard the murmur of voices, and went up more quietly. He stepped lightly along the hall and stood just outside Araminta's door, shamelessly listening.

"You ought to be ashamed of yourself," said an indignant feminine voice. "The idea of a big girl like you not bein' able to stand on a ladder without fallin' off. It's your mother's foolishness cropping out in you, after all I've done for you. I've stood on ladders all my life and never so much as slipped. I believe you did it a purpose, though what you thought you'd get for doin' it puzzles me some. P'raps you thought you'd get out of the housecleanin' but you won't. When it comes time for the Fall cleanin,' you'll do every stroke yourself, to pay for all this trouble and expense. Do you know what it's costin'? Four dollars and a half of good money! I should think you'd be ashamed!"

"But, Aunt Hitty--" began the girl, pleadingly.

"Stop! Don't you 'Aunt Hitty' me," continued the angry voice. "You needn't tell me you didn't fall off that ladder a purpose. Four dollars and a half and all the trouble besides! I hope you'll think of that while you're laying here like a lady and your poor old aunt is slavin' for you, workin' her fingers to the bone."

"If I can ever get the four dollars and a half," cried Araminta, with tears in her voice, "I will give it back to you--oh, indeed I will!"

At this point, Doctor Ralph Dexter entered the room, his eyes snapping dangerously.

"Miss Mehitable," he said with forced calmness, "will you kindly come downstairs a moment? I wish to speak to you."

Dazed and startled, Miss Mehitable rose from her chair and followed him. There was in Ralph's voice a quality which literally compelled obedience. He drew her into the dusty parlour and closed all the doors carefully. Miss Evelina was nowhere to be seen.

"I was standing in the hall," said Ralph, coolly, "and I heard every word you said to that poor, helpless child. You ought to know, if you know anything at all, that nobody ever fell off a step-ladder on purpose. She's hurt, and she's badly hurt, and she's not in any way to blame for it, and I positively forbid you ever to enter that room again."

"Forbid!" bristled Aunt Hitty. "Who are you?" she demanded sarcastically, "to 'forbid' me from nursing my own niece!"

"I am the attending physician," returned Ralph, calmly. "It is my case, and nobody else is going to manage it. I have already arranged with--the lady who lives here--to take care of Araminta, and----"

"Arrange no such thing," interrupted Miss Hitty, violently. Her temper was getting away from her.

"One moment," interrupted Ralph. "If I hear of your entering that room again before I say Araminta is cured, I will charge you just exactly one hundred dollars for my services, and collect it by law."

Miss Hitty's lower jaw dropped, her strong, body shook. She gazed at Ralph as one might look at an intimate friend gone suddenly daft. She had heard of people who lost their reason without warning. Was it possible that she was in the room with a lunatic?

She edged toward the door, keeping her eyes on Ralph.

He anticipated her, and opened it with a polite flourish. "Remember," he warned her. "One step into Araminta's room, one word addressed to her, and it costs you just exactly one hundred dollars." He opened the other door and pointed suggestively down the hill, She lost no time in obeying the gesture, but scudded down the road as though His Satanic Majesty himself was in her wake.

Ralph laughed to himself all the way upstairs but in the hall he paused and his face grew grave again. From Araminta's room came the sound of sobbing.

She did not see him enter, for her face was hidden in her pillow. "Araminta!"

said Ralph, tenderly, "You poor child."

Touched by the unexpected sympathy, Araminta raised her head to look at him. "Oh Doctor--" she began,

"Doctor Ralph," said the young man, sitting down on the bed beside her. "My father is Doctor Dexter and I am Doctor Ralph."

"I'm ashamed of myself for being such a baby," sobbed Araminta. "I didn't mean to cry."

"You're not a baby at all," said Doctor Ralph, soothingly, taking her hot hand in his. "You're hurt, and you've been bothered, and if you want to cry, you can. Here's my handkerchief."

After a little, her sobs ceased. Doctor Ralph still sat there, regarding her with a sort of questioning tenderness which was entirely outside of Araminta's brief experience.

"You're not to be bothered any more," he said. "I've seen your aunt, and she's not to set foot in this room again until you get well. If she even speaks to you from the hall, you're to tell me."

Araminta gazed at him, wide-eyed and troubled. "I can't take care of myself," she said, with a pathetic little smile.

"You're not going to. The lady who lives here is going to take care of you."

"Miss Evelina? She got burned because she was bad and she has to wear a veil all the time."

"How was she bad?" asked Ralph.

"I don't just know," whispered Araminta, cautiously. "Aunt Hitty didn't know, or else she wouldn't tell me, but she was bad. She went to a man's house. She----"

Then Araminta remembered that it was Doctor Dexter's house to which Miss Evelina had gone. In shame and terror, she hid her face again.

"I don't believe anybody ever got burned just for being bad," Ralph was saying, "but your face is hot and I'm going to cool it for you."

He brought a bowl of cold water, and with his handkerchief bathed Araminta's flushed face and her hot hands. "Doesn't that feel good?" he asked, when the traces of tears had been practically removed.

"Yes," sighed Araminta, gratefully, "but I've always washed my own face before. I saw a cat once," she continued. "He was washing his children's faces."

"Must have been a lady cat," observed Ralph, with a smile.

"The little cats," pursued Araminta, "looked to be very soft. I think they liked it."

"They are soft," admitted Ralph. "Don't you think so?"

"I don't know. I never had a little cat."

"Never had a kitten?" cried Ralph. "You poor, defrauded child! What kind of a kitten would you like best?"

"A little grey cat," said Araminta, seriously, "a little grey cat with blue eyes, but Aunt Hitty would never let me have one."

"See here," said Ralph. "Aunt Hitty isn't running this show. I'm stage manager and ticket taker and advance man and everything else, all rolled into one. I can't promise positively, because I'm not posted on the cat supply around here, but if I can find one, you shall have a grey kitten with blue eyes, and you shall have some kind of a kitten, anyhow."

"Oh!" cried Araminta, her eyes shining. "Truly?"

"Truly," nodded Ralph.

"Would--would--" hesitated Araminta--"would it be any more than four dollars and a half if you brought me the little cat? Because if it is, I can't----"

"It wouldn't," interrupted Ralph. "On any bill over a dollar and a quarter, I always throw in a kitten. Didn't you know that?"

"No," answered Araminta, with a happy little laugh. How kind he was, even though he was a man! Perhaps, if he knew how wicked her mother had been, he would not be so kind to her. The stern Puritan conscience rose up and demanded explanation.

"I--I--must tell you," she said, "before you bring me the little cat. My mother--she--" here Araminta turned her crimson face away. She swallowed a lump in her throat, then said, bravely: "My mother was married!"

Doctor Ralph Dexter laughed--a deep, hearty, boyish laugh that rang cheerfully through the empty house. "I'll tell you something," he said. He leaned over and whispered in her ear; "So was mine!"

Araminta's tell-tale face betrayed her relief. He knew the worst now--and he was similarly branded. His mother, too, had been an outcast, beyond Aunt Hitty's pale. There was comfort in the thought, though Araminta had been taught not to rejoice at another's misfortune.

Ralph strolled off down the hill, his hands in his pockets, for the moment totally forgetting the promised kitten. "The little saint," he mused, "she's been kept in a cage all her life. She doesn't know anything except what the dragon has taught her. She looks at life with the dragon's sidewise squint. I'll open the door for her," he continued, mentally, "for I think she's worth saving. Hope to Moses and the prophets I don't forget that cat."

No suspicion that he could forget penetrated Araminta's consciousness. It had been pleasant to have Doctor Ralph sit there and wash her face, talking to her meanwhile, even though he was a man, and men were poison. Like a strong, sure bond between them, Araminta felt their common disgrace.

"His mother was married," she thought, drowsily, "and so was mine. Neither of them knew any better. Oh, Lord," prayed Araminta, with renewed vigour, "keep me from the contamination of marriage, for Thy sake. Amen."

XI
The Loose Link

Seated primly on a chair in Miss Evelina's kitchen, Miss Mehitable gave a full account of her sentiments toward Doctor Ralph Dexter. She began with his birth and remarked that he was a puny infant, and, for a time, it was feared that he was "light headed."

"He got his senses after a while, though," she continued, grudgingly, "that is, such as they are."

She proceeded through his school-days, repeated unflattering opinions which his teachers had expressed to her, gave an elaborate description of the conflict that ensued when she caught him stealing green apples from her incipient, though highly promising, orchard, alluded darkly to his tendency to fight with his schoolmates, suggested that certain thefts of chickens ten years and more ago could, if the truth were known, safely be attributed to Ralph Dexter, and speculated upon the trials and tribulations a scapegrace son might cause an upright and respected father.

All the dead and buried crimes of the small boys of the village were excavated from the past and charged to Ralph Dexter. Miss Mehitable brought the record fully up to the time he left Rushton for college, having been prepared for entrance by his father. Then she began with Araminta.

First upon the schedule were Miss Mehitable's painful emotions when Barbara Smith had married Henry Lee. She croaked anew all her raven-like prophecies of misfortune which had added excitement to the wedding, and brought forth the birth of Araminta in full proof. Full details of Barbara's death were given, and the highly magnified events which had led to her adoption of the child. Condescending for a moment to speak of the domestic virtues, Miss Mehitable explained, with proper pride, how she had "brought up" Araminta. The child had been kept close at the side of her guardian angel, never had been to school, had been carefully taught at home, had not been allowed to play with other children; in short, save at extremely rare intervals, Araminta had seen no one unless in the watchful presence of her counsellor.

"And if you don't think that's work," observed Miss Hitty, piously, "you just keep tied to one person for almost nineteen years, day and night, never lettin' 'em out of your sight, and layin' the foundation of their manners and morals and education, and see how you'll feel when a blackmailing sprig of a play-doctor threatens to collect a hundred dollars from you if you dast to nurse your own niece!"

Miss Evelina, silent as always, was moving restlessly about the kitchen. Unaccustomed since her girlhood to activity of any description, she found her new tasks hard. Muscles, long unused, ached miserably from exertion. Yet Araminta had to be taken care of and her room kept clean.

The daily visits of Doctor Ralph, who was almost painfully neat, had made Miss Evelina ashamed of her house, though he had not appeared to notice that anything was wrong. She avoided him when she could, but it was not always possible, for directions had to be given and reports made. Miss Evelina never looked at him directly. One look into his eyes, so like his father's, had made her so faint that she would have fallen, had not Doctor Ralph steadied her with his strong arm.

To her, he was Anthony Dexter in the days of his youth, though she continually wondered to find it so. She remembered a story she had read, a long time ago, of a young woman who lost her husband of a few weeks in a singularly pathetic manner. In exploring a mountain, he fell into a crevasse, and his body could not be recovered. Scientists calculated that, at the rate the glacier was moving, his body might be expected to appear at the foot of the mountain in about twenty-three years; so, grimly, the young bride set herself to wait.

At the appointed time, the glacier gave up its dead, in perfect preservation, owing to the intense cold. But the woman who had waited for her husband thus was twenty-three years older; she had aged, and he was still young. In some such way had Anthony Dexter come back to her; eager, boyish, knowing none of life except its joy, while she, a quarter of a century older, had borne incredible griefs, been wasted by long vigils, and now stood, desolate, at the tomb of a love which was not dead, but continually tore at its winding sheet and prayed for release.

To Evelina, at times, the past twenty-five years seemed like a long nightmare. This was Anthony Dexter--this boy with the quick, light step, the ringing laugh, the broad shoulders and clear, true eyes. No terror lay between them, all was straight and right; yet the realisation still enshrouded her like a black cloud.

"And," said Miss Hitty, mournfully, "after ail my patience and hard work in bringing up Araminta as a lady should be brought up, and having taught her to beware of men and even of boys, she's took away from me when she's sick, and nobody allowed to see her except a blackmailing play-doctor, who is putting Heaven knows what devilment into her head. I suppose there's nothing to prevent me from finishing the housecleaning, if I don't speak to my own niece as I pass her door?"

She spoke inquiringly, but Miss Evelina did not reply.

"Most folks," continued Miss Hitty, with asperity, "is pleased enough to have their houses cleaned for 'em to say 'thank you,' but I'm some accustomed to ingratitude. What I do now in the way of cleanin' will be payin' for the nursin' of Araminta."

Still Miss Evelina did not answer, her thoughts being far away.

"Maybe I did speak cross to Minty," admitted Miss Hitty, grudgingly, "at a time when I had no business to. If I did, I'm willin' to tell her so, but not that blackmailing play-doctor with a hundred-dollar bill for a club. I was clean out of patience with Minty for falling off the ladder, but I guess, as he says, she didn't go for to do it. 'T ain't in reason for folks to step off ladders or out of windows unless they're walkin' in their sleep, and I've never let Minty sleep in the daytime."

Unceasingly, Miss Mehitable prattled on. Reminiscence, anecdote, and philosophical observations succeeded one another with startling rapidity, ending always in vituperation and epithet directed toward Araminta's physician. Dark allusions to the base ingratitude of everybody with whom Miss Hitty had ever been concerned alternately cumbered her speech. At length the persistent sound wore upon Miss Evelina, much as the vibration of sound may distress one totally deaf.

The kitchen door was open and Miss Evelina went outdoors. Miss Mehitable continued to converse, then shortly perceived that she was alone. "Well, I never!" she gasped. "Guess I'll go home!"

Her back was very stiff and straight when she marched downhill, firmly determined to abandon Evelina, scorn Doctor Ralph Dexter, and leave Araminta to her well-deserved fate. One thought and one only illuminated her gloom. "He ain't got his four dollars and a half, yet," she chuckled, craftily. "Mebbe he'll get it and mebbe he won't. We'll see."

While straying about the garden. Miss Evelina saw her unwelcome guest take her militant departure, and reproached herself for her lack of hospitality. Miss Mehitable had been very kind to her and deserved only kindness in return. She had acted upon impulse and was ashamed.

Miss Evelina meditated calling her back, but the long years of self-effacement and inactivity had left her inert, with capacity only for suffering. That very suffering to which she had become accustomed had of late assumed fresh phases. She was hurt continually in new ways, yet, after the first shock of returning to her old home, not so much as she had expected. It is a way of life, and one of its inmost compensations--this finding of a reality so much easier than our fears.

April had come over the hills, singing, with a tinkle of rain and a rush of warm winds, and yet the Piper had not returned. His tools were in the shed, and the mountain of rubbish was still in the road in front of the house. Half of the garden had not been touched. On one side of the house was the bare brown earth, with tiny green shoots springing up through it, and on the other was a twenty-five years' growth of weeds. Miss Evelina reflected that the place was not unlike her own life; half of it full of promise, a forbidding wreck in the midst of it, and, beyond it, desolation, ended only by a stone wall.

"Did you think," asked a cheerful voice at her elbow, "that I was never coming back to finish my job?"

Miss Evelina started, and gazed into the round, smiling face of Piper Tom, who was accompanied, as always, by his faithful dog.

"'T is not our way," he went on, including the yellow mongrel in the pronoun, "to leave undone what we've set our hands and paws to do, eh, Laddie?"

He waited a moment, but Miss Evelina did not speak.

"I got some seeds for my garden," he continued, taking bulging parcels from the pockets of his short, shaggy coat. "The year's sorrow is at an end."

"Sorrow never comes to an end," she cried, bitterly.

"Doesn't it," he asked. "How old is yours?"

"Twenty-five years," she answered, choking. The horror of it was pressing heavily upon her.

"Then," said the Piper, very gently, "I'm thinking there is something wrong. No sorrow should last more than a year--'t is written all around us so."

"Written? I have never seen it written."

"No," returned the Piper, kindly, "but 't is because you have not looked to see. Have you ever known a tree that failed to put out its green leaves in the Spring, unless it had died from lightning or old age? When a rose blossoms, then goes to sleep, does it wait for more than a year before it blooms again? Is it more than a year from bud to bud, from flower to flower, from fruit to fruit? 'T is God's way of showing that a year of darkness is enough,--at a time."

The Piper's voice was very tender; the little dog lay still at his feet. She leaned against the crumbling wall, and turned her veiled face away.

"'T is not for us to be happy without trying," continued the Piper, "any more than it is for a tree to bear fruit without effort. All the beauty and joy in the world are the result of work--work for each other and in ourselves. When you see a butterfly over a field of clover, 't is because he has worked to get out of his chrysalis. He was not content to abide within his veil."

"Suppose," said Miss Evelina, in a voice that was scarcely audible, "that he couldn't get out?"

"Ah, but he could," answered the Piper. "We can get out of anything, if we try. I'm not meaning by escape, but by growth. You put an acorn into a crevice in a rock. It has no wings, it cannot fly out, nobody will lift it out. But it grows, and the oak splits the rock; even takes from the rock nourishment for its root."

"People are not like acorns and butterflies," she stammered. "We are not subject to the same laws."

"Why not?" asked the Piper. "God made us all, and I'm thinking we're all brothers, having, in a way, the same Father. 'T is not for me to hold myself above Laddie here, though he's a dog and I'm a man. 'T is not for me to say that men are better than dogs; that they're more honest, more true, more kind. The seed that I have in my hand, here, I'm thinking 't is my brother, too. If I plant it, water it, and keep the weeds away from it, 't will give me back a blossom. 'T is service binds us all into the brotherhood."

"Did you never," asked Evelina, thickly, "hear of chains?"

"Aye," said the Piper, "chains of our own making. 'T is like the ancient people in one of my ragged books. When one man killed another, they chained the dead man to the living one, so that he was forever dragging his own sin. When he struck the blow, he made his own chain."

"I am chained," cried Evelina, piteously, "but not to my own sin."

"'T is wrong," said the Piper; "I'm thinking there's a loose link somewhere that can be slipped off."

"I cannot find it," she sobbed; "I've hunted for it in the dark for twenty-five years."

"Poor soul," said the Piper, softly. "'T is because of the darkness, I'm thinking. From the distaff of Eternity, you take the thread of your life, but you're sitting in the night, and God meant you to be a spinner in the sun. When the day breaks for you, you'll be finding the loose link to set yourself free."

"When the day breaks," repeated Evelina, in a whisper. "There is no day."

"There is day. I've come to lead you to it. We'll find the light together and set the thread to going right again."

"Who are you?" cried Evelina, suddenly terror stricken.

The Piper laughed, a low, deep friendly laugh. Then he doffed his grey hat and bowed, sweeping the earth with the red feather, in cavalier fashion. "Tom Barnaby, at your service, but most folks call me Piper Tom. 'T is the flute, you know," he continued in explanation, "that I'm forever playing on in the woods, having no knowledge of the instrument, but sort of liking the sound."

Miss Evelina turned and went into the house, shaken to her inmost soul. More than ever, she felt the chains that bound her. Straining against her bonds, she felt them cutting deep into her flesh. Anthony Dexter had bound her; he alone could set her free. From this there seemed no possible appeal.

Meanwhile the Piper mowed down the weeds in the garden, whistling cheerily. He burned the rubbish in the road, and the smoke made a blue haze on the hill. He spaded and raked and found new stones for the broken wall, and kept up a constant conversation with the dog.

It was twilight long before he got ready to make the flower beds, so he carried the tools back into the shed and safely stored away the seeds. Miss Evelina watched him from the grimy front window as he started downhill, but he did not once look back.

There was something jaunty in the Piper's manner, aside from the drooping red feather which bobbed rakishly as he went home, whistling. When he was no longer to be seen, Miss Evelina sighed. Something seemed to have gone out of her life, like a sunbeam which has suddenly faded. In a safe shadow of the house, she raised her veil, and wiped away a tear.

When out of sight and hearing, the Piper stopped his whistling. "'T is no need to be cheerful, Laddie," he explained to the dog, "when there's none to be saddened if you're not. We don't know about the loose link, and perhaps we can never find it, but we're going to try. We'll take off the chain and put the poor soul in the sun again before we go away, if we can learn how to do it, but I'm thinking 't is a heavy chain and the sun has long since ceased to shine."

After supper, he lighted a candle and absorbed himself in going over his stock. He had made a few purchases in the city and it took some time to arrange them properly.

Last of all, he took out a box and opened it. He held up to the flickering light length after length of misty white chiffon--a fabric which the Piper had never bought before.

"'T is expensive, Laddie," he said; "so expensive that neither of us will taste meat again for more than a week, though we walked both ways, but I'm thinking she'll need more sometime and there was none to be had here. We'll not be in the way of charging for it since her gown is shabby and her shoes are worn."

Twilight deepened into night and still the Piper sat there, handling the chiffon curiously and yet with reverence. It was silky to his touch, filmy, cloud-like. He folded it into small compass, and crushed it in his hands, much surprised to find that it did not crumple. All the meaning of chiffon communicated itself to him--the lightness and the laughter, the beauty and the love. Roses and moonlight seemed to belong with it, youth and a singing heart.

"'T is a rare stuff, I'm thinking, Laddie," he said, at length, not noting that the dog was asleep. "'T is a rare, fine stuff, and well suited to her wearing, because she is so beautiful that she hides her face."

XII
A Grey Kitten

With her mouth firmly set, and assuming the air of a martyr trying to make himself a little more comfortable against the stake, Miss Mehitable climbed the hill. In her capable hands were the implements of warfare--pails, yellow soap, and rags. She carried a mop on her shoulder as a regular carries a gun.

"Havin' said I would clean house, I will clean house," she mused, "in spite of all the ingratitude and not listenin'. 'T won't take long, and it'll do my heart good to see the place clean again. Evelina's got no gumption about a house--never did have. I s'pose she thinks it's clean just because she's swept it and brushed down the cobwebs, but it needs more 'n a broom to take out twenty-five years' dirt."

Her militant demeanour was somewhat chastened when she presented herself at the house. When the door was opened, she brushed past Miss Evelina with a muttered explanation, and made straight for the kitchen stove. She heated a huge kettle of water, filled her pail, and then, for the first time, spoke.

"I've come to finish cleanin' as I promised I would, and I hope it'll offset your nursin' of Minty. And if that blackmailing play-doctor comes while I'm at work, you can tell him that I ain't speakin' to Minty from the hall, nor settin' foot in her room, and that he needn't be in any hurry to make out his bill, 'cause I'm goin' to take my time about payin' it."

She went upstairs briskly, and presently the clatter of moving furniture fairly shook the house over Miss Evelina's head. It sounded as if Miss Mehitable did not know there was an invalid in the house, and found distinct pleasure in making unnecessary noise. The quick, regular strokes of the scrubbing brush swished through the hall. Resentment inspired the ministering influence to speed.

But it was not in Miss Hitty's nature to cherish her wrath long, while the incense of yellow soap was in her nostrils and the pleasing foam of suds was everywhere in sight.

Presently she began to sing, in a high, cracked voice which wavered continually off the key. She went through her repertory of hymns with conscientious thoroughness. Then a bright idea came to her.

"There wa'n't nothin' said about singin'," she said to herself. "I wa'n't to speak to Minty from the hall, nor set foot into her room. But I ain't pledged not to sing in the back room, and I can sing any tune I please, and any words. Reckon Minty can hear."

The moving of the ladder drowned the sound made by the opening of the lower door. Secure upon her height, with her head near the open transom of the back room. Miss Mehitable began to sing.

"Araminta Lee is a bad, un-grate-ful girl," she warbled, to a tune the like of which no mortal had ever heard before. "She fell off of a step-lad-der, and sprained her an-kle, and the play-doc-tor said it was broke in or-der to get more mon-ey, breaks being more val-u-able than sprains. Araminta Lee is lay-ing in bed like a la-dy, while her poor old aunt works her fingers to the bone, to pay for doc-tor's bills and nursin'. Four dollars and a half," she chanted, mournfully, "and no-body to pay it but a poor old aunt who has to work her fin-gers to the bone. Four dollars and a half, four dollars and a half--almost five dollars. Araminta thinks she will get out of work by pretending to be sick, but it is not so, not so. Araminta will find out she is much mis-taken. She will do the Fall clean-ing all alone, alone, and we do not think there will be any sprained an-kles, nor any four dollars--"

Doctor Ralph Dexter appeared in the doorway, his face flaming with wrath. Miss Mehitable continued to sing, apparently unconcerned, though her heart pounded violently against her ribs. By a swift change of words and music, she was singing "Rock of Ages," as any woman is privileged to do, when cleaning house, or at any other time.

But the young man still stood there, his angry eyes fixed upon her. The scrutiny made Miss Mehitable uncomfortable, and at length she descended from the ladder, still singing, ostensibly to refill her pail.

"Let me hide--" warbled Miss Hitty, tremulously, attempting to leave the room.

Doctor Ralph effectually barred the way. "I should think you'd want to hide," he said, scornfully. "If I hear of anything; like this again, I'll send in that bill I told you of. I know a lawyer who can collect it."

"If you do," commented Miss Mehitable, ironically, "you know more 'n I do." She tried to speak with assurance, but her soul was quaking within her. Was it possible that any one knew she had over three hundred dollars safely concealed in the attic?

"I mean exactly what I say," continued Ralph. "If you so much as climb these stairs again, you and I will have trouble,"

Sniffing disdainfully, Miss Mehitable went down into the kitchen, no longer singing. "You'll have to finish your own cleanin'," she said to Miss Evelina. "That blackmailing play-doctor thinks it ain't good for my health to climb ladders. He's afraid I'll fall off same as Minty did and he hesitates to take more of my money."

"I'd much rather you wouldn't do any more," replied Miss Evelina, kindly. "You have been very good to me, ever since I came here, and I appreciate it more than I can tell you. I'm going to clean my own house, for, indeed, I'm ashamed of it."

Miss Hitty grunted unintelligibly, gathered up her paraphernalia, and prepared to depart. "When Minty's well," she said, "I'll come back and be neighbourly."

"I hope you'll come before that," responded Miss Evelina. "I shall miss you if you don't."

Miss Hitty affected not to hear, but she was mollified, none the less.

From his patient's window, Doctor Ralph observed the enemy in full retreat, and laughed gleefully. "What is funny?" queried Araminta, She had been greatly distressed by the recitative in the back bedroom and her cheeks were flushed with fever.

"I was just laughing," said Doctor Ralph, "because your aunt has gone home and is never coming back here any more."

"Oh, Doctor Ralph! Isn't she?" There was alarm in Araminta's voice, but her grey eyes were shining.

"Never any more," he assured her, in a satisfied tone. "How long have you lived with Aunt Hitty?"

"Ever since I was a baby."

"H--m! And how old are you now?"

"Almost nineteen."

"Where did you go to school?"

"I didn't go to school. Aunt Hitty taught me, at home."

"Didn't you ever have anybody to play with?"

"Only Aunt Hitty. We used to play a quilt game. I sewed the little blocks together, and she made the big ones."

"Must have been highly exciting. Didn't you ever have a doll?"

"Oh, no!" Araminta's eyes were wide and reproachful now. "The Bible says 'thou shalt not make unto thee any graven image.'"

Doctor Ralph sighed deeply, put his hands in his pockets, and paced restlessly across Araminta's bare, nun-like chamber. As though in a magic mirror, he saw her nineteen years of deprivation, her cramped and narrow childhood, her dense ignorance of life. No playmates, no dolls--nothing but Aunt Hitty. She had kept Araminta wrapped in cotton wool, mentally; shut her out from the world, and persistently shaped her toward a monastic ideal.

A child brought up in a convent could have been no more of a nun in mind and spirit than Araminta. Ralph well knew that the stern guardianship had not been relaxed a moment, either by night or by day. Miss Mehitable had a well-deserved reputation for thoroughness in whatever she undertook.

And Araminta was made for love. Ralph turned to look at her as she lay on her pillow, her brown, wavy hair rioting about her flushed face. Araminta's great grey eyes were very grave and sweet; her mouth was that of a lovable child. Her little hands were dimpled at the knuckles, in fact, as Ralph now noted; there were many dimples appertaining to Araminta.

One of them hovered for an instant about the corner of her mouth. "Why must you walk?" she asked. "Is it because you're glad your ankle isn't broken?"

Doctor Ralph came back and sat down on the bed beside her. He had that rare sympathy which is the inestimable gift of the physician, and long years of practice had not yet calloused him so that a suffering fellow-mortal was merely a "case". His heart, was dangerously tender toward her.

"Lots of things are worse than broken ankles," he assured her. "Has it been so bad to be shut up here, away from Aunt Hitty?"

"No," said the truthful Araminta. "I have always been with Aunt Hitty, and it seems queer, but very nice. Someway, I feel as if I had grown up."

"Has Miss Evelina been good to you?"

"Oh, so good," returned Araminta, gratefully. "Why?"

"Because," said Ralph, concisely, "if she hadn't been, I'd break her neck."

"You couldn't," whispered Araminta, softly, "you're too kind. You wouldn't hurt anybody."

"Not unless I had to. Sometimes there has to be a little hurt to keep away a greater one."

"You hurt me, I think, but I didn't know just when. It was the smelly, sweet stuff, wasn't it?"

Ralph did not heed the question. He was wondering what would become of Araminta when she went back to Miss Mehitable's, as she soon must. Her ankle was healing nicely and in a very short time she would be able to walk again. He could not keep her there much longer. By a whimsical twist of his thought, he perceived that he was endeavouring to wrap Araminta in cotton wool of a different sort, to prevent Aunt Hitty from wrapping her in her own particular brand.

"The little cat," said Araminta, fondly. "I thought perhaps it would come to-day. Is it coming when I am well?"

"Holy Moses!" ejaculated Ralph. He had never thought of the kitten again, and the poor child had been waiting patiently, with never a word. The clear grey eyes were upon him, eloquent with belief.

"The little cat," replied Ralph, shamelessly perjuring himself, "was not old enough to leave its mother. We'll have to wait until to-morrow or next day. I was keeping it for a surprise; that's why I didn't say anything about it. I thought you'd forgotten."

"Oh, no! When I go back home, you know, I can't have it. Aunt Hitty would never let me."

"Won't she?" queried Ralph. "We'll see!"

He spoke with confidence he was far from feeling, and was dimly aware that Araminta had the faith he lacked. "She thinks I'm a wonder-worker," he said to himself, grimly, "and I've got to live up to it."

It was not necessary to count Araminta's pulse again, but Doctor Ralph took her hand--a childish, dimpled hand that nestled confidingly in his.

"Listen, child," he said; "I want to talk to you. Your Aunt Hitty hasn't done right by you. She's kept you in cotton when you ought to be outdoors. You should have gone to school and had other children to play with."

"And cats?"

"Cats, dogs, birds, rabbits, snakes, mice, pigeons, guinea-pigs--everything."

"I was never in cotton," corrected Araminta, "except once, when I had a bad cold."

"That isn't just what I mean, but I'm afraid I can't make you understand. There's a whole world full of big, beautiful things that you don't know anything about; great sorrows, great joys, and great loves. Look here, did you ever feel badly about anything?"

"Only--only--" stammered Araminta; "my mother, you know. She was--was married."

"Poor child," said Ralph, beginning to comprehend. "Have you been taught that it's wrong to be married?"

"Why, yes," answered Araminta, confidently. "It's dreadful. Aunt Hitty isn't married, neither is the minister. It's very, very wrong. Aunt Hitty told my mother so, but she would do it."

There was a long pause. The little warm hand still rested trustingly in Ralph's. "Listen, dear," he began, clearing his throat; "it isn't wrong to be married. I never before in all my life heard of anybody who thought it was. Something is twisted in Aunt Hitty's mind, or else she's taught you that because she's so brutally self-ish that she doesn't want you ever to be married. Some people, who are unhappy themselves, are so constituted that they can't bear to see anybody else happy. She's afraid of life, and she's taught you to be.

"It's better to be unhappy, Araminta, than never to take any risks. It all lies in yourself at last. If you're a true, loving woman, and never let yourself be afraid, nothing very bad can ever happen to you. Aunt Hitty has been unjust to deny you life. You have the right to love and learn and suffer, to make great sacrifices, see great sacrifices made for you; to believe, to trust--even to be betrayed. It's your right, and it's been kept away from you."

Araminta was very still and her hand was cold. She moved it uneasily.

"Don't, dear," said Ralph, his voice breaking. "Don't you like to have me hold your hand? I won't, if you don't want me to."

Araminta drew her hand away. She was frightened.

"I don't wonder you're afraid," continued Ralph, huskily. "You little wild bird, you've been in a cage all your life. I'm going to open the door and set you free."

Miss Evelina tapped gently on the door, then entered, with a bowl of broth for the invalid. She set it down on the table at the head of the bed, and went out, as quietly as she had come.

"I'm going to feed you now," laughed Ralph, with a swift change of mood, "and when I come to see you to-morrow, I'm going to bring you a book."

"What kind of a hook?" asked Araminta, between spoonfuls.

"A novel--a really, truly novel."

"You mustn't!" she cried, frightened again. "You get burned if you read novels."

"Some of them are pretty hot stuff, I'll admit," returned Ralph, missing her meaning, "but, of course, I wouldn't give you that kind. What sort of stories do you like best?"

"Daniel in the lions' den and about the ark. I've read all the Bible twice to Aunt Hitty while she sewed, and most of the *Pilgrim's Progress*, too. Don't ask me to read a novel, for I can't. It would be wicked."

"All right--we won't call it a novel. It'll be just a story book. It isn't wrong to read stories, is it?"

"No-o," said Araminta, doubtfully. "Aunt Hitty never said it was."

"I wouldn't have you do anything wrong, Araminta--you know that. Good-bye, now, until to-morrow."

Beset by strange emotions, Doctor Ralph Dexter went home. Finding that the carriage was not in use, he set forth alone upon his feline quest, reflecting that Araminta herself was not much more than a little grey kitten. Everywhere he went, he was regarded with suspicion. People denied the possession of cats, even while cats were mewing in defiance of the assertion. Bribes were offered, and sternly refused.

At last, ten miles from home, he found a maltese kitten its owner was willing to part with, in consideration of three dollars and a solemn promise that the cat was not to be hurt.

"It's for a little girl who is ill," he said. "I've promised her a kitten."

"So your father's often said," responded the woman, "but someway, I believe you."

On the way home, he pondered long before the hideous import of it came to him. All at once, he knew.

XIII
The River Comes into its Own

"Father," asked Ralph, "who is Evelina Grey?"

Anthony Dexter started from his chair as though he had heard a pistol shot, then settled back, forcing his features into mask-like calmness. He waited a moment before speaking.

"I don't know," he answered, trying to make his voice even, "Why?"

"She lives in the house with my one patient," explained Ralph; "up on the hill, you know. She's a frail, ghostly little woman in black, and she always wears a thick white veil."

"That's her privilege, isn't it?" queried Anthony Dexter. He had gained control of himself, now, and spoke almost as usual.

"Of course I didn't ask any questions," continued Ralph, thoughtfully, "but, obviously, the only reason for her wearing it is some terrible disfigurement. So much is surgically possible in these days that I thought something might be done for her. Has she never consulted you about it, Father?"

The man laughed--a hollow, mirthless laugh. "No," he said; "she hasn't." Then he laughed once more--in a way that jarred upon his son.

Ralph paced back and forth across the room, his hands in his pockets. "Father," he began, at length, "it may be because I'm young, but I hold before me, very strongly, the ideals of our profession. It seems a very beautiful and wonderful life that is opening before me--always to help, to give, to heal. I--I feel as though I had been dedicated to some sacred calling--some lifelong service. And service means brotherhood."

"You'll get over that," returned Anthony Dexter, shortly, yet not without a certain secret admiration. "When you've had to engage a lawyer to collect your modest wages for your uplifting work, the healed not being sufficiently grateful to pay the healer, and when you've gone ten miles in the dead of Winter, at midnight, to take a pin out of a squalling infant's back, why, you may change your mind."

"If the healed aren't grateful," observed Ralph, thoughtfully, "it must be in some way my fault, or else they haven't fully understood. And I'd go ten miles to take a pin out of a baby's back--yes, I'm sure I would."

Anthony Dexter's face softened, almost imperceptibly. "It's youth," he said, "and youth is a fault we all get over soon enough, Heaven knows. When you're forty, you'll see that the whole thing is a matter of business and that, in the last analysis, we're working against Nature's laws. We endeavour to prolong the lives of the unfit, when only the fittest should survive."

"That makes me think of something else," continued Ralph, in a low tone. "Yesterday, I canvassed the township to get a cat for Araminta--the poor child never had a kitten. Nobody would let me have one till I got far away from home, and, even then, it was difficult. They thought I wanted it for--for the laboratory," he concluded, almost in a whisper.

"Yes?" returned Doctor Dexter, with a rising inflection. "I could have told you that the cat and dog supply was somewhat depleted hereabouts--through my own experiments."

"Father!" cried Ralph, his face eloquent with reproach.

Laughing, yet secretly ashamed, Anthony Dexter began to speak. "Surely, Ralph," he said, "you're not so womanish as that. If I'd known they taught such stuff as that at my old Alma Mater, I'd have sent you somewhere else. Who's doing it? What old maid have they added to their faculty?"

"Oh, I know, Father," interrupted Ralph, waiving discussion. "I've heard all the arguments, but, unfortunately, I have a heart. I don't know by what right we assume that human life is more precious than animal life; by what right we torture and murder the fit in order to prolong the lives of the unfit, even if direct evidence were obtainable in every case, which it isn't. Anyhow, I can't do it, I never have done it, and I never will. I recognise your individual right to shape your life in accordance with the dictates of your own conscience, but, because I'm your son, I can't help being ashamed. A man capable of torturing an animal, no matter for what purpose, is also capable of torturing a fellow human being, for purposes of his own."

Anthony Dexter's face suddenly blanched with anger, then grew livid. "You--" he began, hotly.

"Don't, Father," interrupted Ralph. "We'll not have any words. We'll not let a difference of opinion on any subject keep us from being friends. Perhaps it's because I'm young, as you say, but, all the time I was at college, I felt that I had something to lean on, some standard to shape myself to. Mother died so soon after I was born that it is almost as if I had not had a mother. I haven't even a childish memory of her, and, perhaps for that reason, you meant more to me than the other fellows' fathers did to them.

"When I was tempted to any wrongdoing, the thought of you always held me back. 'Father wouldn't do it,' I said to myself. 'Father always does the square thing, and I'm his son.' I remembered that our name means 'right.' So I never did it."

"And I suppose, now," commented Anthony Dexter, with assumed sarcasm, "your idol has fallen?"

"Not fallen, Father. Don't say that. You have the same right to your opinions that I have, but it isn't square to cut up an animal alive, just because you're the stronger and there's no law to prevent you. You know it isn't square!"

In the accusing silence, Ralph left the room, and was shortly on his way uphill, with Araminta's promised cat mewing in his coat pocket.

The grim, sardonic humour of the situation appealed strongly to Doctor Dexter. "To think," he said to himself, "that only last night, that identical cat was observed as a fresh and promising specimen, providentially sent to me in the hour of need. And if I hadn't wanted Ralph to help me, Araminta's pet would at this moment have been on the laboratory table, having its heart studied--in action."

Repeatedly, he strove to find justification for a pursuit which his human instinct told him had no justification. His reason was fully adequate, but something else failed at the crucial point. He felt definitely uncomfortable and wished that Ralph might have avoided the subject. It was none of his business, anyway. But then, Ralph himself had admitted that.

His experiments were nearly completed along the line in which he had been working. In deference to a local sentiment which he felt to be extremely narrow and dwarfing, he had done his work secretly. He had kept the door of the laboratory locked and the key in his pocket. All the doors and windows had been closely barred. When his subjects had given out under the heavy physical strain, he had buried the pitiful little bodies himself.

He had counted, rather too surely, on the deafness of his old housekeeper, and had also heavily discounted her personal interest in his pursuits and her tendency to gossip. Yet, through this single channel had been disseminated information and conjecture which made it difficult for Ralph to buy a pet for Araminta.

Anthony Dexter shuddered at his narrow escape. Suppose Araminta's cat had been sacrificed, and he had been obliged to tell Ralph? One more experiment was absolutely necessary. He was nearly satisfied, but not quite. It would be awkward to have Ralph make any unpleasant discoveries, and he could not very well keep him out of the laboratory, now, without arousing his suspicion. Very possibly, a man who would torture an animal would also torture a human being, but he was unwilling to hurt Ralph. Consequently, there was a flaw in the logic--the boy's reasoning was faulty, unless this might be the exception which proved the rule.

Who was Evelina Grey? He wondered how Ralph had come to ask the question. Suppose he had told him that Evelina Grey was the name of a woman who haunted him, night and day! In her black gown and with her burned face heavily veiled, she was seldom out of his mental sight.

All through the past twenty-five years, he had continually told himself that he had forgotten. When the accusing thought presented itself, he had invariably pushed it aside, and compelled it to give way to another. In this way, he had acquired an emotional control for which he, personally, had great admiration, not observing that his admiration of himself was an emotion, and, at that, less creditable than some others might have been.

Man walls up a river, and commands it to do his bidding. Outwardly, the river assents to the arrangement, yielding to it with a readiness which, in itself, is suspicious, but man, rapt in contemplation of his own skill, sees little else. By night and by day the river leans heavily against the dam. Tiny, sharp currents, like fingers, tear constantly at the structure, working always underneath. Hidden and undreamed-of eddies burrow beneath the dam; little river animals undermine it, ever so slightly, with tooth and claw.

At last an imperceptible opening is made. Streams rush down from the mountain to join the river; even raindrops lend their individually insignificant aid. All the forces of nature are subtly arrayed against the obstruction in the river channel. Suddenly, with the thunder of pent-up waters at last unleashed, the dam breaks, and the structures placed in the path by complacent and self-satisfied man are swept on to the sea like so much kindling-wood. The river, at last, has come into its own,

A feeling, long controlled, must eventually break its bonds. Forbidden expression, and not spent by expression, it accumulates force. When the dam breaks, the flood is more destructive than the steady, normal current ever could have been. Having denied himself remorse, and having refused to meet the fact of his own cowardice, Anthony Dexter was now face to face with the inevitable catastrophe.

He told himself that Ralph's coming had begun it, but, in his heart, he knew that it was that veiled and ghostly figure standing at twilight in the wrecked garden. He had seen it again on the road, where hallucination was less likely, if not altogether impossible. Then the cold and sinuous necklace of discoloured pearls had been laid at his door--the pearls which had come first from the depths of the sea, and then from the depths of his love. His love had given up its dead as the sea does, maimed past all recognition.

The barrier had been so undermined that on the night of Ralph's return he had been on the point of telling Thorpe everything--indeed, nothing but Ralph's swift entrance had stopped his impassioned speech. Was he so weak that only a slight accident had kept him from utter self-betrayal, after twenty-five years of magnificent control? Anthony Dexter liked that word "magnificent" as it came into his thoughts in connection with himself.

"Father wouldn't do it. Father always does the square thing, and I'm his son." Ralph's words returned with a pang unbearably keen. Had Father always done the square thing, or had Father been a coward, a despicable shirk? And what if Ralph should some day come to know?

The man shuddered at the thought of the boy's face--if he knew. Those clear, honest eyes would pierce him through and through, because "Father always does the square thing."

Remorsely, the need of confession surged upon him. There was no confessional in his church--he even had no church. Yet Thorpe was his friend. What would Thorpe tell him to do?

Then Anthony Dexter laughed, for Thorpe had unconsciously told him what to do--and he was spared the confession. As though written in letters of fire, the words came back:

The honour of the spoken word still holds him. He asked her to marry him, and she consented. He was never released from his promise--did not even ask for it. He slunk away like a cur. In the sight of God he is hound to her by his own word still. He should go to her and either fulfil his promise, or ask for release. The tardy fulfilment of his promise would be the only atonement he could make.

Had Evelina come back to demand atonement? Was this why the vision of her confronted him everywhere? She waited for him on the road in daylight, mocked him from the shadows, darted to meet him from every tree. She followed him on the long and lonely ways he took to escape her, and, as he walked, her step chimed in with his.

In darkness, Anthony Dexter feared to turn suddenly, lest he see that black, veiled figure at his heels. She stood aside on the stairs to let him pass her, entered the carriage with him and sat opposite, her veiled face averted. She stood with him beside the sick-bed, listened, with him, to the heart-beats when he used the stethoscope, waited while he counted the pulse and measured the respiration.

Always disapprovingly, she stood in the background of his consciousness. When he wrote a prescription, his pencil seemed to catch on the white chiffon which veiled the paper he was using. At night, she stood beside his bed, waiting. In his sleep, most often secured in these days by drugs, she steadfastly and unfailingly came. She spoke no word; she simply followed him, veiled--and the phantom presence was driving him mad. He admitted it now.

And "Father always does the square thing." Very well, what was the square thing? If Father always does it, he will do it now. What is it?

Anthony Dexter did not know that he asked the question aloud. From the silence vibrated the answer in Thorpe's low, resonant tones:

The honour of the spoken word still holds him . . . he was never released . . . he slunk away like a cur . . . in the sight of God he is bound to her by his own word still.

Bound to her! In every fibre of his being he felt the bitter truth. He was bound to her--had been bound for twenty-five years--was bound now. And "Father always does the square thing."

Once in a man's life, perhaps, he sees himself as he is. In a blinding flash of insight, he saw what he must do. Confession must be made, but not to any pallid priest in a confessional, not to Thorpe, nor to Ralph, but to Evelina, herself.

He should go to her and either fulfil his promise, or ask for release. The tardy fulfilment of his promise would be the only atonement he could make.

Then again, still in Thorpe's voice:

If the woman is here and you can find your friend, we may help him to wash the stain of cowardice off his soul.

"The stain is deep," muttered Anthony Dexter. "God knows it is deep."

Once again came Thorpe's voice, shrilling at him, now, out of the vibrant silence:

Sometimes I think there is no sin but shirking. I can excuse a liar, I can pardon a thief, I can pity a murderer, but a shirk--no!

"Father always does the square thing."

Evidently, Ralph would like to have his father bring him a stepmother--a woman whose face had been destroyed by fire--and place her at the head of his table, veiled or not, as Ralph chose. Terribly burned, hopelessly disfigured, she must live with them always--because she had saved him from the same thing, if she had not actually saved his life.

The walls of the room swayed, the furniture moved dizzily, the floor undulated. Anthony Dexter reeled and fell--in a dead faint.

"Are you all right now, Father?" It was Ralph's voice, anxious, yet cheery. "Who'd have thought I'd get another patient so soon!"

Doctor Dexter sat up and rubbed his eyes. Memory returned slowly; strength more slowly still.

"Can't have my Father fainting all over the place without a permit," resumed Ralph. "You've been doing too much. I take the night work from this time on."

The day wore into late afternoon. Doctor Dexter lay on the couch in the library, the phantom Evelina persistently at his side. His body had failed, but his mind still fought, feebly.

"There is no one here," he said aloud. "I am all alone. I can see nothing because there is nothing here."

Was it fancy, or did the veiled woman convey the impression that her burned lips distorted themselves yet further by a smile?

At dusk, there was a call. Ralph received from his father a full history of the case, with suggestions for treatment in either of two changes that might possibly have taken place, and drove away.

The loneliness was keen. The empty house, shorne of Ralph's sunny presence, was unbearable. A thousand memories surged to meet him; a thousand voices leaped from the stillness. Always, the veiled figure stood by him, mutely accusing him of shameful cowardice. Above and beyond all was Thorpe's voice, shrilling at him:

The honour of the spoken word still holds him . . . he was never released . . . he slunk away like a cur . . . he is bound to her still . . . there is no sin but shirking . . .

Over and over again, the words rang through his consciousness. Then, like an afterclap of thunder:

Father always does the square thing!

The dam crashed, the barrier of years was broken, the obstructions were swept out to sea. Remorse and shame, no longer denied, overwhelmingly submerged his soul. He struggled up from the couch blindly, and went out--broken in body, crushed in spirit, yet triumphantly a man at last.

XIV
A Little Hour of Triumph

Miss Evelina sat alone in her parlour, which was now spotlessly clean. Araminta had had her supper, her bath, and her clean linen--there was nothing more to do until morning. The hard work had proved a blessing to Miss Evelina; her thoughts had been constantly forced away from herself. She had even learned to love Araminta with the protecting love which grows out of dependence, and, at the same time, she felt herself stronger; better fitted, as it were, to cope with her own grief.

Since coming back to her old home, her thought and feeling had been endlessly and painfully confused. She sat in her low rocker with her veil thrown back, and endeavoured to analyse herself and her surroundings, to see, if she might, whither she was being led. She was most assuredly being led, for she had not come willingly, nor remained willingly; she had been hurt here as she had not been hurt since the very first, and yet, if a dead heart can be glad of anything, she was glad she had come. Upon the far horizon of her future, she dimly saw change.

She had that particular sort of peace which comes from the knowledge that the worst is over; that nothing remains. The last drop of humiliation had been poured from her cup the day she met Anthony Dexter on the road and had been splashed with mud from his wheels as he drove by. It was inconceivable that there should be more.

Dusk came and the west gleamed faintly. The afterglow merged into the first night and at star-break, Venus blazed superbly on high, sending out rays mystically prismatic, as from some enchanted lamp. "Our star," Anthony Dexter had been wont to call it, as they watched for it in the scented dusk. For him, perhaps, it had been indeed the love-star, but she had followed it, with breaking heart, into the quicksands.

To shut out the sight of it, Miss Evelina closed the blinds and lighted a candle, then sat down again, to think.

There was a dull, uncertain rap at the door. Doctor Ralph, possibly--he had sometimes come in the evening,--or else Miss Hitty, with some delicacy for Araminta's breakfast.

Drawing down her veil, she went to the door and opened it, thinking, as she did so, that lives were often wrecked or altered by the opening or closing of a door.

Anthony Dexter brushed past her and strode into the parlour. Through her veil, she would scarcely have recognised him--he was so changed. Upon the instant, there was a transformation in herself. The suffering, broken-hearted woman was strangely pushed aside--she could come again, but she must step aside now. In her place arose a veiled vengeance, emotionless, keen, watchful; furtively searching for the place to strike.

"Evelina," began the man, without preliminary, "I have come back. I have come to tell you that I am a coward--a shirk."

Miss Evelina laughed quietly in a way that stung him. "Yes?" she said, politely. "I knew that. You need not have troubled to come and tell me."

He winced. "Don't," he muttered. "If you knew how I have suffered!"

"I have suffered myself," she returned, coldly, wondering at her own composure. She marvelled that she could speak at all.

"Twenty-five years ago," he continued in a parrot-like tone, "I asked you to marry me, and you consented. I have never been released from my promise--I did not even ask to be. I slunk away like a cur. The honour of the spoken word still holds me. The tardy fulfilment of my promise is the only atonement I can make."

The candle-light shone on his iron-grey hair, thinning at the temples; touched into bold relief every line of his face.

"Twenty-five years ago," said Evelina, in a voice curiously low and distinct, "you asked me to marry you, and I consented. You have never been released from your promise--you did not even ask to be." The silence was vibrant; literally tense with emotion. Out of it leaped, with passionate pride: "I release you now!"

"No!" he cried. "I have come to fulfil my promise--to atone, if atonement can be made!"

"Do you call your belated charity atonement? Twenty-five years ago, I saved you from death--or worse. One of us had to be burned, and it was I, instead of you. I chose it, not deliberately, but instinctively, because I loved you. When you came to the hospital, after three days----"

"I was ill," he interrupted. "The gas----"

"You were told," she went on, her voice dominating his, "that I had been so badly burned that I would be disfigured for life. That was enough for you. You never asked to see me, never tried in any way to help me, never sent by a messenger a word of thanks for your cowardly life, never even waited to be sure it was not a mistake. You simply went away."

"There was no mistake," he muttered, helplessly. "I made sure."

He turned his eyes away from her miserably. Through his mind came detached fragments of speech. The honour of the spoken word still holds him . . . Father always does the square thing . . .

"I am asking you," said Anthony Dexter, "to be my wife. I am offering you the fulfilment of the promise I made so long ago. I am asking you to marry me, to live with me, to be a mother to my son."

"Yes," repeated Evelina, "you ask me to marry you. Would you have a scarred and disfigured wife? A man usually chooses a beautiful woman, or one he thinks beautiful, to sit at the head of his table, manage his house, take the place of a servant when it is necessary, accept gladly what money he chooses to give her, and bear and rear his children. Poor thing that I am, you offer me this. In return, I offer you release. I gave you your life once, I give you freedom now. Take your last look at the woman who would not marry you to save you from--hell!"

The man started forward, his face ashen, for she had raised her veil, and was standing full in the light.

In the tense silence he gazed at her, fascinated. Every emotion that possessed him was written plainly on his face for her to read. "The night of realisation," she was saying, "turned my hair white. Since I left the hospital, no human being has seen my face till now. I think you understand--why?"

Anthony Dexter breathed hard; his body trembled. He was suffering as the helpless animals had suffered on the table in his laboratory. Evelina was merciless, but at last, when he thought she had no pity, she lowered her veil.

The length of chiffon fell between them eternally; it was like the closing of a door. "I understand," he breathed, "oh, I understand. It is my punishment--you have scored at last. Good----"

A sob drowned the last word. He took her cold hand in his, and, bending over it, touched it with his quivering lips.

"Yes," laughed Evelina, "kiss my hand, if you choose. Why not? My hand was not burned!"

His face working piteously, he floundered out into the night and staggered through the gate as he had come--alone.

The night wind came through the open door, dank and cold. She closed it, then bolted it as though to shut out Anthony Dexter for ever.

It was his punishment, he had said. She had scored at last. If he had suffered, as he told her he had, the sight of her face would be torture. Yes, Evelina knew that she had scored. From her hand she wiped away tears--a man's hot, terrible tears.

Through the night she sat there, wide-eyed and sleepless, fearlessly unveiled. The chiffon trailed its misty length unheeded upon the floor. The man she had loved was as surely dead to her as though he had never been.

Anthony Dexter was dead. True, his body and mind still lived, but he was not the man she had loved. The face that had looked into hers was not the face of Anthony Dexter. It had been cold and calm and cruel, until he came to her house. His eyes were fish-like, and, stirred by emotion, he was little less than hideous.

Her suffering had been an obsession--there had been no reason for it, not the shadow of an excuse. A year, as the Piper said, would have been long enough for her to grieve. She saw her long sorrow now as something outside of herself, a beast whose prey she had been. When Anthony Dexter had proved himself a coward, she should have thanked God that she knew him before it was too late. And because she was weak in body, because her hurt heart still clung to her love for him, she had groped in the darkness for more than half of her life.

And now he had come back! The blood of triumph surged hard. She loved him no longer; then, why was she not free? Her chains yet lay heavily upon her; in the midst of victory, she was still bound.

The night waned. She was exhausted by stress of feeling and the long vigil, but the iron, icy hand that had clasped her .heart so long did not for a moment relax its hold. She went to the window and looked out. Stars were paling, the mysterious East had trembled; soon it would be day.

She watched the dawn as though it were for the first time and she was privileged to stand upon some lofty peak when "God said: 'Let there be light,' and there was light." The tapestry of morning flamed splendidly across the night, reflecting its colour back upon her unveiled face.

From far away, in the distant hills, whose summits only as yet were touched with dawn, came faint, sweet music--the pipes o' Pan. She guessed that the Piper was abroad with Laddie, in some fantastic spirit of sun-worship, and smiled.

Her little hour of triumph was over; her soul was once more back in its prison. The prison house was larger, and different, but it was still a prison. For an instant, freedom had flashed before her and dazed her; now it was dark again.

"Why?" breathed Evelina. "Dear God, why?"

As if in answer, the music came back from the hills in uncertain silvery echoes. "Oh, pipes o' Pan," cried Evelina, choking back a sob, "I pray you, find me! I pray you, teach me joy!"

XV
The State of Araminta's Soul

The Reverend Austin Thorpe was in his room at Miss Mehitable's, with a pencil held loosely in his wrinkled hand. On the table before him was a pile of rough copy paper, and at the top of the first sheet was written, in capitals, the one word: "Hell." It was underlined, and around it he had drawn sundry fantastic flourishes and shadings, but the rest of the sheet was blank.

For more than an hour the old man had sat there, his blue, near-sighted eyes wandering about the room. A self-appointed committee from his congregation had visited him and requested him to preach a sermon on the future abode of the wicked. The wicked, as the minister gathered from the frank talk of the committee, included all who did not belong to their own sect.

Try as he might, the minister could find in his heart nothing save charity. Anger and resentment were outside of his nature. He told himself that he knew the world, and had experienced his share of injustice, that he had seen sin in all of its hideous phases. Yet, even for the unrepentant sinner, Thorpe had only kindness.

Of one sin only, Thorpe failed in comprehension. As he had said to Anthony Dexter, he could excuse a liar, pardon a thief, and pity a murderer, but he had only contempt for a shirk.

Persistently, he analysed and questioned himself, but got no further. To him, all sin resolved itself at last into injustice, and he did not believe that any one was ever intentionally unjust. But the congregation desired to hear of hell--"as if," thought Thorpe, whimsically, "I received daily reports."

With a sigh, he turned to his blank sheet. "In the earlier stages of our belief," he wrote, "we conceived of hell as literally a place of fire and brimstone, of eternal suffering and torture. In the light which has come to us later, we perceive that hell is a spiritual state, and realise that the consciousness of a sin is its punishment."

Then he tore the sheet into bits, for this was not what his congregation wanted; yet it was his sincere belief. He could not stultify himself to please his audience-- they must take him as he was, or let him go.

Yet the thought of leaving was unpleasant, for he had found work to do in a field where, as it seemed to him, he was sorely needed. His parishioners had heard much of punishment, but very little of mercy and love. They were tangled in doctrinal meshes, distraught by quibbles, and at swords' points with each other.

He felt that he must in some way temporise, and hold his place until he had led his flock to a loftier height. He had no desire to force his opinions upon any one else, but he wished to make clear his own strong, simple faith, and spread abroad, if he might, his own perfect trust.

A commanding rap resounded upon his door. "Come," he called, and Miss Mehitable entered.

Thorpe was not subtle, but he felt that this errand was of deeper import than usual. The rustle of her stiffly-starched garments was portentous, and there was a set look about her mouth which boded no good to anybody.

"Will you sit down?" he asked, offering her his own chair.

"No," snapped Miss Mehitable, "I won't. What I've got to say, I can say standin'. I come," she announced, solemnly, "from the Ladies' Aid Society."

"Yes?" Thorpe's tone was interrogative, but he was evidently not particularly interested.

"I'm appointed a committee of one," she resumed, "to say that the Ladies' Aid Society have voted unanimously that they want you to preach on hell. The Church is goin' to rack and ruin, and we ain't goin' to stand it no longer. Even the disreputable characters will walk right in and stay all through the sermon--Andy Rogers and the rest. And I was particularly requested to ask whether you wished to have us understand that you approve of Andy Rogers and his goin's on."

"What," temporised Thorpe, "does Andy Rogers do?"

"For the lands sake!" ejaculated Miss Mehitable. "Wasn't he drunk four months ago and wasn't he caught stealing the Deacon's chickens? You don't mean to tell me you never heard of that?"

"I believe I did hear," returned the minister, in polite recognition of the fact that it had been Miss Mehitable's sole conversational topic at the time. "He stole the chickens because he was hungry, and he got drunk because he didn't know any better. I talked with him, and he promised me that he would neither steal nor drink any more. Moreover, he earned the money and paid full price for the chickens. Have you heard that he has broken his promise?"

"No I dunno's I have, but he'll do it again if he gets the chance--you just see!"

Thorpe drummed idly on the table with his pencil, wishing that Miss Mehitable would go. He had for his fellow-men that deep and abiding love which enables one to let other people alone. He was a humanitarian in a broad and admirable sense.

"I was told," said Miss Mehitable, "to get a definite answer."

Thorpe bowed his white head ever so slightly. "You may tell the Ladies' Aid Society, for me, that next Sunday morning I will give my congregation a sermon on hell."

"I thought I could make you see the reason in it," remarked Miss Mehitable, piously taking credit to herself, "and now that it's settled, I want to speak of Araminta."

"She's getting well all right, isn't she?" queried Thorpe, anxiously. He had a tender place in his heart for the child.

"That's what I don't know, not bein' allowed to speak to her or touch her. What I do know is that her immortal soul is in peril, now that she's taken away from my influence. I want you to get a permit from that black-mailing play-doctor that's curing her, or pretending to, and go up and see her. I guess her pastor has a right to see her, even if her poor old aunt ain't. I want you to find out when she'll be able to be moved, and talk to her about her soul, dwellin' particularly on hell."

Thorpe bowed again. "I will be very glad to do anything I can for Araminta."

Shortly afterward, he made an errand to Doctor Dexter's and saw Ralph, who readily gave him permission to visit his entire clientele.

"I've got another patient," laughed the boy. "My practice is increasing at the rate of one case a month. If I weren't too high-minded to dump a batch of germs into the water supply, I'd have a lot more."

"How is Araminta?" asked Thorpe, passing by Ralph's frivolity.

"She's all right," he answered, his sunny face clouding. "She can go home almost any time now. I hate to send her back into her cage--bless her little heart."

It was late afternoon when Thorpe started up the hill, to observe and report upon the state of Araminta's soul. He had struggled vainly with his own problem, and had at last decided to read a fiery sermon by one of the early evangelists, from a volume which he happened to have. The sermon was lurid with flame, and he thought it would satisfy his congregation. He would preface it with the statement that it was not his, but he hoped they would regard it as a privilege to hear the views of a man who was, without doubt, wiser and better than he.

Miss Evelina came to the door when he rapped, and at the sight of her veiled face, a flood of pity overwhelmed him. He introduced himself and asked whether he might see Araminta.

When he was ushered into the invalid's room, he found her propped up by pillows, and her hair was rioting in waves about her flushed face. A small maltese kitten, curled into a fluffy ball, slept on the snowy counterpane beside her. Araminta had been reading the "story book" which Doctor Ralph had brought her.

"Little maid," asked the minister, "how is the ankle?"

"It's well, and to-morrow I'm to walk on it for the first time. Doctor Ralph has been so good to me--everybody's been good."

Thorpe picked up the book, which lay face downward, and held it close to his near-sighted eyes. Araminta trembled; she was afraid he would take it away from her.

All that day, she had lived in a new land, where men were brave and women were fair. Castle towers loomed darkly purple in the sunset, or shone whitely at noon. Kings and queens, knights and ladies, moved sedately across the tapestry, mounted on white chargers with trappings of scarlet and gold. Long lances shimmered in the sun and the armour of the knights gave back the light an hundred fold. Strange music sounded in Araminta's ears--love songs and serenades, hymns of battle and bugle calls. She felt the rush of conflict, knew the anguish of the wounded, and heard the exultant strains of victory.

And all of it--Araminta had greatly marvelled at this--was done for love, the love of man and woman.

A knight in the book had asked the lady of his heart to marry him, and she had not seen that she was insulted, nor guessed that he was offering her disgrace.

Araminta wondered that the beautiful lady could be so stupid, but, of course, she had no Aunt Hitty to set her right. Far from feeling shame, the lady's heart had sung for joy, but secretly, since she was proud. Further on, the same beautiful lady had humbled her pride for the sake of her love and had asked the gallant knight to marry her, since she had once refused to marry him.

"Why, Araminta!" exclaimed Mr. Thorpe, greatly surprised. "I thought Miss Mehitable did not allow you to read novels."

"A novel! Why, no, Mr. Thorpe, it isn't a novel! It's just a story book. Doctor Ralph told me so."

Austin Thorpe laughed indulgently. "A rose by any other name," he said, "is-- none the less a rose. Doctor Ralph was right--it is a story book, and I am right, too, for it is also a novel."

Araminta turned very pale and her eyes filled with tears.

"Mr. Thorpe," she said, in an anguished whisper, "will I be burned?"

"Why, child, what do you mean?"

"I didn't know it was a novel," sobbed Araminta. "I thought it was a story book. Aunt Hitty says people who read novels get burned--they writhe in hell forever in the lake of fire."

The Reverend Austin Thorpe went to the door and looked out into the hall. No one was in sight. He closed the door very gently and came back to Araminta's bed. He drew his chair nearer and leaned over her, speaking in a low voice, that he might not be heard.

"Araminta, my poor child," he said, "perhaps I am a heretic. I don't know. But I do not believe that a being divine enough to be a God could be human enough to cherish so fiendish a passion as revenge. Look up, dear child, look up!"

Araminta turned toward him obediently, but she was still sobbing.

"It is a world of mystery," he went on. "We do not know why we come nor where we go--we only know that we come and that eventually, we go. Yet I do not think that any one of us nor any number of us have the right to say what the rest of us shall believe.

"I cannot think of Heaven as a place sparsely populated by my own sect, with a world of sinners languishing in flames below. I think of Heaven as a sunny field, where clover blooms and birds sing all day. There are trees, with long, cool shadows where the weary may rest; there is a crystal stream where they may forget their thirst. I do not think of Heaven as a place of judgment, but rather of pardon and love.

"Punishment there is, undoubtedly, but it has seemed to me that we are sufficiently punished here for all we do that is wrong. We don't intend to do wrong, Araminta--we get tired, and things and people worry us, and we are unjust. We are like children afraid in the dark; we live in a world of doubting, we are made the slaves of our own fears, and so we shirk."

"But the burning," said Araminta, wiping her eyes. "Is nobody ever to be burned?"

"The God I worship," answered Thorpe, passionately, "never could be cruel, but there are many gods, it seems, and many strange beliefs. Listen, Araminta. Whom do you love most?"

"Aunt Hitty?" she questioned.

"No, you don't have to say that if it isn't so. You can be honest with me. Who, of all the world, is nearest to you? Whom would you choose to be with you always, if you could have only one?"

"Doctor Ralph!" cried Araminta, her eyes shining.

"I thought so," replied Thorpe. "I don't know that I blame you. Now suppose Doctor Ralph did things that hurt you; that there was continual misunderstanding and distrust. Suppose he wronged you, cruelly, and apparently did everything he could to distress you and make you miserable. Could you condemn him to a lake of fire?"

"Why, no!" she cried. "I'd know he never meant to do it!"

"Suppose you knew he meant it?" persisted Thorpe, looking at her keenly.

"Then," said Araminta, tenderly, "I'd feel very, very sorry."

"Exactly, and why? Because, as you say, you love him. And God is love, Araminta. Do you understand?"

Upon the cramped and imprisoned soul of the child, the light slowly dawned. "God is love," she repeated, "and nobody would burn people they loved."

There was an illuminating silence, then Thorpe spoke again. He told Araminta of a love so vast and deep that it could not be measured by finite standards; of infinite pity and infinite pardon. This love was everywhere; it was impossible to conceive of a place where it was not--it enveloped not only the whole world, but all the shining worlds beyond. And this love, in itself and of itself, was God.

"This," said Araminta, touching the book timidly; "is it bad?"

"Nothing is bad," explained Thorpe, carefully, "which does not harm you or some one else. Of the two, it is better to harm yourself than another. How does the book make you feel?"

"It makes me feel as if the world was a beautiful place, and as if I ought to be better, so I could make it still more beautiful by living in it."

"Then, Araminta, it is a good book."

Thorpe went down-stairs strangely uplifted. To him, Truth was not a creed, but a light which illumined all creeds. His soul was aflame with eagerness to help and comfort the whole world. Miss Evelina was waiting in the hall, veiled and silent, as always.

She opened the door, but Thorpe lingered, striving vainly for the right word. He could not find it, but he had to speak.

"Miss Evelina," he stammered, the high colour mounting to his temples, "if there should ever be anything I can do for you, will you let me know?"

She seemed to shrink back into her veil. "Yes," she said, at length, "I will." Then, fearing she had been ungracious, she added: "Thank you."

His mood of exaltation was still upon him, and he wandered long in the woods before going home. His spirit dwelt in the high places, and from the height he gained the broad view.

When he entered the house. Miss Mehitable was waiting for him with a torrent of questions. When he had an opportunity to reply he reported that he had seen Doctor Ralph and Araminta could come home almost any time, now. Yes, he had talked with Araminta about her soul, and she had cried. He thought he had done her good by going, and was greatly indebted to Miss Mehitable for the suggestion.

XVI
The March of the Days

Out in the garden, the Piper was attending to his belated planting. He had cleared the entire place, repaired the wall, and made flower-beds in fantastic shapes that pleased his own fancy. To-day, he was putting in the seeds, while Laddie played about his feet, and Miss Evelina stood by, timidly watchful.

"I do not see," she said, "why you take so much trouble to make me a garden. Nobody was ever so good to me before."

The Piper laughed and paused a moment to wipe his ruddy face. "Did nobody ever care before whether or not you had a garden?"

"Never," returned Evelina, sadly.

"Then 't is time some one did, so Laddie and I have come to make it for you, but I'm thinking 't is largely for ourselves, too, since the doing is the best part of anything."

Miss Evelina made no answer. Speech did not come easily to her after twenty-five years of habitual repression.

"'T will be a brave garden," continued the Piper, cheerily. "Marigolds and lark-spur and mignonette; phlox and lad's love, rosemary, lavender, and verbena, and many another that you'll not guess till the time comes for blossoming."

"Lad's love grew in my garden once," sighed Evelina, after a little. "It was sweet while it lasted--oh, but it was sweet!"

She spoke so passionately that the Piper gathered the underlying significance of her words.

"You're speaking of another garden, I think," he ventured; "the garden in your heart. "'T is meet that lad's love should grow there. Are you sure 't was not a weed?"

"Yes, it was a weed," she replied, bitterly. "The mistake was mine."

The Piper leaned on his rake thoughtfully. "'T is hard, I think," he said, "for us to see that the mistakes are all ours. The Gardener plants rightly, but we are never satisfied. When sweet herbs are meant for us, we ask for roses, and 't is not every garden in which a rose will bloom. If we could keep it clean of weeds, and make it free of all anger and distrust, there'd be heartsease there instead of thorns."

"Heartsease?" asked Evelina, piteously. "I thought there was no more!"

"Lady," said the Piper, "there is heartsease for the asking. I'm thinking 't is you who have spoiled your garden."

"No!" cried Evelina. "Believe me, it was not I!"

"Who else?" queried the Piper, with a look which made her shrink farther back into the shelter of her chiffon. "Ah, I was not asking a question that needed an answer; I do not concern myself with names and things. But ask this of yourself--is there sin on your soul?"

"No," she whispered, "unless it be a sin to suffer for twenty-five years."

"Another's sin, then? You're grieving because another has done wrong?"

"Because another has done wrong to me." The Piper came to her and laid his hand very gently upon hers. There was reassurance in the friendly, human touch. "'T is there," he said, "that the trouble lies. 'T is not for you to suffer because you are wronged, but for the one who has wronged you. He must have been very dear to you, I'm thinking; else you would not hide the beauty of your face."

"Beauty?" repeated Evelina, scornfully. "You do not understand. I was burned--horribly burned."

"Yes," said the Piper, softly, "and what of that? Beauty is of the soul."

He went out to the gate and brought in a small, flat box. "'T is for you," he said. "I got it for you when I went to the city--there was none here."

She opened the box, her fingers trembling, and held up length after length of misty white chiffon. "I ask no questions," said the Piper, proudly, "but I know that because you are so beautiful, you hide your face. Laddie and I, we got more of the white stuff to help you hide it, because you would not let us see how beautiful you are."

The chiffon fluttered in her hand, though there was no wind. "Why?" she asked, in a strange voice; "why did you do this?"

"You gave me a garden," laughed the Piper, "when I had no garden of my own, so why should I not get the white stuff for you? 'T was queer, the day I got it," he went on, chuckling at the recollection, "for I did not know its name. Every place I went, I asked for white stuff, and they showed me many kinds, but nothing like this. At last I said to a young girl: 'What is it that is like a cloud, all white and soft, which one can see through, but through which no one can be seen--the stuff that ladies wear when they are so beautiful that they do not want their faces seen?' She smiled, and told me it was 'chiffon.' And so--" A wave of the hand finished his explanation.

After an interval of silence, the Piper spoke again. "There are chains that bind you," he began, "but they are chains of your own forging. No one else can shackle you--you must always do it yourself. Whatever is past is over, and I'm thinking you have no more to do with it than a butterfly has with the empty chrysalis from which he came. The law of life is growth, and we cannot linger--we must always be going on.

"You stand alone upon a height," he said, dreamily, "like one in a dreary land. Behind you all is darkness, before you all is darkness; there is but one small space of light. In that one space is a day. They come, one at a time, from the night of To-morrow, and vanish into the night of Yesterday.

"I have thought of the days as men and women, for a woman's day is not at all like a man's. For you, I think, they first were children, with laughing eyes and little, dimpled hands. One at a time, they came out of the darkness, and disappeared into the darkness on the other side. Some brought you flowers or new toys and some brought you childish griefs, but none came empty-handed. Each day laid its gift at your feet and went on.

"Some brought their gifts wrapped up, that you might have the surprise of opening them. Many a gift in a bright-hued covering turned out to be far from what you expected when you were opening it. Some of the happiest gifts were hidden in dull coverings you took off slowly, dreading to see the contents. Some days brought many gifts, others only one.

"As the days grew older, some brought you laughter; some gave you light and love. Others came with music and pleasure--and some of them brought pain."

"Yes," sighed Evelina, "some brought pain."

"It is of that," went on the Piper, "that I wished to be speaking. It was one day, was it not, that brought you a long sorrow?"

"Yes."

"Not more than one? Was it only one day?"

"Yes, only one day,"

"See," said The Piper, gently, "the day came with her gift. You would not let her lay it at your feet and pass on into the darkness of Yesterday. You held her by her grey garments and would not let her go. You kept searching her sad eyes to see whether she did not have further pain for you. Why keep her back from her appointed way? Why not let your days go by?"

"The other days," murmured Evelina, "have all been sad."

"Yes, and why? You were holding fast to one day--the one that brought you pain. So, with downcast eyes they passed you, and carried their appointed gifts on into Yesterday, where you can never find them again. Even now, the one day you have been holding is struggling to free herself from the chains you have put upon her. You have no right to keep a day."

"Should I not keep the gifts?" she asked. His fancy pleased her.

"The gifts, yes--even the gifts of tears, but never a day. You cannot hold a happy day, for it goes too quickly. This one sad day that marched so slowly by you is the one you chose to hold. Lady," he pleaded, "let her go!"

"The other days," she whispered, brokenly. "What of them?"

"No man can say. While you have been holding this one, the others have passed you, taking your gifts into Yesterday. Memory guards Yesterday, but there is a veil on the face of To-morrow. Sometimes I think To-morrow is so beautiful that she hides her face."

"God veils her face," cried Evelina, "or else we could not live!"

"Lady," said the Piper, "have you lived so long and never learned this simple thing? Whatever a day may bring you, whatever terrible gifts of woe, if you search her closely, you will always find the strength to meet her face to face. Overshadowed by her burden of bitterness, one fails to find the balm. Concealed within her garments or held loosely in her hand, she always has her bit of consolation; rosemary in the midst of her rue, belief with the doubt, life with the death."

"I found no balm," murmured Evelina, "in the day you say I held."

"Had there been no secret balm, you could never have held her--the thorns would have pierced your hands. Have you not seen that you can never have sorrow until you have first had joy? Happiness is the light and sadness the shade. God sets you right, and you stray from the path, into the shadow of the cypress."

"The cypress casts a long shadow," said Evelina, pointing to the tree at the gate.

The Piper smiled. "The shadow of a sorrow is longer than the sorrow," he answered. "The shadow of one day, with you, has stretched over twenty-five years. 'T is approaching night that makes long shadows; when life is at noon, they are short. When life is at its highest, there are no shadows at all."

Miss Evelina sighed and leaned uneasily against the wall.

"This, I'm thinking," mused the Piper, "is the inmost truth of living--there is always a balance which swings true. A sorrow is precisely equal to a joy, and the shadow can loom no larger unless the light slants. And if you sit always in the sun, the shadow that lies behind a joy can be scarcely seen at all."

A faint breath of Spring stirred Miss Evelina's veil. She caught at it and tied the long floating ends about her neck.

"I would not look," said the Piper, softly. "If your veil should blow away, I would close my eyes and feel my way to the gate. Unless you chose to have me see your beauty, I would never ask, nor take advantage of an accidental opportunity. I'm thinking you are very beautiful, but you need never be afraid of me."

Miss Evelina did not reply; she only leaned more heavily against the wall.

"Lady," he continued, "perhaps you think I do not know. You may think I'm talking blindly, but there are few sorrows in the world that I have not seen face to face. Those I have not had myself, my friends have had, and I have been privileged to share with them. The sorrows of the world are not so many--they are few, and, in essence, the same.

"It's very strange, I'm thinking. The little laughing, creeping days go by us, then the awkward ones that bring us the first footsteps, then childhood comes, and youth, and then maturity. But the days have begun to grow feeble before one learns how to meet them; how to take the gifts humbly, scorning none, and how to make each day give up its secret balm. Memory, the angel who stands at the portal of Yesterday, has always an inscrutable smile. She keeps for us so many things that we would be glad to spare, and pushes headlong into Yesterday so much that we fain would keep. I do not yet know all the ways of Memory--I only know that she means to be kind."

"Kind!" repeated Evelina. Her tone was indescribably bitter.

"Yes," returned the Piper, "Memory means to be kind--she is kind. I have said that I do not know her ways, but of that I am sure. Lady, I would that you could let go of the day you are holding back. Cast her from you, and let her go into the Yesterday from which you have kept her so long. Perhaps Memory will be kinder to you then, for, remember, she stands at the gate."

"I cannot," breathed Evelina. "I have tried and I cannot let her go!"

"Yes," said the Piper, very gently, "you can. 'T is that, I'm thinking, that has set your life all wrong. Unclasp your hands from her rough garments, cease to question her closed eyes. Take her gift and the balm that infallibly comes with it; meet To-day with kindness and To-morrow with a brave heart. Oh, Spinner in the Shadow," he cried, his voice breaking, "I fain would see you a Spinner in the Sun!"

"No," she sighed, "I have been in the dark too long. There is no light for me."

"There is light," he insisted. "When you admit the shadow, you have at the same time acknowledged the light."

Evelina shook her head. "Too late," she said, despairingly; "it is too late."

"Ah," cried the Piper, "if you could only trust me! I have helped many a soul into the sun again."

"I trusted," said Evelina, "and my trust was betrayed."

"Yes," he answered, "I know. I have trusted, too, and I have been betrayed, also, but I know that the one who wronged me must suffer more than I."

She laughed; a wild, fantastic laugh. "The one who wronged me," she said, "has not suffered at all. He married in a year."

"There are different ways of suffering," he explained. "With a woman, it is most often spread out over a long period. The quick, clean-cut stroke is seldom given to a woman--she suffers less and longer than a man. With him, I'm thinking, it has come, or will come, all at once."

"If it does," she cried, her frail body quivering, "what a day for him, oh, what a day!"

Her voice was trembling with the hideous passion for revenge, and the Piper read her, unerringly. "Lady," he said, sadly, "'t is a long way to the light, but I'm here to help | you find it. We'll be going now. Laddie and I, but we'll come back soon."

He whistled to the dog and the two went off downhill together. She watched him from the gate until the bobbing red feather turned a corner at the foot of the hill, and the cheery whistle had ceased.

The stillness was acute, profound. It was so deep that it seemed positive, rather than negative. She went back into the house, her steps dragging painfully.

As in a vision she saw the days passing her while she stood upon a height. All around her were bare rocks and fearful precipices; there was nothing but a narrow path in front. Day by day, they came, peacefully, contentedly; till at last dawned that terrible one which had blasted her life. Was it true that she still held that day by the garment, and could not unclasp her hands?

One by one they had passed her, leaving no gifts, because she still clung to one. If she could let go, what gifts would the others bring? Joy? Never--there was no joy in the world for her.

Sometime that mystical procession must come to an end. When the last day passed on, she would follow, too, and go into the night of Yesterday, where, perhaps, there was peace. As never before, she craved the last gift, praying to see the uplifted head and stately figure of the last Day--grave, silent, unfathomable, tender; the Day with the veiled face, bearing white poppies in her hands.

XVII
Loved by a Dog

Anthony Dexter sat on the porch in front of his house, alone. Ralph had been out since early morning, attending to his calls. It was the last of April and the trees were brave in their panoply of new leaves. Birds were singing and the very air was eloquent with new life.

Between Anthony Dexter and the lilac bush at the gate, there moved perpetually the black, veiled figure of Evelina Grey. He knew she was not there and he was fully certain of the fact that it was an hallucination, but his assurance had not done away with the phantom.

How mercilessly she followed him! Since the night he had flung himself out of her house, tortured in every nerve, she had not for a moment left him. When he walked through the house, she followed him, her stealthy footfall sounding just the merest fraction of a second after his. He avoided the bare polished floors and walked on the rugs whenever possible, that he might not hear that soft, slow step so plainly. Ralph had laughed at him, once, for taking a long, awkward jump from rug to rug.

Within the line of his vision she moved horizontally, but never back and forth. Sometimes her veiled face was averted, and sometimes, through the eternal barrier of chiffon, he could feel her burning eyes fixed pitilessly upon his.

He never slept, now, without drugs. Gradually he had increased the dose, but to no purpose. Evelina haunted his sleep endlessly and he had no respite. Through the dull stupor of the night, she was never for a moment absent, and in every horrible dream, she stood in the foreground, mute, solitary, accusing.

He was fully aware of the fact that he was in the clutches of a drug addiction, but that was nothing to be feared in comparison with his veiled phantom. He had exhausted the harmless soporifics long ago, and turned, perforce, to the swift and deadly ministers of forgetfulness.

The veiled figure moved slowly back and forth across the yard, lifting its skirts daintily to avoid a tiny pool of water where a thirsty robin was drinking. The robin, evidently, did not fear Evelina. He could hear the soft, slow footfalls on the turf, and the echo of three or four steps upon the brick walk, when she crossed. She kept carefully within the line of his vision; he did not have to turn his head to see her. When he did turn his head, she moved with equal swiftness. Not for a single pitying instant was she out of his sight.

Farther on, doubtless, as he thought, she would come closer. She might throw back her veil as she had done on that terrible night, or lay her cold hand on his--she might even speak to him. What hideous conversations they might have--he and the woman he had once loved and to whom he was still bound! Anthony Dexter knew now that even his marriage had not released him and that Evelina had held him, through all the five-and-twenty years.

Such happiness as he had known had been purely negative. The thrill of joyous life had died, for him, the day he took Evelina into the laboratory. He was no longer capable of caring for any one except Ralph. The remnant of his cowardly heart was passionately and wholly given to his son.

He meditated laying his case before Ralph. as one physician to another, then the inmost soul of him shuddered at the very thought. Rather than have Ralph know, he would die a thousand deaths. He would face the uttermost depths of hell, rather than see those clear, honest eyes fixed upon him in judgment.

He might go to the city to see a specialist--it would be an easy matter to accomplish, and Ralph would gladly attend to his work. Yes, he might go--he and Evelina. He could go to a brother physician and say:

"This woman haunts me. She saved my life and continually follows me. I want her kept away. What, do you not see her, too?"

Anthony Dexter laughed harshly, and fancied that the veiled figure paused slightly at the sound. "No," he said, aloud, "you need not prepare for travel, Evelina. We shall not go to the city--you and I."

That was his mate, walking in his garden before him, veiled. She was his and he was hers. They were mated as two atoms of hydrogen and one of oxygen, forming a molecule of water. All these years, her suffering had reacted upon him, kept him from being happy, and made him fight continually to keep her out of his remembrance. For having kept her out, he was paying, now, with compound interest.

Upon a lofty spire of granite stands a wireless telegraph instrument. Fogs are thick about it, wild surges crash in the unfathomable depths below; the silence is that of chaos, before the first day of creation. Out of the emptiness, a world away, comes a message. At the first syllable, the wireless instrument leaps to answer its mate. With the universe between them, those two are bound together, inextricably, eternally bound. One may fancy that a disorder in one might cause vague unrest in the other. In like manner, Evelina's obsession had preyed upon Anthony Dexter for twenty-five years. Now, the line was at work again and there was an unceasing flow of communication.

Perhaps, if he had the strength, he might learn to ignore the phantom as he had ignored memory. Eventually, he might be able to put aside the eternal presence as he had put aside his own cowardice. There was indefinite comfort in the thought.

Having preached the gospel of work for so long, he began to apply it to himself. Work was undoubtedly what he needed--the one thing which could set him right again. After a little, he could make the rounds with Ralph, and dwell constantly in the boy's sunny presence. In the meantime, there was his paper, for the completion of which one more experiment was absolutely essential.

He stirred uneasily in his chair. He wished that Ralph had not been so womanish, or else that he had more diplomatically concealed his own opinions, to which, indeed, Ralph had admitted his right. Condemnation from Ralph was the one thing he could not bear, but, after all, was it needful that Ralph should know?

The experiment would not take long, as he wished to satisfy himself on but one minor point. It could be done, easily, while Ralph was out upon his daily round. Behind the lilac bushes there was yet room for one more tiny grave.

One more experiment, and then, in deference to Ralph's foolish, effeminate sentiments, he would give it up. One more heart in action, the conclusion of his brilliant paper, and then--why, he would be willing to devote the rest of his life, in company with Ralph, to curing whooping-cough, measles, and mumps.

The veiled figure still paced restlessly back and forth, now on the turf and now on the brick walk. He closed his eyes, but he still saw Evelina and noted the slight difference of sound in her footfalls as she crossed the walk. He heard the swish of her skirts as she lifted them when she passed the pool of water--was it possible that his hearing was becoming more keen? He was sure that he had not heard it from that distance before.

It was certainly an inviting yard and the gate stood temptingly ajar. The gravelled highway was rough for a little dog's feet, and Laddie and the Piper had travelled far. For many a mile, there had been no water, and in this cool, green yard, there was a small pool. Laddie whined softly and nosed the gate farther open.

A man sat on the porch, but he was asleep--anyhow, his eyes were closed. Perhaps he had a dog of his own. At any rate, he could not object to a tired yellow mongrel quenching his thirst at his pool. The Piper had gone on without observing that his wayworn companion had stopped.

Except for a mob of boys who had thrown stones at him and broken his leg, humans had been kind to Laddie. It had been a human, Piper Tom, in fact, who had rescued him from the boys and made his leg good again. Laddie cherished no resentment against the mob, for he had that eternal forgiveness of blows and neglect which lives in the heart of the commonest cur.

Opening his eyes, Anthony Dexter noted that a small, rough-coated yellow dog was drinking eagerly at the pool of water past which Evelina continually moved. She went by twice while the dog was drinking, but he took no notice of her. Neither robins nor dogs seemed to fear Evelina--it was only men, or, to be exact, one man, who had hitherto feared nothing save self-analysis.

The turf was cool and soft to a little dog's tired feet. Laddie walked leisurely toward the shrubbery, where there was deep and quiet shade. Under the lilac bush, he lay down to rest, but was presently on his feet again, curiously exploring the place.

He sniffed carefully at the ground behind the lilac bushes, and the wiry hair on his back bristled. There was something uncanny about it, and a guarding instinct warned him away. But what was this that lay on the ground, so soaked with rains that, in the shade, it had not yet dried? Laddie dragged it out into the sunlight to see.

It was small and square and soft on the outside, yet hard within. Except for the soft, damp outer covering, it might have been the block of pine with which Piper Tom and he would play by the hour. The Piper would throw the block of wood far from him, sometimes even into the water, and Laddie would race after it, barking gaily. When he brought it back, he was rewarded with a pat on the head, or, sometimes, a bone. Always, there would be friendly talk. Perhaps the man on the porch had thrown this, and was waiting for him to bring it back.

Laddie took the mysterious thing carefully in his strong jaws, and trotted exultantly up to the porch, wagging his stub of a tail. Strangely enough, just at the steps, the thing opened, and something small and cold and snake-like slipped out. The man could scarcely have seen the necklace of discoloured pearls before, with an oath, he rose to his feet, and, firmly holding Laddie under his arm, strode into the house, entering at the side door.

The Piper had reached home before he missed his dog. He waited a little, then called, but there was no answer. It was not like Laddie to stray, for he was usually close at his master's heels.

"Poor little man," said the Piper to himself, "I'm thinking we went too far."

He retraced his steps over the dusty road, searching the ground. He discovered that Laddie's tracks ended in the road near Doctor Dexter's house, and turned toward the gate. Tales of mysterious horrors, vaguely hinted at, came back to him now with ominous force. He searched the yard carefully, looking in every nook and corner, then a cry of anguish reached his ears.

Great beads of sweat stood out upon Piper Tom's forehead, as he burst in at the laboratory door. On a narrow table, tightly strapped down, lay Laddie, fully conscious, his faithful heart laid bare. The odour of anesthetics was so faint as to be scarcely noticeable. At the dog's side stood Doctor Dexter, in a blood-stained linen coat, with a pad of paper and a short pencil in his white, firm hands. He was taking notes.

With infinite appeal in his agonised eyes, Laddie recognised his master, who at last had come too late. Piper Tom seized the knife from the table, and, with a quick, clean stroke, ended the torture. Doctor Dexter looked up, his mask-like face wearing an expression of insolent inquiry.

"Man," cried the Piper, his voice shaking, "have you never been loved by a dog?"

The silence was tense, but Doctor Dexter had taken out his watch, and was timing the spasmodic pulsations of the heart he had been so carefully studying.

"Aye," said the Piper, passionately, "watch it till the last--you cannot hurt him now. 'T is the truest heart in all the world save a woman's, and you do well to study it, having no heart of your own. A poor beast you are, if a dog has never loved you. Take your pencil and write down on the bit of paper you have there that you've seen the heart of a dog. Write down that you've seen the heart of one who left his own kind to be with you, to fight for you, even against them. Write down that 't is a good honest heart with red blood in it, that never once failed and never could fail.

"When a man's mother casts him off, when his wife forsakes him, when his love betrays him, his dog stays true. When he's poor and his friends pass him by on the other side of the street, looking the other way, his dog fares with him, ready to starve with him for very love of him. 'T is a man and his dog, I'm thinking, against the whole world.

"This little lad here was only a yellow mongrel, there was no fine blood in him; he couldn't bring in the birds nor swim after the ducks men kill to amuse themselves. He was worth no high price to anybody--nobody wanted him but me. When I took him away from the boys who were hurting him, and set his poor broken leg as best I could, he knew me for his master and claimed me then.

"He's walked with me through four States and never whined. He's gone without food for days at a time, and never complained. He's been cold and hungry, and we've slept together, more than once, on the ground in the snow, with only one blanket between us. He's kept me from freezing to death with his warm body, he's suffered from thirst the same as I, and never so much as whimpered. We've been comrades and we've fared together, as only man and dog may fare.

"When every man's face was set against you, did you never have a dog to trust you? When there was never a man nor a woman you could call your friend, did a dog never come to you and lick your hand? When you've been bent with grief you couldn't stand up under, did a dog never come to you and put his cold nose on your face? Did a dog never reach out a friendly paw to tell you that you were not alone--that it was you two together?

"When you've come home alone late at night, tired to death with the world and its ways, was there never a dog to greet you with his bark of welcome? Did a dog never sit where you told him to sit, and guard your property till you came back, though it might be hours? When you could trust no man to guard your treasures, could you never trust a dog? Man, man, the world has fair been cruel if you've never known the love of a dog!

"I've heard these things of you, but I thought folks were prattling, as folks will, but dogs never do. I thought they were lying about you--that such things couldn't be true. They said you were cutting up dogs to learn more of people, and I'm thinking, if we're so much alike as that, 't is murder to kill a dog."

"You killed him," said Anthony Dexter, speaking for the first time. "I didn't."

"Yes," answered the Piper, "I killed him, but 't was to keep him from being hurt. I'd do the same for a man or a woman, if there was need. If 't was a child you had tied down here with your blood-stained straps, cut open to see an innocent heart, your own being black past all pardon, I'd do the same for the child and all the more quickly if it was my own. I never had a child--I've never had a woman to love me, but I've been loved by a dog. I've thought that even yet I might know the love of a woman, for a man who deserves the love of a dog is worthy of a woman, and a man who will torture a dog will torture a woman, too.

"Laddie," said the Piper, laying his hand upon the blood-stained body, "no man ever had a truer comrade, and I'll not insult your kind by calling this brute a cur. Laddie, it was you and I, and now it's I alone. Laddie--" here the Piper's voice broke, and, taking up the knife again, he cut the straps. With the tears raining down his face, he stumbled out of the laboratory, the mutilated body of his pet in his arms.

Anthony Dexter looked after him curiously. The mask-like expression of his face was slightly changed. In a corner of the laboratory, seeming to shrink from him, stood the phantom black figure, closely veiled. Out of the echoing stillness came the passionate accusation: "A man who will torture a dog will torture a woman, too."

He carefully removed the blood stains from the narrow table, and pushed it back in its place, behind a screen. The straps were cut, and consequently useless, so he wrapped them up in a newspaper and threw them into the waste basket. He cleaned his knife with unusual care, and wiped an ugly stain from his forceps.

Then he took off his linen coat, folded it up, and placed it in the covered basket which held soiled linen from the laboratory. He washed his hands and copied the notes he had made, for there was blood upon the page. He tore the original sheet into fine bits, and put the pieces into the waste basket. Then he put on his cuffs and his coat, and went out of the laboratory.

He was dazed, and did not see that his own self-torture had filled him with primeval lust to torture in return. He only knew that his brilliant paper must remain forever incomplete, since his services to science were continually unappreciated and misunderstood. What was one yellow dog, more or less, in the vast economy of Nature? Was he lacking in discernment, because, as Piper Tom said, he had never been loved by a dog?

He sat down in the library to collect himself and observed, with a curious sense of detachment, that Evelina was walking in the hall instead of in the library, as she usually did when he sat there.

An hour--or perhaps two--went by, then, unexpectedly, Ralph came home, having paused a moment outside. He rushed into the library with his face aglow.

"Look, Dad," he cried, boyishly, holding it at arm's length; "see what I found on the steps! It's a pearl necklace, with a diamond in the clasp! Some of the stones are discoloured, but they're good and can be made right again, I've found it, so it's mine, and I'm going to give it to the girl I marry!"

Anthony Dexter's pale face suddenly became livid. He staggered over to Ralph, snatched the necklace out of his hand, and ground the pearls under his heel. "No," he cried, "a thousand times, no! The pearls are cursed!"

Then, for the second time, he fainted.

XVIII
Undine

It's almost as good as new!" cried Araminta, gleefully. She was clad in a sombre calico Mother Hubbard, of Miss Mehitable's painstaking manufacture, and hopping back and forth on the bare floor of her room at Miss Evelina's.

"Yes," answered Doctor Ralph, "I think it's quite as good as new." He was filled with professional pride at the satisfactory outcome of his first case, and yet was not at all pleased with the idea of Araminta's returning to Miss Mehitable's, as, perforce, she soon must do.

"Don't walk any more just now," he said "Come here and sit down. I want to talk to you."

Araminta obeyed him unquestioningly. He settled her comfortably in the hair-cloth easy-chair and drew his own chair closer. There was a pause, then she looked up at him, smiling with childish wistfulness.

"Are you sorry it's well?" he asked.

"I--I think I am," she answered, shyly, the deep crimson dyeing her face.

"I can't see you any more, you know," said Ralph, watching her intently.

The sweet face saddened in an instant and Araminta tapped her foot restlessly upon the floor. "Perhaps," she returned, slowly, "Aunt Hitty will be taken sick. Oh, I do hope she will!"

"You miserable little sinner," laughed Ralph, "do you suppose for a moment that Aunt Hitty would send for me if she were ill? Why, I believe she'd die first!"

"Maybe Mr. Thorpe might be taken sick," suggested Araminta, hopefully. "He's old, and sometimes I think he isn't very strong."

"He'd insist on having my father. You know they're old friends."

"Mr. Thorpe is old and your father is old," corrected Araminta, precisely, "but they haven't been friends long. Aunt Hitty says you must always say what you mean."

"That is what I meant. Each is old and both are friends. See?"

"It must be nice to be men," sighed Araminta, "and have friends. I've never had anybody but Aunt Hitty--and you," she added, in a lower tone,

"'No money, no friends, nothing but relatives,'" quoted Ralph, cynically. "It's hard lines, little maid--hard lines." He walked back and forth across the small room, his hands clasped behind his back--a favourite attitude, Araminta had noted, during the month of her illness.

He pictured his probable reception should he venture to call upon her. Personally, as it was, he stood none too high in the favour of the dragon, as he was wont to term Miss Mehitable in his unflattering thoughts. Moreover, he was a man, which counted heavily against him. Since he had taken up his father's practice, he had heard a great deal about Miss Mehitable's view of marriage, and her determination to shield Araminta from such an unhappy fate.

And Araminta had not been intended, by Dame Nature, for such shielding. Every line of her body, rounding into womanhood, defied Aunt Hitty's well-meant efforts. The soft curve of her cheek, the dimples that lurked unsuspected in the comers of her mouth, the grave, sweet eyes--all these marked Araminta for love. She had, too, a wistful, appealing childishness.

"Did you like the story book?" asked Ralph.

"Oh, so much!"

"I thought you would. What part of it did you like best?"

"It was all lovely," replied Araminta, thoughtfully, "but I think the best part of it was when she went back to him after she had made him go away. It made him so glad to know that they were to talk together again."

Ralph looked keenly at Araminta, the love of man and woman was so evidently outside her ken. The sleeping princess in the tower had been no more set apart. But, as he remembered; the sleeping princess had been wakened by a kiss--when the right man came.

A lump came into his throat and he swallowed hard. Blindly, he went over to her chair. The girl's flower-like face was lifted questioningly to his. He bent over and kissed her, full upon the lips.

Araminta shrank from him a little, and the colour surged into her face, but her eyes, still trustful, still tender, never wavered from his.

"I suppose I'm a brute," Ralph said, huskily, "but God knows I haven't meant to be."

Araminta smiled--a sweet, uncomprehending smile. Ralph possessed himself of her hand. It was warm and steady--his own was cold and tremulous.

"Child," he said, "did any one ever kiss you before?"

"No," replied Araminta; "only Aunt Hitty. It was when I was a baby and she thought I was lost. She kissed me--here." Araminta pointed to her soft cheek. "Did you kiss me because I was well?"

Ralph shook his head despairingly. "The man in the book kissed the lady," went on Araminta, happily, "because he was so glad they were to talk together again, but we--why, I shall never see you any more," she concluded, sadly.

His fingers tightened upon hers. "Yes," he said, in a strange voice, "we shall see each other again."

"They both seem very well," sighed Araminta, referring to Aunt Hitty and Mr. Thorpe, "and even if I fell off of a ladder again, it might not hurt me at all. I have fallen from lots of places and only got black and blue. I never broke before."

"Listen, child," said Ralph. "Would you rather live with Aunt Hitty, or with me?"

"Why, Doctor Ralph! Of course I'd rather live with you, but Aunt Hitty would never let me!"

"We're not talking about Aunt Hitty now. Is there anyone in the world whom you like better than you do me?"

"No," said Araminta, softly, her eyes shining. "How could there be?"

"Do you love me, Araminta?"

"Yes," she answered, sweetly, "of course I do! You've been so good to me!"

The tone made the words meaningless. "Child," said Ralph, "you break my heart."

He walked back and forth again, restlessly, and Araminta watched him, vaguely troubled. What in the world had she done?

Meanwhile, he was meditating. He could not bear to have her go back to her prison, even for a little while. Had he found her only to lose her, because she had no soul?

Presently he came back to her and stood by her chair. "Listen, dear," he said, tenderly. "You told me there was no one in the world for whom you cared more than you care for me. You said you loved me, and I love you--God knows I do. If you'll trust me, Araminta, you'll never be sorry, never for one single minute as long as you live. Would you like to live with me in a little house with roses climbing over it, just us two alone?"

"Yes," returned Araminta, dreamily, "and I could keep the little cat."

"You can have a million cats, if you like, but all I want is you. Just you, sweetheart, to love me, with all the love you can give me. Will you come?"

"Oh," cried Araminta, "if Aunt Hitty would only let me, but she never would!"

"We won't ask her," returned Ralph. "We'll go away to-night, and be married."

At the word, Araminta started out of her chair. Her face was white and her eyes wide with fear. "I couldn't," she said, with difficulty. "You shouldn't ask me to do what you know is wrong. Just because my mother was married, because she was wicked--you must not think that I would be wicked, too."

Hot words were struggling for utterance, but Ralph choked them back. The fog was thick before him and he saw Araminta as through a heavy veil. "Undine," he said, moistening his parched lips, "some day you will find your soul. And when you do, come to me. I shall be waiting."

He went out of the room unsteadily, and closed the door. He stood at the head of the stairs for a long time before he went down. Apparently there was no one in the house. He went into the parlour and sat down, wiping the cold sweat from his forehead, and trying to regain his self-control.

He saw, clearly, that Araminta was not in the least to blame; that almost ever since her birth, she had been under the thumb of a domineering woman who persistently inculcated her own warped ideas. Since her earliest childhood, Araminta had been taught that marriage was wrong--that her own mother was wicked, because she had been married. And of the love between man and woman, the child knew absolutely nothing.

"Good God!" muttered Ralph. "My little girl, oh, my little girl!" Man-like, he loved her more than ever because she had denied him; man-like, he wanted her now as he had never wanted her before. Through the weeks that he had seen her every day, he had grown to feel his need of her, to hunger for the sweetness of her absolute dependence upon him. Yet, until now, he had not guessed how deeply he cared, nor guessed that such caring was possible.

He sat there for the better part of an hour, slowly regaining command of himself. Miss Evelina came through the hall and paused just outside the door, feeling intuitively that some one was in the house. She drew down her veil and went in.

"I thought you had gone," she said. "Did you wish to see me?"

"No," returned Ralph, wearily; "not especially."

She sat down opposite him silently. All her movements were quiet, for she had never been the noisy sort of woman. There was something soothing in the veiled presence.

"I hope I'm not intruding," ventured Ralph, at length. "I'll go, presently. I've just had a--well, a blow. That little saint upstairs has been taught that marriage is wicked."

"I know," returned Miss Evelina, instantly comprehending. "Mehitable has very strange ideas. I'm sorry," she added, in a tone she might have used in speaking to Anthony Dexter, years before.

Her sympathy touched the right chord. It was not obtrusive, it had no hint of pity; it was simply that one who had been hurt fully understood the hurt of another. Ralph felt a mysterious kinship.

"I've wanted for some time to ask you," he began awkwardly, "if there was not something I could do for you. The--the veil, you know--" He stopped, at a loss for further words.

"Yes?" Miss Evelina's voice was politely inquiring. She thought it odd for Anthony Dexter's son to be concerned about her veil. She wondered whether he meditated giving her a box of chiffon, as Piper Tom had done.

"Believe me," he said, impetuously, "I only want to help. I want to make it possible for you to take that--to take that thing off."

"It is not possible," returned Miss Evelina, after a painful interval. "I shall always wear my veil."

"You don't understand," explained Ralph. It seemed to him that he had spent the day telling women they did not understand. "I know, of course, that there was some dreadful accident, and that it happened a long time ago. Since then, wonderful advances have been made in surgery--there is a great deal possible now that was not dreamed of then. Of course I should not think of attempting it myself, but I would find the man who could do it, take you to him, and stand by you until it was over."

The clock ticked loudly and a little bird sang outside, but there was no other sound.

"I want to help you," said Ralph, humbly, as he rose to his feet; "believe me, I want to help you."

Miss Evelina said nothing, but she followed him to the door. At the threshold, Ralph turned back. "Won't you let me help you?" he asked. "Won't you even let me try?"

"I thank you," said Miss Evelina, coldly, "but nothing can be done."

The door closed behind him with a portentous suggestion of finality. As he went down the path, Ralph felt himself shut out from love and from all human service. He did not look back to the upper window, where Araminta was watching, her face stained with tears.

As he went out of the gate, she, too, felt shut out from something strangely new and sweet, but her conscience rigidly approved, none the less. Against Aunt Hitty's moral precepts, Araminta leaned securely, and she was sure that she had done right.

The Maltese kitten was purring upon a cushion, the loved story book lay on the table nearby. Doctor Ralph was going down the road, his head bowed. They would never see each other again--never in all the world.

She would not tell Aunt Hitty that Doctor Ralph had asked her to marry him; she would shield him, even though he had insulted her. She would not tell Aunt Hitty that Doctor Ralph had kissed her, as the man in the story book had kissed the lady who came back to him. She would not tell anybody. "Never in all the world," thought Araminta. "We shall never see each other again."

Doctor Ralph was out of sight, now, and she could never watch for him any more. He had gone away forever, and she had broken his heart. For the moment, Araminta straightened herself proudly, for she had been taught that it did not matter whether one's heart broke or not--one must always do what was right. And Aunt Hitty knew what was right.

Suddenly, she sank on her knees beside her bed, burying her face in the pillow, for her heart was breaking, too. "Oh, Lord," she prayed, sobbing wildly, "keep me from the contamination of marriage, for Thy sake. Amen."

The door opened silently, a soft, slow step came near. The pillow was drawn away and a cool hand was laid upon Araminta's burning cheek. "Child," said Miss Evelina, "what is wrong?"

Araminta had not meant to tell, but she did. She sobbed out, in disjointed fragments, all the sorry tale. Wisely, Miss Evelina waited until the storm had spent itself, secretly wishing that she, too, might know the relief of tears.

"I knew," said Miss Evelina, her cool, quiet hand still upon Araminta's face. "Doctor Ralph told me before he went home."

"Oh," cried Araminta, "does he hate me?"

"Hate you?" repeated Miss Evelina. "Dear child, no. He loves you. Would you believe me, Araminta, if I told you that it was not wrong to be married--that there was no reason in the world why you should not marry the man who loves you?"

"Not wrong!" exclaimed Araminta, incredulously. "Aunt Hitty says it is. My mother was married!"

"Yes," said Miss Evelina, "and so was mine. Aunt Hitty's mother was married, too."

"Are you sure?" demanded Araminta. "She never told me so. If her mother was married, why didn't she tell me?"

"I don't know, dear," returned Miss Evelina, truthfully. "Mehitable's ways are strange." Had she been asked to choose, at the moment, between Araminta's dense ignorance and all of her own knowledge, embracing, as it did, a world of pain, she would have chosen gladly, the fuller life.

The door-bell below rang loudly, defiantly. It was the kind of a ring which might impel the dead to answer it. Miss Evelina fairly ran downstairs.

Outside stood Miss Mehitable. Unwillingly, in her wake, had come the Reverend Austin Thorpe. Under Miss Mehitable's capable and constant direction, he had made a stretcher out of the clothes poles and a sheet. He was jaded in spirit beyond all words to express, but he had come, as Roman captives came, chained to the chariot wheels of the conqueror.

"Me and the minister," announced Miss Mehitable, imperiously, "have come to take Minty home!"

XIX
In the Shadow of the Cypress

The house seemed lonely without Araminta. Miss Evelina missed the child more than she had supposed she could ever miss any one. She had grown to love her, and, too, she missed the work.

Miss Evelina's house was clean, now, and most of the necessary labour had been performed by her own frail hands. The care of Araminta had been an added burden, which she had borne because it had been forced upon her. Slowly, but surely, she had been compelled to take thought for others.

The promise of Spring had come to beautiful fulfilment, and the world was all abloom. Faint mists of May were rising from the earth, and filmy clouds half veiled the moon. The loneliness of the house was unbearable, so Miss Evelina went out into the garden, her veil fluttering, moth-like, about her head.

The old pain was still at her heart, yet, in a way, it was changed. She had come again into the field of service. Miss Mehitable had been kind to her, indeed, more than kind. The Piper had made her a garden, and she had taken care of Araminta. Doctor Ralph, meaning to be wholly kind, had offered to help her, if he could, and she had been on the point of doing a small service for him, when Fate, in the person of Miss Mehitable, intervened. And over and above and beyond all, Anthony Dexter had come back, to offer her tardy reparation.

That hour was continually present with her. She could not forget his tortured face when she had thrown back her veil. What if she had taken him at his word, and gone with him, to be, as he said, a mother to his son? Miss Evelina laughed bitterly.

The beauty of the night brought her no peace as she wandered about the garden. Without knowing it, she longed for human companionship. Piper Tom had finished his work. Doctor Ralph would come no more, Araminta had gone, and Miss Mehitable offered little comfort.

She went to the gate and leaned upon it, looking down the road. Thus she had watched for Anthony Dexter in years gone by. Memories, mercilessly keen, returned to her. As though it were yesterday, she remembered the moonlit night of their betrothal, felt his eager arms about her and his bearded cheek pressed close to hers. She heard again the music of his voice as he whispered, passionately: "I love you, oh, I love you--for life, for death, for all eternity!"

The rose-bush had been carefully pruned and tied up, but it promised little, at best. The cypress had grown steadily, and, at times, its long shadow reached through the door and into the house. Heavily, too, upon her heart, the shadow of the cypress lay, for sorrow seems so much deeper than joy.

A figure came up the road, and she turned away, intending to go into the house. Then she perceived that it was Piper Tom, and, drawing down her veil, turned back to wait for him. He had never come at night before.

Even in the darkness, she noted a change in him; the atmosphere of youth was all gone. He walked slowly, as though he had aged, and the red feather no longer bobbed in his hat.

He went past her silently, and sat down on the steps.

"Will you come in?" asked Evelina.

"No," answered the Piper, sadly, "I'll not be coming in. 'T is selfish of me, perhaps, but I came to you because I had sorrow of my own."

Miss Evelina sat down on the step beside him, and waited for him to speak.

"'T is a small sorrow, perhaps, you'll be thinking," he said, at last. "I'm not knowing what great ones you have seen, face to face, but 't is so ordered That all sorrows are not the same. 'T is all in the heart that bears them. I told you I had known them all, and at the time, I was thinking I spoke the truth. A woman never loved me, and so I have lost the love of no woman, but," he went on with difficulty, "no one had ever killed my dog."

"How?" asked Miss Evelina, dully. It seemed a matter of small moment to her.

"I'll not be paining you with that," the Piper answered, "At the last, 't was I who killed him to save him from further hurt. 'T was the best I could do for the little lad, and I'm thinking he'd take it from me rather than from any one else. I'm missing his cheerful bark and his pleasant ways, but I've taken him away for ever from Doctor Dexter and his kind."

"Doctor Dexter!" Evelina sprang to her feet, her body tense and quivering.

"Aye, Doctor Dexter--not the young man, but the old one."

A deep-drawn breath was her only answer, but the Piper looked up, startled. Slowly he rose to his feet and leaned toward her intently, as though to see her face behind her veil.

"Spinner in the Shadow," he said, with infinite tenderness, "I'm thinking 't was he who hurt you, too!"

Evelina's head drooped, she swayed, and would have fallen, had he not put his arm around her. She sat down on the step again, and hid her veiled face in her hands.

"'T was that, I'm thinking, that brought me to you," he went on. "I knew you did not care much for the little lad--he was naught to any one but me. 'T is this that binds us together--you and I."

The moon climbed higher into the heavens and the clouds were blown away. The shadow of the cypress was thrown toward them, and the dense night of it concealed the half-open door.

"See," breathed Evelina, "the shadow of the cypress is long."

"Aye," answered Piper Tom, "the shadow of the cypress is long and the rose blooms but once a year. 'T is the way of the world."

He loosened his flute from the cord by which it was slung over his shoulder. "I was going to the woods," he said, "but at the last, I could not, for the little lad always fared with me when I went out to play. He would sit quite still when I made the music, so still that he never frightened even the birds. The birds came, too.

"'T is a way I've had for long," he continued. "I never could be learning the printed music, so I made music of my own. So many laughed at it, not hearing any tune, that I've always played by myself. 'T was my own soul breathing into it--perhaps I'm not to blame that it never made a tune.

"Sometimes I'm thinking that there may be tunes and tunes. I was once in a place where there were many instruments, all playing at once, and there was nothing came from it that one could call a tune. But 't was great and beautiful beyond any words of mine to tell you, and the master of them all, standing up in front, knew just when each must play.

"Most, of course, I watched the one who played the flute and listened to the voice of it. 'T is strange how, if you listen, you can pick out one instrument from all the rest. I saw that sometimes he did not play at all, and yet the music went on. Sometimes, again, he was privileged to play just a note or two--not at all like a tune.

"'T was just his part, and, by itself, it would have sounded queer. I might have laughed at it myself if I did not know, and was listening for a tune. But the master of them all was pleased, because the man with the flute made his few notes to sing rightly when they should sing and because he kept still when there was no need of his instrument.

"So I'm thinking," concluded the Piper, humbly, "that these few notes of mine may belong to something I cannot hear, and that the Master himself leads me, when 't is time to play."

He put the instrument to his lips and began to play softly. The low, sweet notes were, as he said, no evident part of a tune, yet they were not without a deep and tender appeal.

Evelina listened, her head still bowed. It did not sound like the pipes o' Pan, but rather like some fragment of a mysterious, heart-breaking melody. Faint, far echoes rang back from the surrounding hills, as though in a distant forest cathedral another Piper sat enthroned.

The sound of singing waters murmured through the night as the Piper's flute breathed of stream and sea. There was the rush of a Summer wind through sway- ing branches, the tinkle of raindrops, the deep notes of rising storm. Moonlight shimmered through it, birds sang in green silences, and there was scent of birch and pine.

Then swiftly the music changed. Through the utter sadness of it came also a hint of peace, as though one had planted a garden of roses and instead there had come up herbs and balm. In the passionate pain, there was also uplifting--a flight on broken wings. Above and beyond all there was a haunting question, to which the answer seemed lost.

At length the Piper laid down his flute. "You do not laugh," he said, "and yet

I'm thinking you may not care for music that has no tune."

"I do care," returned Evelina.

"I remember," he answered, slowly. "It was the day in the woods, when I called you and you came."

"I was hurt," she said. "I had been terribly hurt, only that morning,"

"Yes, many have come to me so. Often when I have played in the woods the music that has no tune, some one who was very sad has come to me. I saw you that day from far and I felt you were sad, so I called you. I called you," he repeated, lingering on the words, "and you came."

"I do not so much care for the printed music," he went on, after an interval, "unless it might be the great, beautiful music which takes so many to play. I have often thought of it and wondered what might happen if the players were not willing to follow the master--if one should play a tune where no tune was written, and he who has the violin should insist on playing the flute.

"I would not want the violin, for I think the flute is best of all. It is made from the trees on the mountains and the silver hidden within, and so is best fitted for the message of the mountains--the great, high music.

"I'm thinking that the life we live is not unlike the players. We have each our own instrument, but we are not content to follow as the Master leads. We do not like the low, long notes that mean sadness; we will not take what is meant for us, but insist on the dancing tunes and the light music of pleasure. It is this that makes the discord and all the confusion. The Master knows his meaning and could we each play our part well, at the right time, there would be nothing wrong in all the world."

Miss Evelina sighed, deeply, and the Piper put his hand on hers.

"I'm not meaning to reproach you," he said, kindly, "though, truly, I do think you have played wrong. In any music I have heard, there has never been any one instrument that has played all the time and sadly. When there is sadness, there is always rest, and you have had no rest."

"No," said Evelina, her voice breaking, "I have had no rest--God knows that!"

"Then do you not see," asked the Piper very gently, "that you cannot help but make the music wrong? The Master gives you one deep note to play, and you hold it, always the same note, till the music is at an end.

"'T is something wrong, I'm thinking, that has made you hold it so. I'm not asking you to tell me, but I think that one day I shall see. Together we shall find what makes the music wrong, and together we shall make it right again."

"Together," repeated Evelina, unconsciously. Once the word had been sweet to her, but now it brought only bitterness.

"Aye, together. 'T is for that I stayed. Laddie and I were going on, that very day we saw you in the wood--the day I called you, and you came. I shall see, some day, what has made it wrong--yes. Spinner in the Shadow, I shall see. I'm grieving now for Laddie and my heart is sore, but when I have forgiven him, I shall be at rest."

"Forgiven who?" queried Evelina.

"Why, the man who hurt Laddie--the same, I'm thinking, who hurt you. But your hurt was worse than Laddie's, I take it, and so 't is harder to forgive."

Evelina's heart beat hard. Never before had she thought of forgiving Anthony Dexter. She put it aside quickly as altogether impossible. Moreover, he had not asked.

"What is it to forgive?" she questioned, curiously.

"The word is not made right," answered the Piper, "I'm thinking 't is wrong end to, as many things in this world are until we move and look at them from another way. It's giving for, that's all. When you have put self so wholly aside that you can be sorry for him because he has wronged you, why, then, you have forgiven."

"I shall never be able to do that," she returned. "Why, I should not even try."

"Ah," cried the Piper, "I knew that some day I should find what was wrong, but I did not think it would be now. 'T is because you have not forgiven that you have been sad for so long. When you have forgiven, you will be free."

"He never asked," muttered Evelina.

"No; 't is very strange, I'm thinking, but those who most need to be forgiven are those who never ask. 'T is hard, I know, for I cannot yet be sorry for him because he hurt Laddie--I can only be sorry for Laddie, who was hurt. But the great truth is there. When I have grown to where I can be sorry for him as well as for Laddie, why, my grieving will be done.

"The little chap," mused the Piper, fondly, "he was a faithful comrade. 'T was a true heart that the brute--ah, what am I saying! I'll not be forgetting how he fared with me in sun and storm, sharing a crust with me, often, as man to man, and not complaining, because we were together. A woman never loved me but a dog has, and I'm thinking that some day I may have the greater love because I've been worthy of the less.

"My mother died when I was born and, because of that, I've tried to make the world easier for all women. I'm not thinking I have wholly failed, yet the great love has not come. I've often thought," went on Piper Tom, simply, "that if a woman waited for me at night when I went home, with love on her face, and if a woman's hand might be in mine when the Master tells me that I am no longer needed for the music, 't would make the leaving very easy, and I should not ask for Heaven.

"I've seen, so often, the precious jewel of a woman's love cast aside by a man who did not know what he had, having blinded himself with tinsel until his true knowledge was lost. You'll forgive me for my rambling talk, I'm thinking, for I'm still grieving for the little chap, and I cannot say yet that I have forgiven."

He rose, slung his flute over his shoulder again, and went slowly toward the gate. Evelina followed him, to the cypress tree.

"See," he said, turning, "the shadow of the cypress is long. 'T is because you have not forgiven. I'm thinking it may be easier for us to forgive together, since it is the same man."

"Yes," returned Evelina, steadily, "the shadow of the cypress is long, and I never shall forgive."

"Aye," said the Piper, "we'll forgive him together--you and I. I'll help you, since your hurt is greater than mine. You have veiled your soul as you have veiled your face, but, through forgiveness, the beauty of the one will shine out again, and, I'm thinking, through love, the other may shine out, too. You have hidden your face because you are so beautiful; you have hidden your soul because you are so sad. I called you in the woods, and I call you now. I shall never cease calling, until you come."

He went out of the gate, and did not answer her faint "good-night." Was it true, as he said, that he should never cease calling her? Something in her spirit stirred strangely at his appeal, as a far, celestial trumpet blown from on high might summon the valiant soul of a warrior who had died in the charge.

XX
The Secret of the Veil

F ather," said Ralph, pacing back and forth, as was his habit, "I have wanted for some time to ask you about Miss Evelina--the woman, you know, in the little house on the hill. She always wears a veil and there can be no reason for it except some terrible disfigurement. Has she never consulted you?"

"Never," answered Anthony Dexter, with dry lips.

"I remember, you told me, but it seems strange. I spoke to her about it the other day. I told her I was sure that something could be done. I offered to find the best available specialist for her, go with her, and stand by her until it was over."

Anthony Dexter laughed--a harsh, unnatural laugh that jarred upon his son.

"I fail to see anything particularly funny about it," remarked Ralph, coldly.

"What did she say?" asked his father, not daring to meet Ralph's eyes.

"She thanked me, and said nothing could be done."

"She didn't show you her face, I take it."

"No."

"I should have thought she would, under the circumstances--under all the circumstances."

"Have you seen her face?" asked Ralph, quickly, "by chance, or in any other way?"

"Yes."

"How is it? Is it so bad that nothing can be done?"

"She was perfectly right," returned Anthony Dexter, slowly. "There is nothing to be done."

At the moment, the phantom Evelina was pacing back and forth between the man and his son. Her veiled face was proudly turned away. "I wonder," thought

Anthony Dexter, curiously, "if she hears. If she did, though, she'd speak, or throw back her veil, so she doesn't hear."

"I may be wrong," sighed Ralph, "but I've always believed that nothing is so bad it can't be made better."

"The unfailing ear-mark of Youth, my son," returned Anthony Dexter, patronisingly. "You'll get over that."

He laughed again, gratingly, and went out, followed by his persistent apparition. "We'll go out for a walk, Evelina," he muttered, when he was half-way to the gate. "We'll see how far you can go without getting tired." The fantastic notion of wearying his veiled pursuer appealed to him strongly.

Ralph watched his father uneasily. Even though he had been relieved of the greater part of his work, Anthony Dexter did not seem to be improving. He was morose, unreasonable, and given to staring vacantly into space for hours at a time. Ralph often spoke to him when he did not hear at all, and at times he turned his head from left to right and back again, slowly, but with the maddening regularity of clock-work. He ate little, but claimed to sleep well.

Whatever it was seemed to be of the mind rather than the body, and Ralph could find nothing in his father's circumstances calculated to worry any one in the slightest degree. He planned, vaguely, to invite a friend who was skilled in the diagnosis of obscure mental disorders to spend a week-end with him, a little later on, and to ask him to observe his father closely. He did not doubt but that Anthony Dexter would see quickly through so flimsy a pretence, but, unless he improved, something of the kind would have to be done soon.

Meanwhile, his heart yearned strangely toward Miss Evelina. It was altogether possible that something, might be done. Ralph was modest, but new discoveries were constantly being made, and he knew that his own knowledge was more abreast of the times than his father's could be. At any rate, he was not so easily satisfied.

He was trying faithfully to forget Araminta, but was not succeeding. The sweet, childish face haunted him as constantly as the veiled phantom haunted his father, but in a different way. Through his own unhappiness, he came into kinship with all the misery of the world. He longed to uplift, to help, to heal.

He decided to try once more to talk with Miss Evelina, to ask her, point blank, if need be, to let him see her face. He knew that his father lacked sympathy, and he was sure that when Miss Evelina once thoroughly understood him, she would be willing to let him help her.

On the way uphill, he considered how he should approach the subject. He had already planned to make an ostensible errand of the book he had loaned Araminta. Perhaps Miss Evelina had read it, or would like to, and he could begin, in that way, to talk to her.

When he reached the gate, the house seemed deserted, though the front door was ajar. It was a warm, sweet afternoon in early Summer, and the world was very still, except for the winged folk of wood and field.

He tapped gently at the door, but there was no answer. He went around to the back door, but it was closed, and there was no sign that the place was occupied, except quantities of white chiffon hung upon the line. Being a man, Ralph did not perceive that Miss Evelina had washed every veil she possessed.

He went back to the front of the house again and found that the door was still ajar. She might have gone away, though it seemed unlikely, or it was not impossible that she might have been taken suddenly ill and was unable to come to the door.

Ralph went in, softly, as he had often done before. Miss Evelina had frequently left the door open for him at the hour he was expected to visit his patient.

He paused a moment in the hall, but heard no sound save slow, deep breathing. He turned into the parlour, but stopped on the threshold as if he had been suddenly changed to stone.

Upon the couch lay Miss Evelina, asleep, and unveiled. Her face was turned toward him--a face of such surpassing beauty that he gasped in astonishment. He had never seen such wondrous perfection of line and feature, nor such a crown of splendour as her lustreless white hair, falling loosely about her shoulders. Her face was as pure and as cold as marble, flawless, and singularly transparent. Her lips were deep scarlet and perfectly shaped; the white slender column of her throat held her head proudly. Long, dark lashes swept her cheek, and the years had left no lines. Feeling the intense scrutiny, Miss Evelina opened her eyes, slowly, like one still half asleep.

Her eyes were violet, so deep in colour as to seem almost black. She stared at Ralph, unseeing, then the light of recognition flashed over her face and she sat up, reaching back quickly for her missing veil.

"Miss Evelina!" cried Ralph. "Why, oh why!"

"Why did you come in?" she demanded, resentfully. "You had no right!"

"Forgive me," he pleaded, coming to her. "I've often come in when the door was open. Why, you've left it open for me yourself, don't you know you have?"

"Perhaps," she answered, a faint colour coming into her cheek. "I had no idea of going to sleep. I am sorry."

"I thought you might be ill," said Ralph. excusing himself further. "Believe me, Miss Evelina, I had no thought of intruding. I only came to help you."

He stood before her, still staring, and her eyes met his clearly in return. In the violet depths was a world of knowledge and pain Suffering had transfigured her face into a noble beauty for which there were no words. Such a face might be the dream of a sculptor, the despair of a painter, and the ecstasy of a lover.

"Why?", cried Ralph, again.

"Because," she answered, simply, "my beauty was my curse."

Ralph did not see that the words were melodramatic; he only sat down, weakly, in a chair opposite her. He never once took his eyes away from her, but stared at her helplessly, like a man in a dream.

"Why?" he questioned, again. "Tell me why!"

"It was in a laboratory," explained Miss Evelina. "I was there with the man I loved and to whom I was to be married the next day. No one knew of our engagement, for, in a small town, you know, people will talk, and we both felt that it was too sacred to be spoken of lightly.

"He was trying an experiment, and I was watching. He came to the retort to put in another chemical, and leaned over it. I heard the mass seething and pushed him away with all my strength. Instantly, there was a terrible explosion. When I came to my senses again, I was in the hospital, wrapped in bandages. I had been terribly burned--see?"

She loosened her black gown at the throat and pushed it down over her right shoulder. Ralph shuddered at the deep, flaming scars.

"My arm is worse," she said, quickly covering her shoulder again. "I need not show you that. My face was burned, too, but scarcely at all. To this day, I do not know how I escaped. I must have thrown up my arm instinctively to shield my face. See, there are no scars."

"I see," murmured Ralph; "and what of him?"

The dark eyes gleamed indescribably. "What of him?" she asked, with assumed lightness. "Why, he was not hurt at all. I saved him from disfigurement, if not from death. I bear the scars; he goes free."

"I know," said Ralph, "but why were you not married? All his life and love would be little enough to give in return for that."

Miss Evelina fixed her deep eyes upon Anthony Dexter's son. In her voice there was no hint of faltering.

"I never saw him again," she said, "until twenty-five years afterward, and then I was veiled. He went away."

"Went away!" repeated Ralph, incredulously. "Miss Evelina, what do you mean?"

"What I said," she replied. "He went away. He came once to the hospital. As it happened, there was another girl there, named Evelyn Grey, burned by acid, and infinitely worse than I. The two names became confused. He was told that I would be disfigured for life--that every feature was destroyed except my sight. That was enough for him. He asked no more questions, but simply went away."

"Coward!" cried Ralph, his face white. "Cur!"

Miss Evelina's eyes gleamed with subtle triumph. "What would you?" she asked unemotionally. "He told me that day of the accident that it was my soul he loved, and not my body, but at the test, he failed. Men usually fail women, do they not, in anything that puts their love to the test? He went away. In a year, he was married, and he has a son."

"A son!" repeated Ralph. "What a heritage of disgrace for a son! Does the boy know?"

There was a significant silence. "I do not think his father has told him," said Evelina, with forced calmness.

"If he had," muttered Ralph, his hands clenched and his teeth set, "his son must have struck him dead where he stood. To accept that from a woman, and then to go away!"

"What would you?" asked Evelina again. A curious, tigerish impulse was taking definite shape in her. "Would you have him marry her?"

"Marry her? A thousand times, yes, if she would stoop so low! What man is worthy of a woman who saves his life at the risk of her own?"

"Disfigured? asked Evelina, in an odd voice.

"Yes," cried Ralph, "with the scars she bore for him!"

There was a tense, painful interval. Miss Evelina was grappling with a hideous temptation. One word from her, and she was revenged upon Anthony Dexter for all the years of suffering. One word from her, and sure payment would be made in the most subtle, terrible way. She guessed that he could not bear the condemnation of this idolised son.

The old pain gnawed at her heart. Anthony Dexter had come back, she had had her little hour of triumph, and still she had not been freed. The Piper had told her that only forgiveness could loosen her chains. And how could Anthony Dexter be forgiven, when even his son said that he was a coward and a cur?

"I--" Miss Evelina's lips moved, then became still.

"And so," said Ralph, "you have gone veiled ever since, for the sake of that beast?"

"No, it was for my own sake. Do you wonder that I have done it? When I first realised what had happened, in an awful night that turned my brown hair white, I knew that Love and I were strangers forevermore.

"When I left the hospital, I was obliged, for a time, to wear it. The new skin was tender and bright red; it broke very easily."

"I know," nodded Ralph.

"There were oils to be kept upon it, too, and so I wore the veil. I became accustomed to the shelter of it. I could walk the streets and see, dimly, without being seen. In those days, I thought that, perhaps, I might meet--him."

"I don't wonder you shrank from it," returned Ralph. His voice was almost inaudible.

"It became harder still to put it by. My heart was broken, and it shielded me as a long, black veil shields a widow. It protected me from curious questions. Never but once or twice in all the twenty-five years have I been asked about it, and then, I simply did not answer. People, after all, are very kind."

"Were you never ill?"

"Never, though every night of my life I have prayed for death. At first, I clung to it without reason, except what I have told you, then, later on, I began to see a further protection. Veiled as I was, no man would ever love me again. I should never be tempted to trust, only to be betrayed. Not that I ever could trust, you understand, but still, sometimes," concluded Miss Evelina, piteously, "I think the heart of a woman is strangely hungry for love."

"I understand," said Ralph, "and, believe me, I do not blame you. Perhaps it was the best thing you could do. Let me ask you of the man. You said, I think, that he still lives?"

"Yes." Miss Evelina's voice was very low.

"He is well and happy--prosperous?"

"Yes."

"Do you know where he lives?"

"Yes."

"Has he ever suffered at all from his cowardice, his shirking?"

"How should I know?"

"Then, Miss Evelina," said Ralph, his voice thick with passion and his hands tightly clenched, "will you let me go to him? For the honour of men, I should like to punish this one brute. I think I could present an argument that even he might understand!"

The temptation became insistent. The sheathed dagger was in Evelina's hands; she had only to draw forth the glittering steel. A vengeance more subtle than she had ever dared to dream of was hers to command.

"Tell me his name," breathed Ralph. "Only tell me his name!"

Miss Evelina threw back her beautiful head proudly. "No," she said, firmly, "I will not. Go," she cried, pointing uncertainly to the door. "For the love of God, go!"

XXI
The Poppies Claim Their Own

It was dusk, and Anthony Dexter sat in the library. Through the day, he had wearied himself to the point of exhaustion, but his phantom pursuer had not tired. The veiled figure of Evelina had kept pace easily with his quick, nervous stride. At the point on the river road, where he had met her for the first time, she had, indeed, seemed to go ahead of him and wait for him there.

Night brought no relief. By a singular fatality, he could see her in darkness as plainly as in sunshine, and even when his eyes were closed, she hovered persistently before him. Throughout his drugged sleep she moved continuously; he never dreamed save of her.

In days gone by, he had been certain that he was the victim of an hallucination, but now, he was not so sure. He would not have sworn that the living Evelina was not eternally in his sight. Time and time again he had darted forward quickly to catch her, but she swiftly eluded him. "If," he thought, gritting his teeth, "I could once get my hands upon her----"

His fists dosed tightly, then, by a supreme effort of will, he put the maddening thought away. "I will not add murder to my sins," he muttered; "no, by Heaven, I will not!"

By a whimsical change of his thought, he conceived himself dead and in his coffin. Would Evelina pace ceaselessly before him then? When he was in his grave, would she wait eternally at the foot of it, and would those burning eyes pierce the shielding sod that parted them? Life had not served to separate them--could he hope that Death would prove potent where Life had failed?

Ralph came in, tired, having done his father's work for the day. The room was wholly dark, but he paused upon the threshold, conscious that some one was there.

"Alone, father?" he called, cheerily.

"No," returned Anthony Dexter, grimly.

"Who's here?" asked Ralph, stumbling into the room. "It's so dark, I can't see."

Fumbling for a match, he lighted a wax candle which stood in an antique candlestick on the library table. The face of his father materialised suddenly out of the darkness, wearing an expression which made Ralph uneasy.

"I thought," he said, troubled, "that some one was with you."

"Aren't you here?" asked Anthony Dexter, trying to make his voice even.

"Oh," returned Ralph. "I see."

With the candle flickering uncertainly between them, the two men faced each other. Sharp shadows lay on the floor and Anthony Dexter's profile was silhouetted upon the opposite wall. He noted that the figure of Evelina, pacing to and fro, cast no shadow. It seemed strange.

In the endeavour to find some interesting subject upon which to talk, Ralph chanced upon the fatal one. "Father," he began, "you know that this morning we were speaking of Miss Evelina?"

The tone was inquiring, but there was no audible answer.

"Well," continued Ralph, "I saw her again to-day. And I saw her face." He had forgotten that his father had seen it, also, and had told him only yesterday.

Anthony Dexter almost leaped from his chair--toward the veiled figure now approaching him. "Did--did she show you her face?" he asked with difficulty.

"No. It was an accident. She often left the front door open for me when I was attending--Araminta--and so, to-day, when I found it open, I went in. She was asleep, on the couch in the parlour, and she wore no veil."

At once, the phantom Evelina changed her tactics. Hitherto, she had walked back and forth from side to side of his vision. Now she advanced slowly toward him and as slowly retreated. Her face was no longer averted; she walked backward cautiously, then advanced. From behind her veil, he could feel her burning, accusing eyes.

"Father," said Ralph, "she is beautiful. She is the most beautiful woman I have ever seen in all my life. Her face is as exquisite as if chiselled in marble, and you never saw such eyes. And she wears that veil all the time."

Anthony Dexter's cold fingers were forced to drum on the table with apparent carelessness. Yes, he knew she was beautiful. He had not forgotten it for an instant since she had thrown back her veil and faced him. "Did--did she tell you why?" he asked.

"Yes," answered Ralph. "She told me why."

A sword, suspended by a single hair, seemed swaying uncertainly over Anthony Dexter's head--a two-edged sword, sure to strike mercilessly if it fell. Ralph's eyes were upon him, but not in contempt. God, in His infinite pity, had made them kind.

"Father," said Ralph, again, "she would not tell the name of the man, though I begged her to." Anthony Dexter's heart began to beat again, slowly at first, then with a sudden and unbearable swiftness. The blood thundered in his ears like the roar of a cataract. He could hardly hear what Ralph was saying.

"It was in a laboratory," the boy continued, though the words were almost lost. "She was there with the man she loved and whom she was pledged to marry. He was trying a new experiment, and she was watching. While he was leaning over the retort to put in another chemical, she heard the mass seethe, and pushed him away, just in time to save him.

"There was an explosion, and she was terribly burned. He was not touched, mind you--she had saved him. They took her to the hospital, and wrapped her in bandages. He went there only once. There was another girl there, named Evelyn Grey, who was so badly burned that every feature was destroyed. The two names became confused, and a mistake was made. They told him she would be disfigured for life, and so he went away."

The walls of the room swayed as though they were of fabric. The floor undulated; his chair rocked dizzily. Out of the accusing silence, Thorpe's words leaped to mock him:

The honour of the spoken word still holds him. He asked her to marry him and she consented . . . he was never released from his promise . . . did not even ask for it. He slunk away like a cur . . . sometimes I think there is no sin but shirking. . . I can excuse a liar . . . I can pardon a thief . . . I can pity a murderer . . . but a shirk, no .

"Father," Ralph was saying, "you do not seem to understand. I suppose it is difficult for you to comprehend such cowardice--you have always done the square thing." The man winced, but the boy did not see it.

"Try to think of a brute like that, Father, and be glad that our name means 'right.' She saved him from terrible disfigurement if not from death. Having instinctively thrown up her right arm, she got the worst of it there, and on her shoulder. Her face was badly burned, but not so deeply as to be scarred. She showed me her shoulder--it is awful. I never had seen anything like it. She said her arm was worse, but she did not show me that."

"He never knew?" asked Anthony Dexter, huskily. Ralph seemed to be demanding something of him, and the veiled figure, steadily advancing and retreating, demanded more still.

"No," answered Ralph, "he never knew. He went to the hospital only once. He had told her that very day that he loved her for the beautiful soul she had, and at the test, his love failed. He never saw her again. He went away, and married, and he has a son. Think of the son, Father, only think of the son! Suppose he knew it! How could he ever bear a disgrace like that!"

"I do not know," muttered Anthony Dexter. His lips were cold and stiff and he did not recognise his own voice.

"When she understood what had happened," Ralph continued, "and how he had deserted her for ever, after taking his cowardly life from her as a gift, her hair turned white. She has wonderful hair. Father--it's heavy and white and dull--it does not shine. She wore the veil at first because she had to, because her face was healing, and before it had wholly healed she had become accustomed to the shelter of it. Then, too, as she said, it kept people away from her--she could not be tempted to love or trust again."

There was an interval of silence, though the very walls seemed to be crying out: "Tell him! Tell him! Confess, and purge your guilty soul!" The clock ticked loudly, the blood roared in his ears. His hands were cold and almost lifeless; his body seemed paralysed, but he heard, so acutely that it was agony.

"Miss Evelina said," resumed Ralph, "that she did not think he had told his son. Do you know what I was thinking, Father, while she was talking? I was thinking of you, and how you had always done the square thing."

It seemed to Anthony Dexter that all the tortures of his laboratory had been chemically concentrated and were being poured out upon his head. "Our name means 'right,'" said the boy, proudly, and the man writhed in his chair.

For a moment, the ghostly Evelina went to Ralph, her hands outstretched in disapproval. Immediately she returned to her former position, advancing, retreating, advancing, retreating, with the regularity of the tide.

"I begged her," continued Ralph, "to tell me the man's name, but she would not. He still lives, she said, he is happy and prosperous and he has not suffered at all. For the honour of men, I want to punish that brute. Father, do you know that when I think of a cur like that, I believe I could rend him with my own hands?"

Anthony Dexter got to his feet unsteadily. The mists about him cleared and the veiled figure whisked suddenly out of his sight. He went up to Ralph as he might walk to the scaffold, but his head was held high. All the anguish of his soul crystallised itself into one passionate word:

"Strike!"

For an instant the boy faced him, unbelieving. Then he remembered that his father had seen Miss Evelina's face, that he must have known she was beautiful-- and why she wore the veil. "Father!" he cried, shrilly. "Oh, never you!"

Anthony Dexter looked into the eyes of his son until he could bear to look no more. The veiled figure no longer stood between them, but something else was there, infinitely more terrible. As he had watched the beating of the dog's bared heart, the man watched the boy's face. Incredulity, amazement, wonder, and fear resolved themselves gradually into conviction. Then came contempt, so deep and profound and permanent that from it there could never be appeal. With all the strength of his young and knightly soul, Ralph despised his father--and Anthony Dexter knew it.

"Father," whispered the boy, hoarsely, "it was never you! Tell me it isn't true! Just a word, and I'll believe you! For the sake of our manhood, Father, tell me it isn't true!"

Anthony Dexter's head drooped, his eyes lowered before his son's. The cold sweat dripped from his face; his hands groped pitifully, like those of a blind man, feeling his way in a strange place.

His hands fumbled helplessly toward Ralph's and the boy shrank back as though from the touch of a snake. With a deep-drawn breath of agony, the man flung himself, unseeing, out of the room. Ralph reeled like a drunken man against his chair. He sank into it helplessly and his head fell forward on the table, his shoulders shaking with that awful grief which knows no tears.

"Father!" he breathed. "Father! Father!"

Upstairs, Anthony Dexter walked through the hall, followed, or occasionally preceded, by the ghostly figure of Evelina. Her veil was thrown back now, and seemed a part of the mist which surrounded her. Sometimes he had told a patient that there was never a point beyond which human endurance could not be made to go. He knew now that he had lied.

Ralph's unspoken condemnation had hurt him cruelly. He could have borne words, he thought, better than that look on his son's face. For the first time, he realised how much he had cared for Ralph; how much--God help him!--he cared for him still.

Yet above it all, dominant, compelling, was man's supreme passion--that for his mate. As Evelina moved before him in her unveiled beauty, his hungry soul leaped to meet hers. Now, strangely, he loved her as he had loved her in the long ago, yet with an added grace. There was an element in his love that had never been there before--the mysterious bond which welds more firmly into one, two who have suffered together.

He hungered for Ralph--for the strong young arm thrown about his shoulders in friendly fashion, for the eager, boyish laugh, the hearty word. He hungered for Evelina, radiant with a beauty no woman had ever worn before. Far past the promise of her girlhood, the noble, transfigured face, with its glory of lustreless white hair, set his pulses to throbbing wildly. And subtly, unconsciously, but not the less surely, he hungered for death.

Anthony Dexter had cherished no sentiment about the end of life; to him it had seemed much the same as the stopping of a clock, and of as little moment. He had failed to see why such a fuss was made about the inevitable, though he had at times been scientifically interested in the hysterical effect he had produced in a household by announcing that within an hour or so a particular human clock might be expected to stop. It had never occurred to him, either, that a man had not a well-defined right to stop the clock of his own being whenever it seemed desirable or expedient.

Now he thought of death as the final, beautiful solution of all mundane problems. If he were dead, Ralph could not look at him with contempt; the veiled--or unveiled--Evelina could not haunt him as she had, remorselessly, for months. Yes, death was beautiful, and he well knew how to make it sure.

By an incredibly swift transition, his pain passed into an exquisite pleasure. The woman he loved was walking in the hall before him; the son he loved was downstairs. What man could have more?

"For sudden the worst turns the best to the brave,   The black minute's at end,
And the elements' rage, the fiend voices that rave,   Shall dwindle, shall blend,
Shall change, shall become first a peace out of pain,   Then a light, then thy breast--
Oh thou soul of my soul, I shall clasp thee again,   And with God be the rest!"

The wonderful words sang themselves over in his consciousness. He smiled and the unveiled Evelina smiled back at him, with infinite tenderness, infinite love. To-night he would sleep as he had not slept before--in the sleep that knows no waking.

He had the tiny white tablets, plenty of them, but the fancy seized him to taste this last bitterness to the full. He took a wine glass from his chiffonier--those white, blunt fingers had never been more steady than now. He lifted the vial on high and poured out the laudanum, faltering no more than when he had guided the knife in an operation that made him famous throughout the State.

"Evelina," he said, his voice curiously soft, "I pledge you now, in a bond that cannot break!" Was it fancy, or did the violet eyes soften with tears, even though the scarlet lips smiled?

He drank. The silken petals of the poppies, crushed into the peace that passeth all understanding, began their gentle ministry. He made his way to his bed, put out his candle, and lay down. The Spirit of the Poppies stood before him--a woman with a face like Evelina's, but her garments were scarlet, and Evelina always wore black.

In the darkness, he could not distinguish clearly. "Evelina," he called, aloud, "come! Come to me, and put your hand in mine!"

At once she seemed to answer him, wholly tender, wholly kind. Was he dreaming, or did Evelina come and kneel beside him? He groped for her hand, but it eluded him.

"Evelina," he said, again, "dear heart! Come! Forgive," he breathed, drowsily. "Ah, only forgive!"

Then, as if by a miracle, her hand slipped into his and he felt his head drawn tenderly to man's first and last resting place--a woman's breast.

And so, after a little, Anthony Dexter slept. The Spirit of the Poppies had claimed her own at last.

XXII
Forgiveness

Haggard and worn, after a sleepless night, Ralph went down-stairs. Heavily upon his young shoulders, he bore the burden of his father's disgrace. Through their kinship, the cowardice and the shirking became a part of his heritage.

There was nothing to be done, for he could not raise his hand in anger against his own father. They must continue to live together, and keep an unbroken front to the world, even though the bond between them had come to be the merest pretence. He despised his father, but no one must ever know it--not even the father whom he despised. Ralph did not guess that his father had read his face.

He saw, now, why Miss Evelina had refused to tell him the man's name, and he honoured her for her reticence. He perceived, too, the hideous temptation with which she was grappling when she begged him to leave her. She had feared that she would tell him, and he must never let her suspect that he knew.

The mighty, unseen forces that lie beneath our daily living were surging through Ralph's troubled soul. Love, hatred, shame, remorse, anger, despair--the words are but symbols of things that work devastation within.

Behold a man, in all outward seeming a gentleman. Observe his courtesy, refinement, and consideration, his perfect self-control. Note his mastery of the lower nature, and see the mind in complete triumph over the beast. Remark his education, the luxury of his surroundings, and the fine quality of his thought. Wonder at the high levels whereon his life is laid, and marvel at the perfect adjustment between him and his circumstances. Subject this man to the onslaught of some vast, cyclonic passion, and see the barriers crumble, then fall. See all the artifice of civilisation swept away at one fell stroke, and behold your gentleman, transformed in an instant into a beast, with all a beast's primeval qualities.

Under stress like this Ralph was fighting to regain his self mastery. He knew that he must force himself to sit opposite his father at the table, and exchange the daily, commonplace talk. No one must ever suspect that anything was amiss--it is this demand of Society which keeps the structure in place and draws the line between civilisation and barbarism. He knew that he never again could look his father straight in the face, that he must always avoid his eyes. It would be hard at first, but Ralph had never given up anything simply because it was difficult.

It was a relief to find that he was downstairs first. Hearing his father's step upon the stair, he thought, would enable him to steel himself more surely to the inevitable meeting. After they had once spoken together, it would be easier. At length they might even become accustomed to the ghastly thing that lay between them and veil it, as it were, with commonplaces.

Ralph took up the morning paper and pretended to read, though the words danced all over the page. The old housekeeper brought in his breakfast, and, likewise, he affected to eat. An hour went by, and still the dreaded step did not sound upon the stair. At length the old housekeeper said, with a certain timid deference:

"Your father's very late this morning, Doctor Ralph. He has never been so late before."

"He'll be down, presently. He's probably overslept."

"It's not your father's way to oversleep. Hadn't you better go up and see?"

Thus forced, Ralph went leisurely up-stairs, intending only to rap upon the door, which was always closed. Perhaps, with the closed door between them, the first speech might be easier.

He rapped once, with hesitation, then again, more definitely. There was no answer. Wholly without suspicion, Ralph opened the door, and went in.

Anthony Dexter lay upon his bed, fully dressed. On his face was a smile of ineffable peace. Ralph went to him quickly, shook him, and felt his pulse, but vainly. The heart of the man made no answer to the questioning fingers of his son. The eyes were closed and, his hands trembling now, Ralph forced them open. The contracted pupils gave him all the information he needed. He found the wineglass, which still smelled of laudanum. He washed it carefully, put it away, then went down-stairs.

His first sensation was entirely relief. Anthony Dexter had chosen the one sure way out. Ralph had a distinct sense of gratitude until he remembered that death did not end disgrace. Never again need he look in his father's eyes; there was no imperative demand that he should conceal his contempt. With the hiding of Anthony Dexter's body beneath the shriving sod, all would be over save memory. Could he put by this memory as his father had his? Ralph did not know.

The sorrowful preliminaries were all over before Ralph's feeling was in any way changed. Then the pity of it all overwhelmed him in a blinding flood.

Searching for something or some one to lean upon, his thought turned to Miss Evelina. Surely, now, he might go to her. If comfort was to be had, of any sort, he could find it there. At any rate, they were bound, much as his father had been bound to her before, by the logic of events.

He went uphill, scarcely knowing how he made his way. Miss Evelina, veiled, as usual, opened the door for him. Ralph stumbled across the threshold, crying out:

"My father is dead! He died by his own hand!"

"Yes," returned Miss Evelina, quietly. "I have heard. I am sorry--for you."

"You need not be," flashed Ralph, quickly. "It is for us, my father and I, to be sorry for you--to make amends, if any amends can be made by the living or the dead."

Miss Evelina started. He knew, then? And it had not been necessary for her to draw out the sheathed dagger which only yesterday she had held in her hand. The glittering vengeance had gone home, through no direct agency of hers.

"Miss Evelina!" cried the boy. "I have come to ask you to forgive my father!"

A silence fell between them, as cold and forbidding as Death itself. After an interval which seemed an hour, Miss Evelina spoke.

"He never asked," she said. Her tone was icy, repellent.

"I know," answered Ralph, despairingly, "but I, his son, ask it. Anthony Dexter's son asks you to forgive Anthony Dexter--not to let him go to his grave unforgiven."

"He never asked," said Miss Evelina again, stubbornly.

"His need is all the greater for that," pleaded the boy, "and mine. Have you thought of my need of it? My name meant 'right' until my father changed its meaning. Don't you see that unless you forgive my father, I can never hold up my head again?"

What the Piper had said to Evelina came back to her now, eloquent with appeal;

The word is not made right. I'm thinking 't is wrong end to, as many things in this world are until we move and look at them from another way. It's giving for, that's all. When you have put self so wholly aside that you can he sorry for him because he has wronged you, why, then you have forgiven.

She moved about restlessly. It seemed to her that she could never be sorry for Anthony Dexter because he had wronged her; that she could never grow out of the hurt of her own wrong.

"Come with me," said Ralph, choking. "I know it's a hard thing I ask of you. God knows I haven't forgiven him myself, but I know I've got to, and you'll have to, too. Miss Evelina, you've got to forgive him, or I never can bear my disgrace."

She let him lead her out of the house. On the long way to Anthony Dexter's, no word passed between them. Only the sound of their footfalls, and Ralph's long, choking breaths, half sobs, broke the silence.

At the gate, the usual knot of curious people had gathered. They were wondering, in undertones, how one so skilful as Doctor Dexter had happened to take an overdose of laudanum, but they stood by, respectfully, to make way for Ralph and the mysterious, veiled woman in black. The audible whispers followed them up to the very door: "Who is she? What had she to do with him?"

As yet, Anthony Dexter's body lay in his own room. Ralph led Miss Evelina in, and closed the door. "Here he is," sobbed the boy. "He has gone and left the shame for me. Forgive him, Miss Evelina! For the love of God, forgive him!"

Evelina sighed. She was standing close to Anthony Dexter now without fear. She had no wish to torture him, as she once had, with the sight of her unveiled face. It was the man she had loved, now--the emotion which had made him hideous to her was past and gone. To her, as to him the night before, death seemed the solution of all problems, the supreme answer to all perplexing questions.

Ralph crept out of the room and closed the door so softly that she did not hear. She was alone, as every woman some day is; alone with her dead.

She threw back her veil. The morning sun lay strong upon Anthony Dexter's face, revealing every line. Death had been kind to him at last, had closed the tortured eyes, blotted out the lines of cruelty around his mouth, and changed the mask-like expression to a tender calm.

A hint of the old, loving smile was there; once again he was the man she had loved, but the love itself had burned out of her heart long ago. He was naught to her, nor she to him.

The door knob turned, and, quickly, she lowered her veil. Piper Tom came in, with a soft, slow step. He did not seem to see Miss Evelina; one would have said he did not know she was in the room. He went straight to Anthony Dexter, and laid his warm hand upon the cold one.

"Man," he said, "I've come to say I forgive you for hurting Laddie. I'm not thinking, now, that you would have done it if you had known. I'm sorry for you because you could do it. I've forgiven you as I hope God will forgive you for that and for everything else."

Then he turned to Evelina, and whispered, as though to keep the dead from hearing: "'T was hard, but I've done it. 'T is easier, I'm thinking, to forgive the dead than the living." He went out again, as silently as he had come, and closed the door.

Was it, in truth, easier to forgive the dead? In her inmost soul, Evelina knew that she could not have cherished lifelong resentment against any other person in the world. To those we love most, we are invariably most cruel, but she did not love him now. The man she had loved was no more than a stranger--and from a stranger can come no intentional wrong.

"O God," prayed Evelina, for the first time, "help me to forgive!"

She threw back her veil once more. They were face to face at last, with only a prayer between. His mute helplessness pleaded with her and Ralph's despairing cry rang in her ears. The estranging mists cleared, and, in truth, she put self aside.

Intuitively, she saw how he had suffered since the night he came to her to make it right, if he could. He must have suffered, unless he were more than human. "Dear God," she prayed, again, "oh, help me forgive!"

All at once there was a change. The light seemed thrown into the uttermost places of her darkened soul. She illumined, and a wave of infinite pity swept her from head to foot. She leaned forward, her hands seeking his, and upon Anthony

Dexter's dead face there fell the forgiving baptism of her tears.

In the hall, as she went out, she encountered Miss Mehitable. That face, too, was changed. She had not come, as comes that ghoulish procession of merest acquaintances, to gloat, living, over the helpless dead.

At the sight of Evelina, she retreated. "I'll go back," murmured Miss Mehitable, enigmatically. "You had the best right."

Evelina went down-stairs and home again, but Miss Mehitable did not enter that silent room.

The third day came, and there was no resurrection. Since the miracle of Easter, the world has waited its three days for the dead to rise again. Ralph sat in the upper hall, just beyond the turn of the stair, and beside him, unveiled, was Miss Evelina.

"It's you and I," he had pleaded, "don't you see that? Have you never thought that you should have been my mother?"

From below, in Thorpe's deep voice, came the words of the burial service: "I am the resurrection and the life. He that believeth on me, though he were dead, yet shall he live."

For a few moments, Thorpe spoke of death as the inevitable end of life, and our ignorance of what lies beyond. He spoke of that mystic veil which never parts save for a passage, and from behind which no word ever comes. He said that life was a rainbow spanning brilliantly the two silences, that man's ceasing was no more strange than his beginning, and that the God who ordained the beginning had also ordained the end. He said, too, that the love which gave life might safely be trusted with that same life, at its mysterious conclusion. At length, he struck the personal note.

"It is hard for me," Thorpe went on, "to perform this last service for my friend. All of you are my friends, but the one who lies here was especially dear. He was a man of few friendships, and I was privileged to come close, to know him as he was.

"His life was clean, and upon his record there rests no shadow of disgrace." At this Ralph, in the upper hall, buried his face in his hands. Miss Evelina sat quietly, to all intents and purposes unmoved.

"He was a brave man," Thorpe was saying; "a valiant soldier on the great battle-field of the world. He met his temptations face to face, and conquered them. For

him, there was no such thing as cowardice--he never shirked. He met every re-
sponsibility like a man, and never swerved aside. He took his share, and more, of
the world's work, and did it nobly, as a man should do.

"His brusque manner concealed a great heart. I fear that, at times, some of
you may have misunderstood him. There was no man in our community more
deeply and lovingly the friend of us all, and there is no man among us more noble
in thought and act than he.

"We who have known him cannot but be the better for the knowing. It would
be a beautiful world, indeed, if we were all as good as he. We cannot fail to be inspired by his example. Through knowing him, each of us is better fitted for life. We
can conquer cowardice more easily, meet our temptations more valiantly, and more
surely keep from the sin of shirking, because Anthony Dexter has lived.

"To me," said Thorpe, his voice breaking, "it is the greatest loss, save one, that
I have ever known. But it is only through our own sorrow that we come to understand the sorrow of others, only through our own weaknesses that we learn to pity
the weakness of others, and only through our own love and forgiveness that we can
ever comprehend the infinite love and forgiveness of God. If any of you have ever
thought he wronged you, in some small, insignificant way, I give you my word that
it was entirely unintentional, and I bespeak for him your pardon.

"He goes to his grave to-day, to wait, in the great silence, for the final solution
of God's infinite mysteries, and, as you and I believe, for God's sure reward. He goes
with the love of us all, with the forgiveness of us all, and with the hope of us all that
when we come to die, we may be as certain of Heaven as he."

Perceiving that his grief was overmastering him, Thorpe proceeded quickly to
the benediction. In the pause that followed, Ralph leaned toward the woman who
sat beside him.

"Have you," he breathed, "forgiven him--and me?"

Miss Evelina nodded, her beautiful eyes shining with tears.

"Mother!" said Ralph, thickly. Like a hurt child, he went to her, and sobbed his
heart out, in the shelter of her arms.

XXIII
Undine Finds Her Soul

The year was at its noon. Every rose-bush was glorious with bloom, and even the old climbing rose which clung, in its decay, to Miss Mehitable's porch railing had put forth a few fragrant blossoms.

Soon after Araminta had been carried back home, she discovered that she had changed since she went away. Aunt Hitty no longer seemed infallible. Indeed, Araminta had admitted to herself, though with the pangs of a guilty conscience, that it was possible for Aunt Hitty to be mistaken. It was probable that the entire knowledge of the world was not concentrated in Aunt Hitty.

Outwardly, things went on as usual. Miss Mehitable issued orders to Araminta as the commander in chief of an army issues instructions to his subordinates, and Araminta obeyed as faithfully as before, yet with a distinct difference. She did what she was told to do out of gratitude for lifelong care, and not because she felt that she had to.

She went, frequently, to see Miss Evelina, having disposed of objections by the evident fact that she could not neglect any one who had been so kind to her as Miss Evelina had. Usually, however, the faithful guardian went along, and the three sat in the garden, Evelina with her frail hands listlessly folded, and the others stitching away at the endless and monotonous patchwork.

Miss Mehitable had a secret fear that the bloom had been brushed from her rose. Until the accident, Araminta had scarcely been out of her sight since she brought her home, a toddling infant. Miss Mehitable's mind had unerringly controlled two bodies until Araminta fell off the ladder. Now, the other mind began to show distressing signs of activity.

By dint of extra work, Araminta's eighth patchwork quilt was made for quilting, and the Ladies' Aid Society was invited to Miss Mehitable's for the usual Summer revelry of quilting and gossip. Miss Evelina was invited, but refused to go.

After the festivity was over, Miss Mehitable made a fruitful excavation into a huge chest in the attic, and emerged, flushed but happy, with enough scraps for three quilts.

"This here next quilt, Minty," she said, with the air of one announcing a pleasant surprise, "will be the Risin' Sun and Star pattern. It's harder 'n the others, and that's why I've kep' it until now. You've done all them other quilts real good," she added, grudgingly.

Araminta had her own surprise ready, but it was not of a pleasant nature. "Thank you, Aunt Hitty," she replied, "but I'm not going to make any more quilts, for a while, at any rate."

Miss Mehitable's lower jaw dropped in amazement. Never before had Araminta failed to obey her suggestions. "Minty," she said, anxiously, "don't you feel right? It was hot yesterday, and the excitement, and all--I dunno but you may have had a stroke."

Araminta smiled--a lovable, winning smile. "No, I haven't had any 'stroke,' but I've made all the quilts I'm going to until I get to be an old woman, and have nothing else to do."

"What are you layin' out to do, Minty?" demanded Miss Mehitable.

"I'm going to be outdoors all I want to, and I'm going up to Miss Evelina's and play with my kitten, and help you with the housework, or do anything else you want me to do, but--no more quilts," concluded the girl, firmly.

"Araminta Lee!" cried Miss Mehitable, speech having returned. "If I ain't ashamed of you! Here's your poor old aunt that's worked her fingers to the bone, slaving for you almost ever since the day you was born, and payin' a doctor's outrageous bill of four dollars and a half--or goin' to pay," she corrected, her conscience reproaching her, "and you refusin' to mind!

"Haven't I took good care of you all these eighteen years? Haven't I set up with you when you was sick and never let you out of my sight for a minute, and taught you to be as good a housekeeper as any in Rushton, and made you into a first-class seamstress, and educated you myself, and looked after your religious training, and made your clothes? Ain't I been father and mother and sister and brother and teacher and grandparents all rolled into one? And now you're refusin' to make quilts!"

Araminta's heart reproached her, but the blood of some fighting ancestor was in her pulses now. "I know, Aunt Hitty," she said, kindly, "you've done all that and more, and I'm not in the least ungrateful, though you may think so. But I'm not going to make any more quilts!"

"Araminta Lee," said Miss Mehitable, warningly, "look careful where you're steppin'. Hell is yawning in front of you this very minute!"

Araminta smiled sweetly. Since the day the minister had gone to see her, she had had no fear of hell. "I don't see it, Aunt Hitty," she said, "but if everybody who hasn't pieced more than eight quilts by hand is in there, it must be pretty crowded."

"Araminta Lee," cried Miss Mehitable, "you're your mother all over again. She got just as high-steppin' as you before her downfall, and see where she ended at. She was married," concluded the accuser, scornfully, "yes, actually married!"

"Aunt Hitty," said Araminta, her sweet mouth quivering ever so little, "your mother was married, too, wasn't she?" With this parting shaft, the girl went out of the room, her head held high.

Miss Mehitable stared after her, uncomprehending. Slowly it dawned upon her that some one had been telling tales and undoing her careful work. "Minty! Minty!" she cried, "how can you talk to me so!"

But 'Minty' was outdoors and on her way to Miss Evelina's, bareheaded, this being strictly forbidden, so she did not hear. She was hoping against hope that some day, at Miss Evelina's, she might meet Doctor Ralph again and tell him she was sorry she had broken his heart.

Since the day he went away from her, Araminta had not had even a glimpse of him. She had gone to his father's funeral, as everyone else in the village did, and had wondered that he was not in the front seat, where, in her brief experience of funerals, mourners usually sat.

She admitted, to herself, that she had gone to the funeral solely for the sake of seeing Doctor Ralph. Araminta was wholly destitute of curiosity regarding the dead, and she had not joined the interested procession which wound itself around Anthony Dexter's coffin before passing out, regretfully, at the front door. Neither had Miss Mehitable. At the time, Araminta had thought it strange, for at all previous occasions of the kind, within her remembrance. Aunt Hitty had been well up among the mourners and had usually gone around the casket twice.

At Miss Evelina's, she knocked in vain. There was white chiffon upon the line, but all the doors were locked. Doctor Ralph was not there, either, and even the kitten was not in sight, so, regretfully, Araminta went home again.

Throughout the day, Miss Mehitable did not speak to her erring niece, but Araminta felt it to be a relief, rather than a punishment. In the afternoon, the emancipated young woman put on her best gown--a white, cross-barred muslin which she had made herself. It was not Sunday, and Araminta was forbidden to wear the glorified raiment save on occasions of high state.

She added further to her sins by picking a pink rose--Miss Mehitable did not think flowers were made to pick--and fastening it coquettishly in her brown hair. Moreover, Araminta had put her hair up loosely, instead of in the neat, tight wad which Miss Mehitable had forced upon her the day she donned long skirts. When Miss Mehitable beheld her transformed charge she would have broken her vow of silence had not the words mercifully failed. Aunt Hitty's vocabulary was limited, and she had no language in which to express her full opinion of the wayward one, so she assumed, instead, the pose of a suffering martyr.

The atmosphere at the table, during supper, was icy, even though it was the middle of June. Thorpe noticed it and endeavoured to talk, but was not successful. Miss Mehitable's few words, which were invariably addressed to him, were so acrid in quality that they made him nervous. The Reverend Austin Thorpe, innocent as he was of all intentional wrong, was made to feel like a criminal haled to the bar of justice.

But Araminta glowed and dimpled and smiled. Her eyes danced with mischief, and the colour came and went upon her velvety cheeks. She took pains to ask Aunt Hitty for the salt or the bread, and kept up a continuous flow of high-spirited talk. Had it not been for Araminta, the situation would have become openly strained.

Afterward, she began to clear up the dishes as usual, but Miss Mehitable pushed her out of the room with a violence indicative of suppressed passion. So, humming a hymn at an irreverent tempo, Araminta went out and sat down on the front porch, spreading down the best rug in the house that she might not soil her gown.

This, also, was forbidden.

When the dishes were washed and put away, Miss Mehitable came out, clad in her rustling black silk and her best bonnet. "Miss Lee," she said very coldly, "I am going out."

"All right, Aunt Hitty" returned Araminta, cheerfully. "As it happens, I'm not."

Miss Mehitable repressed an exclamation of horror. Seemingly, then, it had occurred to Araminta to go out in the evening--alone!

Miss Mehitable's feet moved swiftly away from the house. She was going to the residence of the oldest and most orthodox deacon in Thorpe's church, to ask for guidance in dealing with her wayward charge, but Araminta never dreamed of this.

Dusk came, the sweet, June dusk, starred with fireflies and clouded with great white moths. The roses and mignonette and honeysuckle made the air delicately fragrant. To the emancipated one, it was, indeed, a beautiful world.

Austin Thorpe came out, having found his room unbearably close. As the nearsighted sometimes do, he saw more clearly at twilight than at other times.

"You here, child?" he asked.

"Yes, I'm here," replied Araminta, happily. "Sit down, won't you?" Having taken the first step, she found the others comparatively easy, and was rejoicing in her new freedom. She felt sure, too, that some day she should see Doctor Ralph once more and all would be made right between them.

The minister sat down gladly, his old heart yearning toward Araminta as toward a loved and only child. "Where is your aunt?" he asked, timidly.

"Goodness knows," laughed Araminta, irreverently. "She's gone out, in all her best clothes. She didn't say whether she was coming back or not."

Thorpe was startled, for he had never heard speech like this from Araminta. He knew her only as a docile, timid child. Now, she seemed suddenly to have grown up.

For her part, Araminta remembered how the minister had once helped her out of a difficulty, and taken away from her forever the terrible, haunting fear of hell. Here was a dazzling opportunity to acquire new knowledge.

"Mr. Thorpe," she demanded, eagerly, "what is it to be married?"

"To be married," repeated Austin Thorpe, dreamily, his eyes fixed upon a firefly that flitted, star-tike, near the rose, "is, I think, the nearest this world can come to Heaven."

"Oh!" cried Araminta, in astonishment. "What does it mean?"

"It means," answered Thorpe, softly, "that a man and a woman whom God meant to be mated have found each other at last. It means there is nothing in the world that you have to face alone, that all your joys are doubled and all your sorrows shared. It means that there is no depth into which you can go alone, that one other hand is always in yours; trusting, clinging, tender, to help you bear whatever comes.

"It means that the infinite love has been given, in part, to you, for daily strength and comfort. It is a balm for every wound, a spur for every lagging, a sure dependence in every weakness, a belief in every doubt. The perfect being is neither man nor woman, but a merging of dual natures into a united whole. To be married gives a man a woman's tenderness; a woman, a man's courage. The long years stretch before them, and what lies beyond no one can say, but they face it, smiling and serene, because they are together."

"My mother was married," said Araminta, softly. All at once, the stain of disgrace was wiped out.

"Yes, dear child, and, I hope, to the man she loved, as I hope that some day you will be married to the man who loves you."

Araminta's whole heart yearned toward Ralph--yearned unspeakably. In something else, surely, Aunt Hitty was wrong.

"Araminta," said Thorpe, his voice shaking; "dear child, come here."

She followed him into the house. His trembling old hands lighted a candle and she saw that his eyes were full of tears. From an inner pocket, he drew out a small case, wrapped in many thicknesses of worn paper. He unwound it reverently, his face alight with a look she had never seen there before.

"See!" he said. He opened the ornate case and showed her an old daguerreotype. A sweet, girlish face looked out at her, a woman with trusting, loving eyes, a sweet mouth, and dark, softly parted hair.

"Oh," whispered Araminta. "Were you married--to her?"

"No," answered Thorpe, hoarsely, shutting the case with a snap and beginning to wrap it again in the many folds of paper. "I was to have been married to her." His voice lingered with inexpressible fondness upon the words. "She died," he said, his lips quivering.

"Oh," cried the girl, "I'm sorry!" A sharp pang pierced her through and through.

"Child," said Thorpe, his wrinkled hand closing on hers, "to those who love, there is no such thing as Death. Do you think that just because she is dead, I have ceased to care? Death has made her mine as Life could never do. She walks beside me daily, as though we were hand in hand. Her tenderness makes me tender, her courage gives me strength, her great charity makes me kind. Her belief has made my own faith more sure, her steadfastness keeps me from faltering, and her patience enables me to wait until the end, when I go, into the Unknown, to meet her. Child, I do not know if there be a Heaven, but if God gives me her, and her love, as I knew it once, I shall not ask for more."

Unable to say more, for the tears, Thorpe stumbled out of the room. Araminta's own eyes were wet and her heart was strangely tender to all the world. Miss Evelina, the kitten, Mr. Thorpe, Doctor Ralph--even Aunt Hitty--were all included in a wave of unspeakable tenderness.

Never stopping to question, Araminta sped out of the house, her feet following where her heart led. Past the crossroads, to the right, down into the village, across the tracks, then sharply to the left, up to Doctor Dexter's, where, only a few weeks before, she had gone in the hope of seeing Doctor Ralph, Araminta ran like some young Atalanta, across whose path no golden apples were thrown.

The door was open, and she rushed in, unthinking, turning by instinct into the library, where Ralph sat alone, leaning his head upon his hand.

"Doctor Ralph!" she cried, "I've come!"

He looked up, then started forward. One look into her glorified face told him all that he needed to know. "Undine," he said, huskily, "have you found your soul?"

"I don't know what I've found," sobbed Araminta, from the shelter of his arms, "but I've come, to stay with you always, if you'll let me!"

"If I'll let you," murmured Ralph, kissing away her happy tears. "You little saint, it's what I want as I want nothing else in the world."

"I know what it is to be married," said Araminta, after a little, her grave, sweet eyes on his. "I asked Mr. Thorpe to-night and he told me. It's to be always with the one you love, and never to mind what anybody else says or does. It's to help each other bear everything and be twice as happy because you're together. It means that somebody will always help you when things go wrong, and there'll always be something you can lean on. You'll never be afraid of anything, because you're together. My mother was married, your mother was married, and I've found out that Aunt Hitty's mother was married, too.

"And Mr. Thorpe--he would have been married, but she died. He told me and he showed me her picture, and he says that it doesn't make any difference to be dead, when you love anybody, and that Heaven, for him, will be where she waits for him and puts her hand in his again. He was crying, and so was I, but it's because he has her and I have you!"

"Sweetheart! Darling!" cried Ralph, crushing her into his close embrace. "It's God Himself who brought you to me now!"

"No," returned Araminta, missing the point, "I came all by myself. And I ran all the way. Nobody brought me. But I've come, for always, and I'll never leave you again. I'm sorry I broke your heart!"

"You've made it well again," he said, fondly, "and so we'll be married--you and I."

"Yes," repeated Araminta, her beautiful face alight with love, "we'll be married, you and I!"

"Sweet," he said, "do you think I deserve so much?"

"Being married is giving everything," she explained, "but I haven't anything at all. Only eight quilts and me! Do you care for quilts?"

"Quilts be everlastingly condemned. I'm going to tell Aunt Hitty."

"No," said Araminta, "I'm going to tell her my own self, so now! And I'll tell her to-morrow!"

It was after ten when Ralph took Araminta home. From the parlour window Miss Mehitable was watching anxiously. She had divested herself of the rustling black silk and was safely screened by the shutters. She had been at home an hour or more, and though she had received plenty of good advice, of a stern nature, from her orthodox counsellor, her mind was far from at rest. Having conjured up all sorts of dire happenings, she was relieved when she heard voices outside.

Miss Mehitable peered out eagerly from behind the shutters. Up the road came Araminta--may the saints preserve us!--with a man! Miss Mehitable quickly placed him as that blackmailing play-doctor who now should never have his four dollars and a half unless he collected it by law. Only in the last ditch would she surrender.

They were talking and laughing, and Ralph's black-coated arm was around Araminta's white-robed waist. They came slowly to the gate, where they stopped. Araminta laid her head confidingly upon Ralph's shoulder and he held her tightly in his arms, kissing her repeatedly, as Miss Mehitable guessed, though she could not see very well.

At last they parted and Araminta ran lightly into the house, saying, in a low, tender voice: "To-morrow, dear, to-morrow!"

She went up-stairs, singing. Even then Miss Mehitable observed that it was not a hymn, but some light and ungodly tune she had picked up, Heaven knew where!

She went to her room, still humming, and presently her light was out, but her guardian angel was too stiff with horror to move.

"O Lord," prayed Araminta, as she sank to sleep, "keep me from the contamination of--not being married to him, for Thy sake, Amen."

XXIV
Telling Aunt Hitty

Araminta woke with the birds. As yet, it was dark, but from afar came the cheery voice of a robin, piping gaily of coming dawn. When the first ray of light crept into her room, and every bird for miles around was swelling his tiny throat in song, it seemed to her that, until now, she had never truly lived.

The bird that rocked on the maple branch, outside her window, carolling with all his might, was no more free than she. Love had rolled away the stone Aunt Hitty had set before the door of Araminta's heart, and the imprisoned thing was trying its wings, as joyously as the birds themselves.

Every sense was exquisitely alive and thrilling. Had she been older and known more of the world, Love would not have come to her so, but rather with a great peace, an unending trust. But having waked as surely as the sleeping princess in the tower, she knew the uttermost ecstasy of it--heard the sound of singing trumpets and saw the white light.

Her fear of Aunt Hitty had died, mysteriously and suddenly. She appreciated now, as never before, all that had been done for her. She saw, too, that many things had been done that were better left undone, but in her happy heart was no condemnation for anybody or anything.

Araminta dressed leisurely. Usually, she hurried into her clothes and ran down-stairs to help Aunt Hitty, who was always ready for the day's work before anybody else was awake but this morning she took her time.

She loved the coolness of the water on her face, she loved her white plump arms, her softly rounded throat, the velvety roses that blossomed on her cheeks, and the wavy brown masses of her hair, touched by the sun into tints of copper and gold. For the first time in all her life, Araminta realised that she was beautiful. She did not know that Love brings beauty with it, nor that the light in her eyes, like a new star, had not risen until last night.

She was seriously tempted to slide down the banister--this also having been interdicted since her earliest remembrance--but, being a grown woman, now, she compromised with herself by taking two stairs at a time in a light, skipping, perilous movement that landed her, safe but breathless, in the lower hall.

In the kitchen, wearing an aspect distinctly funereal, was Miss Mehitable. Her brisk, active manner was gone and she moved slowly. She did not once look up as Araminta came in.

"Good-morning, Aunt Hitty!" cried the girl, pirouetting around the bare floor. "Isn't this the beautifullest morning that ever was, and aren't you glad you're alive?"

"No," returned Miss Mehitable, acidly; "I am not."

"Aren't you?" asked Araminta, casually, too happy to be deeply concerned about anybody else; "why, what's wrong?"

"I should think, Araminta Lee, that you 'd be the last one on earth to ask what's wrong!" The flood gates were open now. "Wasn't it only yesterday that you broke away from all restraint and refused to make any more quilts? Didn't you put on your best dress in the afternoon when 't want Sunday and I hadn't told you that you could? Didn't you pick a rose and stick it into your hair, and have I ever allowed you to pick a flower on the place, to say nothing of doing anything so foolish as to put it in your hair? Flowers and hair don't go together."

"There's hair in the parlour," objected Araminta, frivolously, "made up into a wreath of flowers, so I thought as long as you had them made out of dead people's hair, I'd put some roses in mine, now, while I'm alive."

Miss Mehitable compressed her lips sternly and went on.

"Didn't you take a rug out of the parlour last night and spread it on the porch, and have I ever had rugs outdoor except when they was being beat? And didn't you sit down on the front porch, where I've never allowed you to sit, it not being modest for a young female to sit outside of her house?"

"Yes," admitted Araminta, cheerfully, "I did all those things, and I put my hair up loosely instead of tightly, as you've always taught me. You forgot that."

"No, I didn't," denied Miss Mehitable, vigorously; "I was coming to that. Didn't you go up to Miss Evelina's without asking me if you could, and didn't you go bareheaded, as I've never allowed you to do?"

"Yes," laughed Araminta, "I did."

"After I went away," pursued Miss Mehitable, swiftly approaching her climax, "didn't you go up to Doctor Dexter's like a shameless hussy?"

"If it makes a shameless hussy of me to go to Doctor Dexter's, that's what I am."

"You went there to see Doctor Ralph Dexter, didn't you?"

"Yes, I did," sang Araminta, "and oh, Aunt Hitty, he was there! He was there!"

"Ain't I told you," demanded Miss Mehitable, "how one woman went up there when she had no business to go and got burnt so awful that she has to wear a veil all the rest of her life?"

"Yes, you told me, Aunt Hitty, but, you see, I didn't get burned."

"Araminta Lee, you're going right straight to hell, just as fast as you can get there. Perdition is yawning at your feet. Didn't that blackmailing play-doctor come home with you?"

"Ralph," Said Araminta--and the way she spoke his name made it a caress--"Ralph came home with me."

"I saw you comin' home," continued Miss Mehitable, with her sharp eyes keenly fixed upon the culprit. "I saw his arm around your waist and you leanin' your head on his shoulder."

"Yes," laughed Araminta, "I haven't forgotten. I can feel his arms around me now."

"And at the gate--you needn't deny it, for I saw it all--he KISSED you!"

"That's right, Aunt Hitty. At his house, he kissed me, too, lots and lots of times. And," she added, her eyes meeting her accuser's clearly, "I kissed him."

"How do you suppose I feel to see such goin's on, after all I've done for you?"

"You needn't have looked, Aunty, if you didn't like to see it."

"Do you know where I went when I went out? I went up to Deacon Robinson's to lay your case before him." Miss Mehitable paused, for the worthy deacon was the fearsome spectre of young sinners.

Araminta executed an intricate dance step of her own devising, but did not seem interested in the advice he had given.

"He told me," went on Miss Mehitable, in the manner of a judge pronouncing sentence upon a criminal, "that at any cost I must trample down this godless uprising, and assert my rightful authority. 'Honour thy father and thy mother,' the Bible says, and I'm your father and mother, rolled into one. He said that if I couldn't make you listen in any other way, it would be right and proper for me to shut you up in your room and keep you on bread and water until you came to your senses."

Araminta giggled. "I wouldn't be there long," she said. "How funny it would be for Ralph to come with a ladder and take me out!"

"Araminta Lee, what do you mean?"

"Why," explained the girl, "we're going to be married--Ralph and I."

A nihilist bomb thrown into the immaculate kitchen could not have surprised Miss Mehitable more. She had no idea that it had gone so far. "Married!" she gasped. "You!"

"Not just me alone, Aunty, but Ralph and I. There has to be two, and I'm of age, so I can if I want to." This last heresy had been learned from Ralph, only the night before.

"Married!" gasped Miss Mehitable, again.

"Yes," returned Araminta, firmly, "married. My mother was married, and Ralph's mother was married, and your mother was married. Everybody's mother is married, and Mr. Thorpe says it's the nearest there is to Heaven. He was going to be married himself, but she died.

"Dear Aunt Hitty," cooed Araminta, with winning sweetness, "don't look so frightened. It's nothing dreadful, it's only natural and right, and I'm the happiest girl the sun shines on to-day. Don't be selfish, Aunty--you've had me all my life, and it's his turn now. I'll come to see you every day and you can come and see me. Kiss me, and tell me you're glad I'm going to be married!"

At this juncture, Thorpe entered the kitchen, not aware that he was upon forbidden ground. Attracted by the sound of voices, he had come in, just in time to hear Araminta's last words.

"Dear child!" he said, his fine old face illumined. "And so you're going to be married to the man you love! I'm so glad! God bless you!" He stooped, and kissed

Araminta gently upon the forehead.

Having thus seen, as it were, the sanction of the Church placed upon Araminta's startling announcement, Miss Mehitable could say no more. During breakfast she did not speak at all, even to Thorpe. Araminta chattered gleefully of everything under the blue heaven, and even the minister noted the liquid melody of her voice.

Afterward, she went out, as naturally as a flower turns toward the sun. It was a part of the magic beauty of the world that she should meet Ralph, just outside the gate, with a face as radiant as her own.

"I was coming," he said, after the first rapture had somewhat subsided, "to tell Aunt Hitty."

"I told her," returned the girl, proudly, "all by my own self!"

"You don't mean it! What did she say?"

"She said everything. She told me hell was yawning at my feet, but I'm sure it's Heaven. She said that she was my father and mother rolled into one, and I was obliged to remind her that I was of age. You thought of that," she said, admiringly. "I didn't even know that I'd ever get old enough not to mind anybody but myself--or you."

"You won't have to 'mind' me," laughed Ralph. "I'll give you a long rope."

"What would I do with a rope?" queried Araminta, seriously.

"You funny, funny girl! Didn't you ever see a cow staked out in a pasture?"

"Yes. Am I a cow?"

"For the purposes of illustration, yes, and Aunt Hitty represents the stake. For eighteen or nineteen years, your rope has been so short that you could hardly move at all. Now things are changed, and I represent the stake. You've got the longest rope, now, that was ever made in one piece. See?"

"I'll come back," answered Araminta, seriously. "I don't think I need any rope at all."

"No, dear, I know that. I was only joking. You poor child, you've lived so long with that old dragon that you scarcely recognise a joke when you see one. A sense of humour, Araminta, is a saving grace for anybody. Next to Love, it's the finest gift of the gods."

"Have I got it?"

"I guess so. I think it's asleep, but we'll wake it up. Look here, dear--see what

I brought you."

From his pocket, Ralph took a small purple velvet case, lined with white satin. Within was a ring, set with a diamond, small in circumference, but deep, and of unusual brilliancy. By a singular coincidence, it fitted Araminta's third finger exactly.

"Oh-h!" she cried, her cheeks glowing. "For me?"

"Yes, for you--till I get you another one. This was my mother's ring, sweetheart. I found it among my father's things. Will you wear it, for her sake and for mine?"

"I'll wear it always," answered Araminta, her great grey eyes on his, "and I don't want any other ring. Why, if it hadn't been for her, I never could have had you."

Ralph took her into his arms. His heart was filled with that supreme love which has no need of words.

Meanwhile Miss Mehitable was having her bad quarter of an hour. Man-like, Thorpe had taken himself away from a spot where he felt there was about to be a display of emotion. She was in the house alone, and the acute stillness of it seemed an accurate foreshadowing of the future.

Miss Mehitable was not among those rare souls who are seldom lonely. Her nature demanded continuous conversation, the subject alone being unimportant. Every thought that came into her mind was destined for a normal outlet in speech. She had no mental reservoir.

Araminta was going away--to be married. In spite of her trouble, Miss Mehitable noted the taint of heredity. "It's in her blood," she murmured, "and maybe Minty ain't so much to blame."

In this crisis, however, Miss Mehitable had the valiant support of her conscience. She had never allowed the child to play with boys--in fact, she had not had any playmates at all. As soon as Araminta was old enough to understand, she was taught that boys and men--indeed all human things that wore trousers, long or short--were rank poison, and were to be steadfastly avoided if a woman desired peace of mind. Miss Mehitable frequently said that she had everything a husband could have given her except a lot of trouble.

Daily, almost hourly, the wisdom of single blessedness had been impressed upon Araminta. Miss Mehitable neglected no illustration calculated to bring the lesson home. She had even taught her that her own mother was an outcast and had brought disgrace upon her family by marrying; she had held aloft her maiden standard and literally compelled Araminta to enlist.

Now, all her work had gone for naught. Nature had triumphantly reasserted itself, and Araminta had fallen in love. The years stretched before Miss Mehitable in a vast and gloomy vista illumined by no light. No soft step upon the stair, no sunny face at her table, no sweet, girlish laugh, no long companionable afternoons with patchwork, while she talked and Araminta listened. At the thought, her stern mouth quivered, ever so slightly, and, all at once, she found the relief of tears.

An hour or so afterward, she went up to the attic, walking with a stealthy, cat-like tread, though there was no one in the house to hear. In a corner, far back under the eaves, three trunks were piled, one on top of the other. Miss Hitty lifted off the two top trunks without apparent effort, for her arms were strong, and drew the lowest one out into the path of sunlight that lay upon the floor, maple branches swaying across it in silhouette.

In another corner of the attic, up among the rafters, was a box apparently filled with old newspapers. Miss Hitty reached down among the newspapers with accustomed fingers and drew out a crumpled wad, tightly wedged into one corner of the box.

She listened carefully at the door, but there was no step in the house. She was absolutely alone. None the less, she bolted the door of the attic before she picked the crumpled paper apart, and took out the key of the trunk.

The old lock opened readily, and from the trunk came the musty odour of long-dead lavender and rosemary, lemon verbena and rose geranium. On top was Barbara Lee's wedding gown. Miss Hitty always handled it with reverence not un-mixed with awe, never having had a wedding gown herself.

Underneath were the baby clothes which the girl-wife had begun to make when she first knew of her child's coming. The cloth was none too fine and the little garments were awkwardly cut and badly sewn, but every stitch had been guided by a great love.

Araminta's first shoes were there, too--soft, formless things of discoloured white kid. Folded in a yellowed paper was a tiny, golden curl, snipped secretly, and marked on the outside: "Minty's hair." Farther down in the trunk were the few relics of Miss Mehitable's far-away girlhood.

A dog-eared primer, a string of bright buttons, a broken slate, a ragged, disreputable doll, and a few blown birds' eggs carefully packed away in a small box of cotton--these were her treasures. There was an old autograph album with a gay blue cover which the years in the trunk had not served to fade. Far down in the trunk was a package which Miss Mehitable took out reverently. It was large and flat and tied with heavy string in hard knots. She untied the knots patiently--her mother had taught her never to cut a string.

Underneath was more paper, and more string. It took her half an hour to bring to light the inmost contents of the package, bound in layer after layer of fine muslin, but not tied. She unrolled the yellowed cloth carefully, for it was very frail. At last she took out a photograph--Anthony Dexter at three-and-twenty--and gazed at it long.

On one page of her autograph album was written an old rhyme. The ink had faded so that it was scarcely legible, but Miss Hitty knew it by heart:

"'If you love me as I love you   No knife can cut our love in two.'
Your sincere friend,
ANTHONY DEXTER."

Like a tiny sprig of lavender taken from a bush which has never bloomed, this bit of romance lay far back in the secret places of her life. She had a knot of blue ribbon which Anthony Dexter had once given her, a lead pencil which he had gallantly sharpened, and which she had never used.

Her life had been barren--Miss Mehitable knew that, and in her hours of self-analysis, admitted it. She would gladly have taken Evelina's full measure of suffering in exchange for one tithe of Araminta's joy. After Anthony Dexter had turned from her to Evelina, Miss Mehitable had openly scorned him. She had spent the rest of her life, since, in showing him and the rest that men were nothing to her and that he was least of all.

She had hovered near his patients simply for the sake of seeing him--she did not care for them at all. She sat in the front window that she might see him drive by, and counted that day lost which brought her no sight of him. This was her one tenderness, her one vulnerable point.

The afternoon shadows grew long and the maple branches ceased to sway. Outside a bird crooned a lullaby to his nesting mate. An oriole perched on the topmost twig of an evergreen in a corner of the yard, and opened his golden throat in a rapture of song.

Love was abroad in the world that day. Bees hummed it, birds sang it, roses breathed it. The black and gold messengers of the fields bore velvety pollen from flower to flower, moving lazily on shimmering, gossamer wings. A meadow-lark rose from a distant clover field, dropping exquisite, silvery notes as he flew. The scent of green fields and honeysuckles came in at the open window, mingled inextricably with the croon of the bees, but Miss Mehitable knew only that it was Summer, that the world was young, but she was old and alone and would be alone for the rest of her life.

She leaned forward to look at the picture, and Anthony Dexter smiled back at her, boyish, frank, eager, lovable. A tear dropped on the pictured face--not the first one, for the photograph was blistered oddly here and there.

"I've done all I could," said Miss Mehitable to herself, as she wrapped it up again in its many yellowed folds of muslin. "I thought Minty would be happier so, but maybe, after all, God knows best."

XXV
Redeemed

Miss Evelina sat alone, in her house, at peace with Anthony Dexter and with all the world. The surging flood of forgiveness and compassion which had swept over her as she gazed at his dead face, had broken down all barriers, abrogated all reserves. She saw that Piper Tom was right; had she forgiven him, she would have been free long ago.

She shrank no longer from her kind, but yearned, instead, for friendly companionship. Once she had taken off her veil and started down the road to Miss Mehitable's, but the habit of the years was strong upon her, and she turned back, affrighted, when she came within sight of the house.

Since she left the hospital, no human being had seen her face, save Anthony Dexter and his son. She had crept, nun-like, into the shelter of her chiffon, dimly taking note of a world which could not, in turn, look upon her. She clung to it still, yet perceived that it was a lie.

She studied herself in the mirror, no longer hating the sight of her own face. She was not now blind to her own beauty, nor did she fail to see that transfiguring touch of sorrow and peace. These two are sculptors, one working both from within and without, and the other only from within.

Why should she not put her veil forever away from her now? Why should she not meet the world face to face, as frankly as the world met her? Why should she delay?

She had questioned herself continually, but found no answer. Since she came back to her old home, she had been mysteriously led. Perhaps she was to be led further through the deep mazes of life--it was not only possible, but probable.

"I'll wait," she said to herself, "for a sign."

She had not seen the Piper since the day they met so strangely, with Anthony Dexter lying dead between them. Quite often, however, she had heard the flute, usually at sunrise or sunset, afar off in the hills. Once, at the hour of the turning night, the melody had come to her on the first grey winds of dawn.

A robin had waked to answer it, for the Piper's fluting was wondrously like his own voice.

Contrasting her present peace with her days of torment. Miss Evelina thrilled with gratitude to Piper Tom, who had taken the weeds out of her garden in more senses than one. His hand had guided her, slowly, yet surely, to the heights of calm. She saw her life now as a desolate valley lying between two peaks. One was sunlit, yet opaline with the mists of morning; the other was scarcely a peak, but merely a high and grassy plain upon which the afternoon shadows lay long.

Ah, but there were terrors in the dark valley which lay between! Sharp crags and treeless wastes, tortuous paths and abysmal depths, with never a rest for the wayfarer who struggled blindly on. She was not yet so secure upon the height that she could contemplate the valley unmoved.

Her house was immaculate, now, and was kept so by her own hands. At first, she had not cared, and the dust and the cobwebs had not mattered at all. Miss Mehitable, in the beginning, had inspired her to housewifely effort, and Doctor Ralph's personal neatness had made her ashamed. She worked in the garden, too, keeping the brick-bordered paths free from weeds, and faithfully attending to every plant.

Yet life seemed strangely empty, lifted above its all-embracing pain. The house and garden did not occupy her fully, and she had few books. These were all old ones, and she knew them by heart, though she had found some pleasure in reading again the well-thumbed fairy books of her childhood.

She had read the book which Ralph had brought Araminta, and thought of asking him to lend her more--if she ever saw him again. She knew that he was very busy, but she felt that, surely, he would come again before long.

Araminta danced up the path, singing, and rapped at Miss Evelina's door. When she came in, it was like a ray of sunlight in a gloomy place.

"Miss Evelina!" she cried; "Oh, Miss Evelina! I'm going to be married!"

"I'm glad," said Evelina, tenderly, yet with a certain wistfulness. Once the joy of it had been in her feet, too, and the dread valley of desolation had opened before her.

"See!" cried Araminta, extending a dimpled hand. "See my ring! It's my engagement ring," she added, proudly.

Miss Evelina winced a little behind her veil, for the ring was the one Anthony Dexter had given her soon after their betrothal. Fearing gossip, she had refused to wear it until after they were married. So he had taken it, to have it engraved, but, evidently, the engraving had never been done. Otherwise Ralph would not have given it to Araminta--she was sure of that.

"It was his mother's ring, Miss Evelina, and now it's mine. His father loved his mother just as Ralph loves me. It's so funny not to have to say 'Doctor Ralph.' Oh, I'm so glad I broke my ankle! He's coming, but I wanted to come first by myself. I made him wait for five minutes down under the elm because I wanted to tell you first. I told Aunt Hitty, all alone, and I wasn't a bit afraid. Oh, Miss Evelina, I wish you had somebody to love you as he loves me!"

"So do I," murmured Evelina, grateful for the chiffon that hid her tears.

"Wasn't there ever anybody?"

"Yes."

"I knew it--you're so sweet nobody could help loving you. Did he die?"

"Yes."

"It was that way with Mr. Thorpe," mused Araminta, reminiscently. "They loved each other and were going to be married, but she died. He said, though, that death didn't make any difference with loving. There's Ralph, now."

"Little witch," said the boy, fondly, as she met him at the door; "did you think I could wait a whole five minutes?"

They sat in the parlour for half an hour or more, and during this time it was not necessary for their hostess to say a single word. They were quite unaware that they were not properly conducting a three-sided conversation, and Miss Evelina made no effort to enlighten them. Youth and laughter and love had not been in her house before for a quarter of a century.

"Come again," she begged, when they started home. Joy incarnate was a welcome guest--it did not mock her now.

Half-way down the path, Ralph turned back to the veiled woman who stood wistfully in the doorway. Araminta was swinging, in childish fashion, upon the gate. Ralph took Miss Evelina's hand in his.

"I wish I could say all I feel," he began, awkwardly, "but I can't. With all my heart, I wish I could give some of my happiness to you!"

"I am content--since I have forgiven."

"If you had not, I could never have been happy again, and even now, I still feel the shame of it. Are you going to wear that--veil--always?"

"No," she whispered, shrinking back into the shelter of it, "but I am waiting for a sign."

"May it soon come," said Ralph, earnestly.

"I am used to waiting. My life has been made up of waiting. God bless you," she concluded, impulsively.

"And you," he answered, touching his lips to her hand. He started away, but she held him back. "Ralph," she said, passionately, "be true to her, be good to her, and never let her doubt you. Teach her to trust you, and make yourself worthy of her trust. Never break a promise made to her, though it cost you everything else you have in the world. I am old, and I know that, at the end, nothing counts for an instant beside the love of two. Remember that keeping faith with her is keeping faith with God!"

"I will," returned Ralph, his voice low and uneven. "It is what my own mother would have said to me had she been alive to-day. I thank you."

The house was very lonely after they had gone, though the echoes of love and laughter seemed to have come back to a place where they once held full sway. The afternoon wore to its longest shadows and the dense shade of the cypress was thrown upon the garden. Evelina smiled to herself, for it was only a shadow.

The mignonette breathed fragrance into the dusk. Scent of lavender and rosemary filled the stillness with balm. Drowsy birds chirped sleepily in their swaying nests, and the fairy folk of field and meadow set up a whirr of melodious wings. White, ghostly moths fluttered, cloud-like, over the quiet garden, and here and there a tiny lamp-bearer starred the night. A flaming meteor sped across the uncharted dark of the heavens, where only the love-star shone. The moon had not yet risen.

From within, Evelina recognised the sturdy figure of Piper Tom, and went out to meet him as he approached. She had drawn down her veil, but her heart was strangely glad.

"Shall we sit in the garden?" she asked.

"Aye, in the garden," answered the Piper, "since 't is for the last time."

His voice was sad, and Evelina yearned to help him, even as he had helped her. "What is it?" she asked. "Is it anything you can tell me?"

"Only that I'll be trudging on to-morrow. My work here is done. I can do no more."

"Then let me tell you how grateful I am for all you have done for me. You made me see things in their true relation and taught me how to forgive. I was in bondage, and you made me free."

The Piper sprang to his feet. "Spinner in the Sun," he cried, "is it true? Just as I thought your night was endless, has the light come? Tell me again," he pleaded, "ah, tell me 't is true!"

"It is true," said Evelina, with solemn joy. "In all my heart there is nothing but forgiveness. The anger and resentment are gone--all gone."

"Spinner in the Sun!" breathed the Piper, scarcely conscious that he spoke the words aloud. "My Spinner in the Sun!"

Slowly the moon climbed toward the zenith, and still, because there was no need, they spoke no word. Dew rose whitely from the clover fields beyond, veiling them as with white chiffon. It was the Piper, at last, who broke the silence.

"When I trudge on to-morrow," he said, "'t will be with a glad heart, even though the little chap is no longer with me. 'T is a fair, brave world, I'm thinking, since I've set your threads to going right again. I called you," he added, softly, "and you came."

"Yes," said Evelina, happily, "you called me, and I came."

"Spinner in the Sun," said the Piper, tenderly, "have you guessed my work?"

"Why, keeping the shop, isn't it?" asked Evelina, wonderingly; "the needles and thread and pins and buttons and all the little trifles that women need? A pedler's pack, set up in a house?"

The Piper laughed. "No," he replied, "I'm thinking that is not my work, nor yet the music that has no tune, which I'm for ever playing on my flute. Lady, I have travelled far, and seen much, and always there has been one thing that is strangest of all. In every place that I have been in yet, there has been a church and a minister, whose business was to watch over human souls.

"He's told them what was right according to his own thinking, which I'm far from saying isn't true for him, and never minded anything more. In spite of blood and tears and agony, he's always held up the one standard, and, I'm thinking, has always pointed to the hardest way to reach it. The way has been so hard that many have never reached it at all, and those who have--I've not seen that they are the happiest or the kindest, nor that they are loved the most.

"In the same place, too, there is always a doctor, whose business it is to watch over the body. If you have a broken leg or a broken arm, or a fever, he can set you right again. Blind eyes can be made to see, and deaf ears made to hear, but, Lady, who is there to care about a broken heart?

"I have taken in my pedler's pack the things that women need, because 't is women, mostly, who bear the heartaches of the world, and I come closer to them so. What you say I have done for you, I have done for many more. I'm trying to make the world a bit easier for all women because a woman gave me life. And because I love another woman in another way," he added, his voice breaking, "I'll be trudging on to-morrow alone, though 't would be easier, I'm thinking, to linger here."

Evelina's heart leaped with a throb of the old pain. "Tell me about her," she said, because it seemed the only thing to say.

"The woman I love," answered the Piper, "is not for me. She'd never be thinking of stooping to such as I, and I'd not be insulting her by asking. She's very proud, but she could be tender if she chose, and she's the bravest soul I ever knew--so brave that she fears neither death nor life, though life itself has not been kind.

"Her little feet have been set upon the rough pathways, almost since the beginning, and her hands catch at my heart-strings, they are so frail. They're fluttering always like frightened birds, and the fluttering is in her voice, too."

"And her face?"

"Ah, but I've dreamed of her face! I've thought it was noble beyond all words, with eyes like the first deep violets of Spring, but filled with compassion for all the world. So brave, so true, so tender it might be that I'm thinking if I could see it once, with love on it for me, that I'd never be asking more."

"Why haven't you seen her face?" asked Evelina, idly, to relieve an awkward pause. "Is she only a dream-woman?"

"Nay, she's not a dream-woman. She lives and breathes as dreams never do, but she hides her face because she is so beautiful. She veils her face from me as once she veiled her soul."

Then, at last, Evelina understood. She felt the hot blood mantling her face, and was thankful, once more, for the shelter of her chiffon.

"Spinner in the Sun," said the Piper, with suppressed tenderness, "were you thinking I could see you more than once or twice and not be caring? Were you thinking I could have the inmost soul of me torn because you'd been hurt, and never be knowing what lay beyond it, for me? Were you thinking I could be talking to you day after day, without having the longing to talk with you always? And now that I've done my best for you, and given you all that rests with me for giving, do you see why I'll be trudging on to-morrow, alone?

"'T is not for me to be asking it, for God knows I could never be worthy, but I've thought of Heaven as a place where you and I might fare together always, with me to heal your wounds, help you over the rough places, and guide you through the dark. That part of it, I'm to have, I'm thinking, for God has been very good to me. I'm to know that wherever you are, you re happy at last, because it's been given me to lead you into the light. I called you, and you came."

"Yes," said Evelina, her voice lingering upon the words, "you called me and I came, and was redeemed. Tell me, in your thought of Heaven, have you ever asked to see my face?"

"Nay," cried the Piper, "do you think I'd be asking for what you hide from me? I know that 't is because you are so beautiful, and such beauty is not for my eyes to see."

"Piper Tom," she answered; "dear Piper Tom! I told you once that I had been terribly burned. I was hurt so badly that when the man I was pledged to marry, and whose life I had saved, was told that every feature of mine was destroyed except my sight, he went away, and never came back any more."

"The brute who hurt Laddie," he said, in a low tone. "I told him then that a man who would torture a dog would torture a woman, too. I'd not be minding the scars," he added, "since they're brave scars, and not the marks of sin or shame. I'm thinking that 't is the brave scars that have made you so beautiful--so beautiful," he repeated, "that you hide your face."

Into Evelina's heart came something new and sweet--that perfect, absolute, unwavering trust which a woman has but once in her life and of which Anthony Dexter had never given her the faintest hint. All at once, she knew that she could not let him go; that he must either stay, or take her, too.

She leaned forward. "Piper Tom," she said, unashamed, "when you go, will you take me with you? I think we belong together--you and I."

"Belong together?" he repeated, incredulously. "Ah, 't is your pleasure to mock me. Oh, my Spinner in the Sun, why would you wish to hurt me so?"

Tears blinded Evelina so that, through her veil, and in the night, she could not see at all. When the mists cleared, he was gone.

XXVI
The Lifting of the Veil

From afar, at the turn of night, came the pipes o' Pan--the wild, mysterious strain which had first summoned Evelina from pain to peace. At the sound, she sat up in bed, her heavy, lustreless white hair falling about her shoulders. She guessed that Piper Tom was out upon the highway, with his pedler's pack strapped to his sturdy back. As in a vision, she saw him marching onward from place to place, to make the world easier for all women because a woman had given him life, and because he loved another woman in another way.

Was it always to be so, she wondered; should she for ever thirst while others drank? While others loved, must she eternally stand aside heart-hungry? Unyielding Fate confronted her, veiled inscrutably, but she guessed that the veil concealed a mocking smile.

Out of her Nessus-robe of agony, Evelina had emerged with one truth. Whatever is may not be right, but it is the outcome of deep and far-reaching forces with which our finite hands may not meddle. The problem has but one solution--adjustment. Hedged in by the iron bars of circumstance as surely as a bird within his cage, it remains for the individual to choose whether he will beat his wings against the bars until he dies, or take his place serenely on the perch ordained for him--and sing.

Within his cage, the bird may do as he likes. He may sleep or eat or bathe, or whet his beak uselessly against the cuttlebone thrust between the bars. He may hop about endlessly and chirp salutations to other birds, likewise caged, or he may try his eager wings in a flight which is little better than no flight at all. His cage may be a large one, yet, if he explores far enough, he will most surely bruise his body against the bars of circumstance. With beak and claws and constant toil he may, perhaps, force an opening in the bars wide enough to get through, slowly, and with great discomfort. He has gained, however, only a larger cage.

If he is a wise bird, he settles down and tries to become satisfied with his surroundings; even to gather pleasure from the gilt wires and the cuttlebone thrust picturesquely between them. When the sea gull wings his majestic way past his habitation, free as the wind itself, the wise bird will close his eyes, and affect not to see. So, also, will the gull, for there is no loneliness comparable with unlimited freedom.

Upon the heights, the great ones stand--alone. To the dweller in the valley, those distant peaks are clad in more than mortal splendour. Time and distance veil the jagged cliffs and hide the precipices. Day comes first to the peaks and lingers there longest; while it is night in the valley, there is still afterglow upon the hills.

Perhaps, some dweller in the valley longs for the height, and sets forth, heeding not the eager hands that, selfishly, as it seems, would keep him within their loving reach. Having once turned his face upward, he does not falter, even for the space of a backward look. He finds that the way is steep, that there is no place to rest, and that the comfort and shelter of the valley are unknown. The sun burns him, and the cold freezes his very blood, for there are only extremes on the way to the peak. Glittering wastes of ice dazzle him and snow blinds him, with terror and not with beauty as from below. The opaline mists are gone, and he sees with dreadful clearness the path which lies immediately ahead.

Beyond, there is emptiness, vast as the desert. At the timber line, he pauses, and, for the first time, looks back. Ah, how fair the valley lies below him! The silvery ribbon of the river winds through a pageantry of green and gold. Upon the banks are woodland nooks, fragrant with growing things and filled with a tender quiet broken only by the murmer of the stream. The turf is soft and cool to the wayfarer's tired feet, and there is crystal water in abundance to quench his thirst.

But, from the peak, no traveller returns, for the way is hopelessly cut off. Above the timber line there is only a waste of rock, worn by vast centuries in which every day is an ordinary lifetime, into small, jagged stones that cut the feet. The crags are thunder-swept and blown by cataclysmic storms of which the dwellers in the valley have never dreamed. In the unspeakable loneliness, the pilgrim abides for ever with his mocking wreath of laurel, cheered only by a rumbling, reverberant "All

Hail!" which comes, at age-long intervals, from some peak before whose infinite distance his finite sight fails.

At intervals throughout the day, Miss Evelina heard the Piper's flute, always from the hills. Each time it brought her comfort, for she knew that, as yet, he had not gone. Once she fancied that he had gone long ago, and some woodland deity, magically transported from ancient Greece, had taken his place. Late in the afternoon, she heard it once, but so far and faintly that she guessed it was for the last time.

In her garden there were flowers, blooming luxuriantly. From their swaying censers, fragrant incense filled the air. The weeds had been taken out and no trace was left. From the garden of her heart the weeds were gone, too, but there were no flowers. Rue and asphodel had been replaced by lavender and rosemary; the deadly black poppy had been uprooted, and where it had grown there were spikenard and balm. Yet, as the Piper had said, she asked for roses, and it is not every garden in which roses will bloom.

At dusk she went out into her transformed garden. Where once the thorns had held her back, the paths were straight and smooth. Dense undergrowth and clinging vines no longer made her steps difficult. Piper Tom had made her garden right, and opened before her, clearly, the way of her soul.

In spite of the beauty there was desolation, because the cheery presence had gone to return no more. Her loneliness was so acute that it was almost pain, and yet the pain was bearable, because he had taught her how to endure and to look beyond.

Fairy-like, the white moths fluttered through the garden, and the crickets piped cheerily. Miss Evelina stopped her ears that she might not hear their piping, rude reminder, as it was, of music that should come no more, but, even so, she could not shut out remembrance.

With a flash of her old resentment, she recalled how everything upon which she had ever depended had been taken away from her, almost immediately. No sooner had she learned the sweetness of clinging than she had been forced to stand alone. One by one the supports had been removed, until she stood alone, desolate and wretched, indeed, but alone. Of such things as these self-reliance is made.

Suddenly, the still air seemed to stir. A sound that was neither breath nor music, so softly was it blown, echoed in from the hills. Then came another and another--merest hints of melody, till at last she started up, trembling. Surely these distant flutings were the pipes o' Pan!

She set herself to listen, her tiny hands working convulsively. Nearer and nearer the music came, singing of wind and stream and mountain--the "music that had no tune." No sooner had it become clear than it ceased altogether.

But, an hour or so afterward, when the moon had risen, there was a familiar step upon the road outside. Veiled, Evelina went to the gate and met Piper Tom, whose red feather was aloft in his hat again and whose flute was slung over his shoulder by its accustomed cord. His pedler's pack was not to be seen.

"I thought you had gone," she said.

"I had," he answered, "but 't is not written, I'm thinking, that a man may not change his mind as well as a woman. My heart would not let my feet go away from you until I knew for sure whether or not you were mocking me last night."

"Mocking you? No! Surely you know I would never do that?"

"No, I did not know. The ways of women are strange, I'm thinking, past all finding out. In truth, 't would be stranger if you were not mocking me than it ever could be if you were. Tell me," he pleaded, "ah, tell me what you were meaning, in words so plain that I can understand!"

"Come," said Evelina; "come to where we were sitting last night and I will tell you." He followed her back to the maple beside the broken wall, where the two chairs still faced each other. He leaned forward, resting his elbows on his knees, and looked at her so keenly that she felt, in spite of the darkness and her veil, that he must see her face.

"Piper Tom," she said, "when you came to me, I was the most miserable woman on earth. I had been most cruelly betrayed, and sorrow seized upon me when I was not strong enough to stand it. It preyed upon me until it became an obsession--it possessed me absolutely, and from it there was no escape but death."

"I know," answered the Piper. "I found the bottle that had held the dreamless sleep. I'm thinking you had thrown it away."

"Yes, I had thrown it away, but only because I was too proud to die at his door--do you understand?"

"Yes, I'm thinking I understand, but go on. You've not told me whether or no you mocked me. What did you mean?"

"I meant," said Evelina, steadfastly, "that if you cared for the woman you had led out of the shadow of the cypress, and for all that was in her heart to give you, she was yours. Not only out of gratitude, but because you have put trust into a heart that has known no trust since its betrayal, and because, where trust is, there may some day come--more."

Her voice sank almost to a whisper, but Piper Tom heard it. He took her hand in his own, and she felt him tremble--she was the strong one, now.

"Spinner in the Sun," he began, huskily, "were you meaning that you'd go with me when I took the highway again, and help me make the world easier for everybody with a hurt heart?"

"Yes," she answered. "You called me and I came--for always."

"Were you meaning that you'd face the storms and the cold with me, and take no heed of the rain--that you'd live on the coarse fare I could pick up from day to day, and never mind it?"

"Yes, I meant all that."

"Were you meaning, perhaps, that you'd make a home for me? Ah, Spinner in the Sun, it takes a woman to make a home!"

"Yes, I'd make a home, or go gypsying with you, just as you chose."

The Piper laughed, with inexpressible tenderness. "You know, I'm thinking, that 't would be a home, and not gypsying--that I'd not let you face anything I could shield you from."

Evelina laughed, too--a low, sweet laugh. "Yes, I know," she said.

The Piper turned away, struggling with temptation. At length he came back to her. "'T is wrong of me, I'm thinking, but I take you as a man takes Heaven, and we'll do the work together. 'T is as though I had risen from the dead and the gates of pearl were open, with all the angels of God beckoning me in."

In the exaltation that was upon him, he had no thought of profaning her by a touch. She stood apart from him as something high and holy, enthroned in a sacred place.

"Beloved," he pleaded, "will you be coming; with me now to the place where I saw you first? 'T is night now, and then 'twas day, but I'm thinking the words are wrong. 'T is day now, with the sun and moon and stars all shining at once and suns that I never saw before. Will you come?"

"I'll go wherever you lead me," she answered. "While you hold my hand in yours, I can never be afraid."

They went through the night together, taking the shorter way over the hills. She stumbled and he took her hand, his own still trembling. "Close your beautiful eyes," he whispered, "and trust me to lead you."

Though she did not close her eyes, she gave herself wholly to his guidance, noting how he chose for himself the rougher places to give her the easier path. He pushed aside the undergrowth before her, lifted her gently over damp hollows, and led her around the stones.

At last they came to the woods that opened out upon the upper river road, where she had stood the day she had been splashed with mud from Anthony Dexter's wheels, and, at the same instant, had heard the mysterious flutings from afar. They entered near the hill to which her long wandering had led her, and at the foot of it, the Piper paused.

"You'll have no fear, I'm thinking, since the moon makes the clearing as bright as day, and I'll not be letting you out of my sight. I have a fancy to stand upon yonder level place and call you as I called you once before. Only, this time, the heart of me will dance to my own music, for I know you'll be coming all the while I play."

He left her and clambered up the hill to the narrow ledge which sloped back, and was surrounded with pines. He kept in the open spaces, so that the moonlight was always upon him, and she did not lose sight of him more than once or twice, and then only for a moment. The hill was not a high one and the ascent was very gradual. Within a few minutes, he had gained his place.

Clear and sweet through the moonlit forest rang out the pipes o' Pan, singing of love and joy. Never before had the Piper's flute given forth such music as this. The melody was as instinctive as the mating-call of a thrush, as crystalline as a mountain stream, and as pure as the snow from whence the stream had come.

Evelina climbed to meet him, her face and heart uplifted. The silvery notes dropped about her like rain as she ascended, strangely glad and strangely at peace. When she reached the level place where he was standing, his face illumined with unspeakable joy. He dropped his flute and opened his arms.

"My Spinner in the Sun," he whispered, "I called you, and you came."

"Yes," she answered, from his close embrace, "you called me, and I have come--for always."

At last, he released her and they stood facing each other. The Piper was stirred to the depths of his soul. "Last night I dreamed," he said, "and 't was the dream that brought me back. It was a little place, with a brook close by, and almost too small to be called a house, but 'twas a home, I'm thinking, because you were there. It was night, and I had come back from making the world a bit easier for some poor woman-soul, and you were standing in the door, waiting.

"The veil was gone, and there was love on your face--ah, I've often dreamed a woman was waiting for me so, but because you hide your beauty from me, 't is not for me to be asking more. God knows I have enough given me, now.

"Since the first, I've known you were very beautiful, and very brave. I knew, too, that you were sad--that you had been through sorrows no man would dare to face. I've dreamed your eyes were like the first violets of Spring, your lips deep scarlet like the Winter berries, and I know the wonder of your hair, for The veil does not hide it all. I've dreamed your face was cold and pure, as if made from marble, yet tender, too, and I well know that it's noble past all words of mine, because it bears brave scars.

"I've told you I would never ask, and I'll keep my word, for I know well 't is not for the likes of me to see it, but only to dream. Don't think I'm asking, for I never will, but, Spinner in the Sun, because you said you would fare with me on the highway and face the cold and storm, it gives me courage to ask for this.

"If I close my eyes, will you lift your veil, and let me kiss the brave scars, that were never from sin or shame? The brave scars, Beloved--ah, if you would let me, only once, kiss the brave scars!"

Evelina laughed--a laugh that was half a sob--and leaning forward, full into the moonlight, she lifted her veil--for ever.

The Codes Of Hammurabi And Moses
W. W. Davies

QTY

The discovery of the Hammurabi Code is one of the greatest achievements of archaeology, and is of paramount interest, not only to the student of the Bible, but also to all those interested in ancient history...

Religion   **ISBN:** *1-59462-338-4*   **Pages:132**
MSRP *$12.95*

The Theory of Moral Sentiments
Adam Smith

QTY

This work from 1749. contains original theories of conscience amd moral judgment and it is the foundation for systemof morals.

Philosophy **ISBN:** *1-59462-777-0*   **Pages:536**
MSRP *$19.95*

Jessica's First Prayer
Hesba Stretton

QTY

In a screened and secluded corner of one of the many railway-bridges which span the streets of London there could be seen a few years ago, from five o'clock every morning until half past eight, a tidily set-out coffee-stall, consisting of a trestle and board, upon which stood two large tin cans, with a small fire of charcoal burning under each so as to keep the coffee boiling during the early hours of the morning when the work-people were thronging into the city on their way to their daily toil...

Pages:84

Childrens   **ISBN:** *1-59462-373-2*   **MSRP** *$9.95*

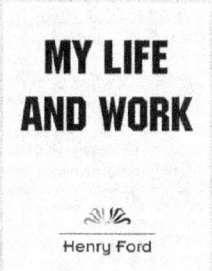

My Life and Work
Henry Ford

QTY

Henry Ford revolutionized the world with his implementation of mass production for the Model T automobile. Gain valuable business insight into his life and work with his own auto-biography... "We have only started on our development of our country we have not as yet, with all our talk of wonderful progress, done more than scratch the surface. The progress has been wonderful enough but..."

Pages:300

Biographies/   **ISBN:** *1-59462-198-5*   **MSRP** *$21.95*

The Art of Cross-Examination
Francis Wellman

QTY

I presume it is the experience of every author, after his first book is published upon an important subject, to be almost overwhelmed with a wealth of ideas and illustrations which could readily have been included in his book, and which to his own mind, at least, seem to make a second edition inevitable. Such certainly was the case with me; and when the first edition had reached its sixth impression in five months, I rejoiced to learn that it seemed to my publishers that the book had met with a sufficiently favorable reception to justify a second and considerably enlarged edition. ..

Pages:412

Reference   **ISBN:** *1-59462-647-2*   *MSRP $19.95*

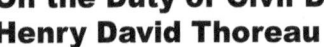

On the Duty of Civil Disobedience
Henry David Thoreau

QTY

Thoreau wrote his famous essay, On the Duty of Civil Disobedience, as a protest against an unjust but popular war and the immoral but popular institution of slave-owning. He did more than write—he declined to pay his taxes,   and was hauled off to gaol in consequence. Who can say how much this refusal of his hastened the end of the war and of slavery ?

Law   **ISBN:** *1-59462-747-9*   **Pages:48**

MSRP $7.45

Dream Psychology Psychoanalysis for Beginners
Sigmund Freud

QTY

Sigmund Freud, born Sigismund Schlomo Freud (May 6, 1856 - September 23, 1939), was a Jewish-Austrian neurologist and psychiatrist who co-founded the psychoanalytic school of psychology. Freud is best known for his theories of the unconscious mind, especially involving the mechanism of repression; his redefinition of sexual desire as mobile and directed towards a wide variety of objects; and his therapeutic techniques, especially his understanding of transference in the therapeutic relationship and the presumed value of dreams as sources of insight into unconscious desires.

Pages:196

Psychology   **ISBN:** *1-59462-905-6*   *MSRP $15.45*

The Miracle of Right Thought
Orison Swett Marden

QTY

Believe with all of your heart that you will do what you were made to do. When the mind has once formed the habit of holding cheerful, happy, prosperous pictures, it will not be easy to form the opposite habit. It does not matter how improbable or how far away this realization may see, or how dark the prospects may be, if we visualize them as best we can, as vividly as possible, hold tenaciously to them and vigorously struggle to attain them, they will gradually become actualized, realized in the life. But a desire, a longing without endeavor, a yearning abandoned or held indifferently will vanish without realization.

Pages:360

Self Help   **ISBN:** *1-59462-644-8*   *MSRP $25.45*

The Rosicrucian Cosmo-Conception Mystic Christianity *by Max Heindel*   ISBN: *1-59462-188-8*   **$38.95**
The Rosicrucian Cosmo-conception is not dogmatic, neither does it appeal to any other authority than the reason of the student. It is: not controversial, but is: sent forth in the, hope that it may help to clear...   New Age/Religion Pages 646

Abandonment To Divine Providence *by Jean-Pierre de Caussade*   ISBN: *1-59462-228-0*   **$25.95**
"The Rev. Jean Pierre de Caussade was one of the most remarkable spiritual writers of the Society of Jesus in France in the 18th Century. His death took place at Toulouse in 1751. His works have gone through many editions and have been republished...   Inspirational/Religion Pages 400

Mental Chemistry *by Charles Haanel*   ISBN: *1-59462-192-6*   **$23.95**
Mental Chemistry allows the change of material conditions by combining and appropriately utilizing the power of the mind. Much like applied chemistry creates something new and unique out of careful combinations of chemicals the mastery of mental chemistry...   New Age Pages 354

The Letters of Robert Browning and Elizabeth Barret Barrett 1845-1846 vol II   ISBN: *1-59462-193-4*   **$35.95**
by Robert Browning and Elizabeth Barrett   Biographies Pages 596

Gleanings In Genesis (volume I) *by Arthur W. Pink*   ISBN: *1-59462-130-6*   **$27.45**
Appropriately has Genesis been termed "the seed plot of the Bible" for in it we have, in germ form, almost all of the great doctrines which are afterwards fully developed in the books of Scripture which follow...   Religion/Inspirational Pages 420

The Master Key *by L. W. de Laurence*   ISBN: *1-59462-001-6*   **$30.95**
In no branch of human knowledge has there been a more lively increase of the spirit of research during the past few years than in the study of Psychology, Concentration and Mental Discipline. The requests for authentic lessons in Thought Control, Mental Discipline and...   New Age/Business Pages 422

The Lesser Key Of Solomon Goetia *by L. W. de Laurence*   ISBN: *1-59462-092-X*   **$9.95**
This translation of the first book of the "Lemegton" which is now for the first time made accessible to students of Talismanic Magic was done, after careful collation and edition, from numerous Ancient Manuscripts in Hebrew, Latin, and French...   New Age/Occult Pages 92

Rubaiyat Of Omar Khayyam *by Edward Fitzgerald*   ISBN:*1-59462-332-5*   **$13.95**
Edward Fitzgerald, whom the world has already learned, in spite of his own efforts to remain within the shadow of anonymity, to look upon as one of the rarest poets of the century, was born at Bredfield, in Suffolk, on the 31st of March, 1809. He was the third son of John Purcell...   Music Pages 172

Ancient Law *by Henry Maine*   ISBN: *1-59462-128-4*   **$29.95**
The chief object of the following pages is to indicate some of the earliest ideas of mankind, as they are reflected in Ancient Law, and to point out the relation of those ideas to modern thought.   Religiom/History Pages 452

Far-Away Stories *by William J. Locke*   ISBN: *1-59462-129-2*   **$19.45**
"Good wine needs no bush, but a collection of mixed vintages does. And this book is just such a collection. Some of the stories I do not want to remain buried for ever in the museum files of dead magazine-numbers an author's not unpardonable vanity..."   Fiction Pages 272

Life of David Crockett *by David Crockett*   ISBN: *1-59462-250-7*   **$27.45**
"Colonel David Crockett was one of the most remarkable men of the times in which he lived. Born in humble life, but gifted with a strong will, an indomitable courage, and unremitting perseverance...   Biographies/New Age Pages 424

Lip-Reading *by Edward Nitchie*   ISBN: *1-59462-206-X*   **$25.95**
Edward B. Nitchie, founder of the New York School for the Hard of Hearing, now the Nitchie School of Lip-Reading, Inc, wrote "LIP-READING Principles and Practice". The development and perfecting of this meritorious work on lip-reading was an undertaking...   How-to Pages 400

A Handbook of Suggestive Therapeutics, Applied Hypnotism, Psychic Science   ISBN: *1-59462-214-0*   **$24.95**
by Henry Munro   Health/New Age/Health/Self-help Pages 376

A Doll's House: and Two Other Plays *by Henrik Ibsen*   ISBN: *1-59462-112-8*   **$19.95**
Henrik Ibsen created this classic when in revolutionary 1848 Rome. Introducing some striking concepts in playwriting for the realist genre, this play has been studied the world over.   Fiction/Classics/Plays 308

The Light of Asia *by sir Edwin Arnold*   ISBN: *1-59462-204-3*   **$13.95**
In this poetic masterpiece, Edwin Arnold describes the life and teachings of Buddha. The man who was to become known as Buddha to the world was born as Prince Gautama of India but he rejected the worldly riches and abandoned the reigns of power when...   Religion/History/Biographies Pages 170

The Complete Works of Guy de Maupassant *by Guy de Maupassant*   ISBN: *1-59462-157-8*   **$16.95**
"For days and days, nights and nights, I had dreamed of that first kiss which was to consecrate our engagement, and I knew not on what spot I should put my lips..."   Fiction/Classics Pages 240

The Art of Cross-Examination *by Francis L. Wellman*   ISBN: *1-59462-309-0*   **$26.95**
Written by a renowned trial lawyer, Wellman imparts his experience and uses case studies to explain how to use psychology to extract desired information through questioning.   How-to/Science/Reference Pages 408

Answered or Unanswered? *by Louisa Vaughan*   ISBN: *1-59462-248-5*   **$10.95**
Miracles of Faith in China   Religion Pages 112

The Edinburgh Lectures on Mental Science (1909) *by Thomas*   ISBN: *1-59462-008-3*   **$11.95**
This book contains the substance of a course of lectures recently given by the writer in the Queen Street Hail, Edinburgh. Its purpose is to indicate the Natural Principles governing the relation between Mental Action and Material Conditions...   New Age/Psychology Pages 148

Ayesha *by H. Rider Haggard*   ISBN: *1-59462-301-5*   **$24.95**
Verily and indeed it is the unexpected that happens! Probably if there was one person upon the earth from whom the Editor of this, and of a certain previous history, did not expect to hear again...   Classics Pages 380

Ayala's Angel *by Anthony Trollope*   ISBN: *1-59462-352-X*   **$29.95**
The two girls were both pretty, but Lucy who was twenty-one who supposed to be simple and comparatively unattractive, whereas Ayala was credited, as her Bombwhat romantic name might show, with poetic charm and a taste for romance. Ayala when her father died was nineteen...   Fiction Pages 484

The American Commonwealth *by James Bryce*   ISBN: *1-59462-286-8*   **$34.45**
An interpretation of American democratic political theory. It examines political mechanics and society from the perspective of Scotsman James Bryce   Politics Pages 572

Stories of the Pilgrims *by Margaret P. Pumphrey*   ISBN: *1-59462-116-0*   **$17.95**
This book explores pilgrims religious oppression in England as well as their escape to Holland and eventual crossing to America on the Mayflower, and their early days in New England...   History Pages 268

QTY

The Fasting Cure *by Sinclair Upton*   ISBN: *1-59462-222-1*   **$13.95**
*In the Cosmopolitan Magazine for May, 1910, and in the Contemporary Review (London) for April, 1910, I published an article dealing with my experi-
ences in fasting. I have written a great many magazine articles, but never one which attracted so much attention... New Age/Self Help/Health Pages 164*

Hebrew Astrology *by Sepharial*   ISBN: *1-59462-308-2*   **$13.45**
*In these days of advanced thinking it is a matter of common observation that we have left many of the old landmarks behind and that we are now pressing
forward to greater heights and to a wider horizon than that which represented the mind-content of our progenitors... Astrology Pages 144*

Thought Vibration or The Law of Attraction in the Thought World   ISBN: *1-59462-127-6*   **$12.95**

by William Walker Atkinson   *Psychology/Religion Pages 144*

Optimism *by Helen Keller*   ISBN: *1-59462-108-X*   **$15.95**
*Helen Keller was blind, deaf, and mute since 19 months old, yet famously learned how to overcome these handicaps, communicate with the world, and
spread her lectures promoting optimism. An inspiring read for everyone... Biographies/Inspirational Pages 84*

Sara Crewe *by Frances Burnett*   ISBN: *1-59462-360-0*   **$9.45**
*In the first place, Miss Minchin lived in London. Her home was a large, dull, tall one, in a large, dull square, where all the houses were alike, and all the
sparrows were alike, and where all the door-knockers made the same heavy sound... Childrens/Classic Pages 88*

The Autobiography of Benjamin Franklin *by Benjamin Franklin*   ISBN: *1-59462-135-7*   **$24.95**
*The Autobiography of Benjamin Franklin has probably been more extensively read than any other American historical work, and no other book of its kind
has had such ups and downs of fortune. Franklin lived for many years in England, where he was agent... Biographies/History Pages 332*

Name	
Email	
Telephone	
Address	
City, State ZIP	

☐ **Credit Card**   ☐ **Check / Money Order**

Credit Card Number	
Expiration Date	
Signature	

Please Mail to: Book Jungle
PO Box 2226
Champaign, IL 61825
or Fax to: 630-214-0564

ORDERING INFORMATION

web*: www.bookjungle.com*
email*: sales@bookjungle.com*
fax*: 630-214-0564*
mail*: Book Jungle PO Box 2226 Champaign, IL 61825*
or PayPal *to sales@bookjungle.com*

Please contact us for bulk discounts

DIRECT-ORDER TERMS

**20% Discount if You Order
Two or More Books**
Free Domestic Shipping!
Accepted: Master Card, Visa,
Discover, American Express

www.ingramcontent.com/pod-product-compliance
Lightning Source LLC
Chambersburg PA
CBHW080905020726
47502CB00008B/2353